PRAISE F   MW00990514

"...Savannah Carlisle is now one of my go-to authors for heartwarming, Kleenex-clutching, feel-good romance!"— **Annie Rains**, *USA Today* bestselling author

"Carlisle's novel is thoughtful, with well-developed characters who move beyond common small-town girl and big-city boy tropes. Instead, she pulls together two characters who turn out to have far more in common than they think."—***Kirkus Reviews*** on *The Library of Second Chances*

"I was completely enchanted by this charmingly sweet beach read and just adored the letters exchanged in the Little Free Library."—**Teri Wilson**, *New York Times* bestselling author on *The Library of Second Chances*

"Fans of 'You've Got Mail' will swoon over Lucy and Logan in this charming romance that celebrates the splendor of small-town living."—**KJ Micciche**, author of *The Book Proposal* on *The Library of Second Chances*

"...Savannah Carlisle's debut is sure to delight. The author's vivid descriptions put me right in Heron Isle along with the characters and had this city girl longing for the cozy and picturesque small-town life she masterfully depicted."— **Meredith Schorr**, author of *As Seen on TV* and *Someone Just Like You* on *The Library of Second Chances*

"100% recommend this for your summer (or anytime) TBR!"

—**The Book Nerd Momma** on *The Library of Second Chances*

ALSO BY SAVANNAH CARLISLE

The Library of Second Chances

The Summer of Starting Over

Meredith —
I hope you enjoy this
mental vacation!

The Summer of Starting Over

SAVANNAH CARLISLE

Fen

HR
HARPETH ROAD
PRESS
Nashville

HARPETH ROAD PRESS

Published by Harpeth Road Press (USA)
P.O. Box 158184
Nashville, TN 37215

eBook: 978-1-963483-20-8
Paperback: 978-1-963483-21-5
Library of Congress Control Number: 2025933050

The Summer of Starting Over: A Wonderfully Romantic Beach Read

Cover Design by Kristen Ingebretson
Cover Images © Shutterstock

Harpeth Road Press, May 2025

To my nieces and the other little girls in my life: Azylinn, Ophelia, Julie, Maddy, Caroline, Maddie, Elaina, Finley, Poppy, Courtney, Montana, Chelsea, and June.

May your dreams be audacious and your pursuit of them be fearless.

CHAPTER ONE
CALLIE

Welcome to Big Dune Island, Florida
Home of Callie Jackson

The white paint on the sign was cracked and faded from years of the Northeast Florida sun beating down on it. Seeing her name on the giant wooden board, greeting visitors as they approached the bridge to the island, had once filled Callie with pride. She still remembered coming home from Nashville two years after signing her first record contract at sixteen and having her debut album go gold. Her mother had pulled over on the side of the road to show her the new sign and they'd giggled as Callie struck poses next to it.

But now the feeling bubbling to the surface at the sight of it definitely wasn't pride.

Her cell phone rang, and she looked down to see it was her childhood best friend, Gigi Franklin, calling. Although Callie had mixed emotions about returning to Big Dune Island, she was looking forward to some long overdue time with her.

"You almost here?" Gigi asked in lieu of a greeting.

"Driving over the bridge now. Are you leaving work?"

"Ugh," Gigi grunted. "Yes, but I have to run to the city council meeting. One of my clients called last minute. I'll text you the code to the front door and hopefully be home in a couple of hours. I can't believe you haven't even seen my house yet."

When Callie last left the island, almost a decade earlier, she hadn't looked back. In fact, she hadn't been sure she could ever come back. But things had changed. She'd bet on herself —like her parents had always taught her to do—and she'd lost.

"I can't wait to see what you've done with your place," Callie said. Gigi had purchased an older house on the beach and renovated it over the last couple of years.

As Callie reached the other side of the bridge, she could see Breakwaters, the local watering hole, and the sun-worn siding of Captain Keller's Seafood Shack, a business that had passed through the generations and was now owned by the original Captain Keller's grandson.

Even with the car windows rolled up, Callie could smell the salt marsh that stretched under the bridge. Visitors said it smelled like rotten eggs, but to her it was the aroma of her childhood. She could almost picture herself down below chasing crabs in the mud at low tide, or casting a line from her father's boat toward the shore to snag a fish for dinner. With summer nearing, all the marsh grass shone bright green in the late-afternoon sunlight.

"I'm excited to give you the tour," Gigi said. "Of course, who knows how long the meeting will go. Last time half the town showed up for the public comment portion."

As Gigi vented about the development she was trying to stop at tonight's city council meeting, Callie eased off the bridge onto Sunset Drive, the weathered and aging commercial signs laying out a familiar path. She passed the plumber who'd been her dad's poker buddy, the sewing shop where her mom had bought dress patterns, and Gigi's father's dental practice. Crossing over Main Street, Callie made a left on Palmetto Avenue, and as she eased the car down the tree-lined road, Spanish moss dripped almost low enough to touch the roof of her Audi convertible.

On autopilot, she turned right onto 6th and slowed to a stop across from a two-story Victorian, complete with a wrap-around porch and turret. When she looked up at her child-hood home, however, she let out a gasp. Several windows were boarded up, and the spindles holding up the porch railing looked like a game of Jenga, as if removing one small piece might topple the whole thing.

Tears sprung to her eyes as she thought of her mom painstakingly repainting the gingerbread trim every spring until it gleamed white. Then she'd always clean out the window boxes and plant them full of purple pansies, her own mother's favorite. She'd been so proud to raise her family in the same home where she'd grown up.

Now Callie looked at the peeling paint, broken shutters, and overgrown lawn and fought back the fresh waves of grief washing over her.

"The house—" Callie choked back, interrupting Gigi's long diatribe on the lack of teeth in the town's tree ordinance.

"Oh, honey, you're there already?"

"Why didn't you tell me?" Callie's voice was barely above a whisper.

"Uncle Lonnie asked me not to." Regret crept into Gigi's voice. "I take it that means he didn't?"

"No," Callie said as she climbed out of the car, sliding up her sunglasses to hold her blonde curls off her face. "I mean, I knew it needed some work, but it's worse than I imagined."

The house looked like a shell of its former self, which was ironic since she felt the same way.

"I think it's all cosmetic. Just some wind damage from the

last hurricane that went by offshore," Gigi said, sounding hopeful. "Really, it looks worse than it is. That house has great bones."

"If you say so." Callie was skeptical; it was no wonder Uncle Lonnie had decided it was time to sell.

"I do. I also suggest you go see Uncle Lonnie sooner than later."

"He's always at the American Legion on Tuesday nights." Callie sighed. "I'll go in the morning. Besides, I'm exhausted from the drive." She didn't have the heart to be mad at him, not after she'd saddled him with all the responsibility of caring for the house. He should have let her spend some of the money she'd offered over the years to make his life easier, but he was too stubborn and proud for that.

"Okay, well I'm heading into the meeting," said Gigi. "But I'll be home in a couple of hours, and we can catch up then."

As they said their goodbyes and ended the conversation, Callie began walking down the driveway to the house, wanting a closer look at the sagging porch. Maybe Thomas Wolfe was right; you can't go home again. Or at least, maybe you shouldn't.

She'd only made it a few steps up the drive when a dog came running around from the backyard, letting out friendly barks at the sight of her as if to let someone know company had arrived.

"Coop?" she asked as she walked toward it, realizing as soon as she said it that it couldn't be true. Cooper, Coop for short, couldn't possibly still be alive. He had already been an old dog when she moved to Nashville thirteen years ago, leaving him and his owner, Jesse Thomas, behind.

Bending over to pet the German shepherd, she glanced around the yard, looking for who he belonged to, but she was alone. The dog was wearing a collar, but it had no tags.

"What's your name, pretty boy?" She continued to look for a distraught owner running to the rescue.

The dog lapped up her attention, tail wagging as he sat on the grass and rubbed his head on her hand. His resemblance to Coop was uncanny.

The last time she saw Coop, she and Jesse were throwing a ball for him in the front yard. It was her final weekend on the island before moving to Nashville after she got her record deal. She'd choked back tears as she watched Jesse put a leash on Coop for the short walk back to his house, knowing it was the last time she'd see them for a while.

She'd cried herself to sleep every night for months in Nashville, but the songs she wrote to ease her heartache quickly filled the gaps on her debut album, which had started with a few of the songs about the island and Jesse she couldn't convince the label to ditch. One music critic wrote, "*Packed Up Promises ripped the scars on my heart from my own childhood sweetheart open again and left them to bleed.*" That's because the scars on Callie's heart had been brand new.

Sometimes she still wondered what it would have been like if Jesse had moved to Nashville to attend Vanderbilt, as they'd initially planned, but she knew her lifestyle wasn't built to include someone else. Not that he would have held her back, but they wouldn't have gotten enough time together to build a lasting relationship. In the early years, it helped to think of it this way.

Her trip down memory lane was interrupted by the dog, now circling and barking to get her attention because it wanted to play.

"Where's your house, huh?" She looked to either side of the yard again. Not seeing anyone, she grabbed him by the collar and started walking him around the back to see if he had come from the house behind hers, or if anyone in another yard was looking for him. He clearly belonged to someone.

As she rounded the corner into the backyard, she stopped in her tracks at the sight of lumber and tools strewn across the expanse of grass behind the back deck. Uncle Lonnie had promised some exterior repairs before closing on the sale, but she hadn't expected to find someone here.

A familiar male voice came from behind her.

"Fen, you old scoundrel, are you bothering this nice lady?"

Startled, she turned, and her heart leaped into her throat. The dog might not be Coop, but they definitely had the same owner.

CHAPTER TWO
JESSE

J esse had been trying to caulk the inside of a window when he saw a convertible pull up across the street and stop directly in front of the house. It didn't matter that he hadn't seen Callie since her parents' funeral nearly a decade earlier, or that he had no idea what kind of car she drove. He'd know that blonde curly hair anywhere.

As she came into view and confirmed what his gut had already told him, he froze, caulk gun poised midair. He hadn't even realized he was holding his breath until his body involuntarily inhaled deeply, returning him to the present as Fenway ran into the front yard to her side. He'd wanted to hide inside the house, to devise a game plan before coming face to face with her, but the dog hadn't given him that chance.

Now that she was standing in front of him, mouth agape as she tried to process his presence, he could see she'd barely changed at all. He'd had his doubts after seeing images splashed across magazine covers of her in leather catsuits with straight hair that elongated her face, making her look as if she'd missed one too many meals. But this Callie was merely an older version of the teenage girl who'd once stood on the same wooden deck behind him and pretended it was a stage, belting out Dolly Parton, her blonde curls bouncing, big eyes lit up with excitement.

"Jesse? Wha-what are you doing here? Did they hire you to fix things up before the sale?"

Clearly Lonnie hadn't yet told her Jesse was the one buying the house. Just like he hadn't mentioned to Jesse that Callie was coming home.

Jesse's eyes scanned every feature on her face, from her bright-blue eyes that contrasted with her pale skin, to her delicate frame that he could remember fitting perfectly in the crook under his arm. She was still so beautiful, her mere presence making his heart race like it had as a teenager. He tore his gaze away, looking back toward the house so he could bottle up his emotions before she saw them on his face.

He thought he'd known exactly what he'd say to her when she came back to pack up the house, but now she was in front of him, he couldn't get the words out. Instead, he bought himself some time.

"Does Uncle Lonnie know you're here?" he asked.

"I haven't seen him yet, but he's expecting me."

He wondered how she felt about the sale, searching her face for clues. She hadn't been home since the funeral, so he'd assumed she'd felt there was nothing left here for her. The house, the island, him, they were all chapters she'd closed. Remembering how she'd refused to let him move to Nashville with her, the warm feelings he'd been fighting were replaced with the stinging reminders of how she'd walked away from him and never looked back.

"Why does Uncle Lonnie have you over here fixing things? I told him that wasn't necessary. He said they're buying as is." She moved slowly in Jesse's direction, closing the gap between them to less than ten feet before she stopped and surveyed the gaping hole at the back of the house where the door had been. "Of course, it's a little more 'as is' than I was expecting."

She took in the twin sawhorses with the back door sitting on top. The sander was lying on the door, its orange cord snaking down from the sawhorse and across the thick green expanse to the outlet beside the empty doorframe.

"It's not so bad. Mostly cosmetic and some seriously overdue repairs." He hadn't meant for the last part to be a dig at her, but he noticed how her eyes fell to the ground as she shifted her weight from foot to foot.

"You know, I could have fixed all of this." She made a big sweeping motion in the direction of the house. "I could have hired someone years ago if Uncle Lonnie had told me what it needed, but he's too stubborn to take any money from me."

"It's not about money. The old girl just needs someone who cares about her and can put the time in to fix her up."

She visibly winced at his words, and he recognized a flash of hurt clouding her eyes before she bent down to pet Fenway, hiding her face from him. He almost apologized, but what for? It was true. She'd hardly been back since she signed her first record deal, which proved she cared for this place about as much as she had him. Heck, she'd just assumed he was the hired help. Never even questioned if he might be the buyer.

He was ready to get rid of her. He had work to do, so he started up the sander again, hoping she'd get the hint. At that same moment, Fen suddenly took off across the yard toward a squirrel, yanking the cord of the tool as he went, causing it to crash to the ground. Jesse yelled at the dog to scare him away from the sander, running the short distance to where it lay buzzing to turn it off.

"I didn't mean to bother you. I just stopped by to see the place on my way to Gigi's." Callie's voice was wistful as she glanced at the double windows in the upper left corner of the house that had been her childhood bedroom.

He couldn't count how many times in the last couple of weeks he'd looked up at it in the same way. He always half expected to see her there, sitting in her window seat, writing a song.

Her bright-blue eyes were glazed over, lost in a memory, so he waited for her to continue.

"I never came back after..." Her voice trailed as she choked on the words. "Well, I haven't been able to come back since then."

Although he still wanted to ask her why she'd never come back to see him after she moved to Nashville, he understood why she'd stayed away after her parents died. The entire town mourned their passing after the car accident.

"Uncle Lonnie says an investor bought it to flip. It just feels so—" She searched for the right word. "—transactional."

He thought he could see tears welling in her eyes. She was more torn up over the sale of the house than he'd thought she would be, and for a moment he considered telling her the truth.

Before he could make a decision, she was already moving on to another subject.

"He sure looks like Coop." She motioned toward Fen as she started up the short staircase leading onto the deck.

That had always been her style: avoid tough conversations by changing the subject. It was probably why she'd avoided Big Dune Island all these years, which had suited him fine. He preferred her out of sight so he could keep her out of mind too.

He remembered the time she'd sent him to check the cast list for their high school's production of *Wizard of Oz*. He'd agonized over how he was going to tell her she hadn't gotten the lead role of Dorothy, but instead Glinda. Everyone knew Mr. Winston never gave the lead to a freshman, but Callie thought she'd be the first. She'd hardly even registered the news before she was rambling on about the new burger place going in the old Citgo station.

Jesse followed her onto the deck at a safe distance, sensing he needed to give her space both physically and emotionally.

"Yeah, German shepherds are kind of like that. They all look the same." He found himself teasing her now. "His name is Fenway—like Fenway Park in Boston—but I call him Fen."

Would she remember that, as a kid, he'd dreamed of playing for the Red Sox one day, his dad's favorite team?

"Where the Red Sox play." She didn't meet his eyes. "I know."

So she did remember something about him. Although remembering where a baseball team played wasn't the same as the memories he'd been battling since being back inside her childhood home. His were filled with fingers intertwined and whispered declarations of love while promising to be together forever, not sports trivia.

He sat on the sun-faded bench built into the porch railing and watched her squat next to Fen and pet him gently down the length of his body. The dog relished the attention and rolled over to display his furry belly, indicating she should focus her petting there. She obliged, causing Fen to lean his head back against the deck in complete doggy bliss.

"You're the sweetest boy in the whole world, aren't you?" she cooed, only faint traces of her accent slipping in. She glanced up at Jesse before he could look away. "What? Why are you looking at me like that?"

He was embarrassed she'd caught him openly staring at her, but he couldn't stop. He still hadn't gotten over the shock of seeing her again, or the way it made his heart pound in his ears. He was finding it difficult to hang on to all the anger that had kept him company in the years since she left.

"Just surprised to see you after all this time, that's all." He brushed off her question and forced himself to concentrate on a cardinal perched in an oleander tree in the backyard.

"So you must still be working with your dad's construction firm, huh?" She didn't wait for him to reply. "What's Lonnie got you doing here?" She sat cross-legged on the deck next to Fen, facing Jesse on the bench.

"Oh, you know. This and that." He was trying to avoid the subject for as long as possible.

"I see the back door is missing." She motioned to the gaping entryway to the kitchen.

"It needed sanding. You know how wooden doors swell around here when it starts heating up."

"I still don't understand why Lonnie thinks he needs to fix things before the closing. Isn't that the whole point of selling to a flipper?" She shook her head in confusion.

She didn't understand, and he wasn't sure she would even when she learned the truth.

CHAPTER THREE
CALLIE

Callie was still reeling from the unexpected encounter with Jesse when she awoke the next morning. She'd heard Gigi rise and leave early for a hearing, but she'd promised Callie she could take off after lunch so they could spend more time together. Callie hadn't told Gigi about running into Jesse yet because she was still sorting out how she felt about it. Instead, they'd spent the evening talking about all the work Gigi had done on the little 1940s cottage she'd bought upon her return to Big Dune Island.

Callie couldn't stop thinking about how her heart quickened when Jesse's green eyes locked with hers, as if he could still read her mind. It hadn't been like that with her ex, Andrew, which she'd chalked up to being an adult instead of a hormone-riddled teenager. There was a lot to be said for someone who knew the industry and understood her lifestyle, and whose life was headed in the same direction. Unfortunately, that direction had been straight downhill.

Forcing the image of Jesse and the rippling muscles under his tight t-shirt from her mind, Callie got dressed and left to see Uncle Lonnie. As painful as it was to come home and

13

confront the absence of her parents, she'd been looking forward to spending some real time with her uncle, the only family she had left.

Uncle Lonnie's house was a short distance from Callie's childhood home, a walk she'd made on countless occasions. For maybe the first time ever, she pulled up in her car and parked in front. It felt foreign, as if she'd only imagined once living in the big Victorian down the street. A cobblestone path led to Uncle Lonnie's white clapboard cottage with the robin's-egg-blue front door, and she stopped to admire the hydrangeas that bordered the property, ballooning like cotton candy toward the windows in varying hues of blue and purple. She remembered what Uncle Lonnie had taught her as a child, about how the blooms get their color from the pH in the soil. The more acid, the more likely you were to get shades of blue, whereas the pinker blooms were caused by more alkaline. Aunt Doris, who died of cancer when Callie was twelve, had loved the blue ones, so Uncle Lonnie painstakingly monitored the dirt around the hydrangeas, keeping it at the proper level of acidity to maintain the range of blues and purples.

"Well, look what the cat dragged in. You comin' inside, or are you just going to stand there and stare?" Uncle Lonnie cracked open the screen door, a broad smile creating deep wrinkles on his face that curved down to outline his chin.

Callie noticed how he gingerly stepped down onto the porch with his left leg. Her mother had been a bit of a surprise pregnancy, so there was a large age gap between Callie's mother and her older brother. Lonnie was only in his midsixties, but a life of blue-collar labor at the local paper mill had been tough on his body.

His cowboy boots clicked along the cement porch as he walked a few paces toward her. From the boots to the music, she'd gotten her love of all things country from her uncle.

"Hey, Uncle Lonnie." She was starting to pick up her old

Southern drawl after only one night back in town. She'd had to work with a vocal coach for months to get rid of it for her first crossover album, the one that turned her into a pop star—for a few years, at least.

She bounded up the two front stairs to the porch the way she'd done a million times as a kid. Uncle Lonnie wrapped his arms around her in a bear hug that felt warmer and more loving than anything she could remember experiencing in months, maybe years.

"You sit here." He motioned to a pair of matching white wooden rocking chairs. "I'll get us some tea."

"I can get it—" she began to say, but he was already retreating into the house, still with that slight hitch in his stride.

Often she'd wondered if her uncle went inside his house for anything other than the kitchen, the bathroom, and bed. Ever since she was a kid, Uncle Lonnie could almost always be found in his rocking chair on the front porch, either picking on a guitar or whittling away at a piece of wood as he turned random discards into beautiful birds and turtles and other creatures. Judging by the shavings beside one rocker and the basket of wood blocks next to it, little had changed.

Callie knew the chair closest to the door was his favorite, so she took the other. When she was a kid, Uncle Lonnie always put a fresh coat of paint on the rockers and concrete floor every spring. Today, however, the chairs and the porch showed some age. The same way she noticed Uncle Lonnie was beginning to show his years. The guilt when she first saw him was like a punch in the gut. It had only been a few years since she'd seen him at one of her concerts in nearby Jacksonville. "Out of sight, out of mind" had been her guiding principle after losing her parents, but now she knew whatever short-term comfort that line of thinking had provided had come at a steep cost.

Her heart pounding, and her breathing coming more quickly, she forced herself to lean back in the chair, letting her feet fall into an easy rhythm, rocking her back and forth. She closed her eyes so she could listen to the light wind blowing through the oak trees that towered around the sides and back of the little house. With summer drawing closer, everything had new growth or was in full bloom already. Uncle Lonnie's house, and every house on this street, could grace the cover of *Southern Living* right now, no Photoshop necessary.

Her breathing had almost returned to normal when she heard Uncle Lonnie's boots clicking in their uneven rhythm on the porch, the screen door slamming behind him.

"Here ya go." He handed her a tall, clear glass filled with square cubes of ice, tea threatening to spill over the top. She leaned forward to sip it down so it wouldn't end up in her lap, and her mouth puckered the instant the cool liquid hit her tongue.

"Wow, I forgot what real sweet tea tasted like."

"Y'all don't have sweet tea in Nashville?"

"Oh, we have it. I just don't get to have any." She laughed. She'd switched to unsweetened years ago. Andrew had been appalled at the amount of sugar she was consuming daily. He was from up north, so of course he didn't understand.

"Don't get to?" Uncle Lonnie frowned in her direction. "Since when does my Callie let anyone tell her what to do?"

"Did you know this stuff has more than thirty grams of sugar in it?" She held the glass up to him as if he could see the mound of sugar inside.

"I don't guess I really ever cared enough to ask." He shook his head and laughed. Clearly, he thought her newfound disdain for sugar ridiculous. But then Uncle Lonnie didn't have to fit into skintight leather pants every night on tour either. She silently prayed he hadn't seen what she'd been talked into wearing on stage the past couple of years in the name of appealing to an "edgier" audience.

Ready to change the subject, because she felt guilty shaming him for drinking the same thing people all over town were sipping on right this very moment, she tiptoed her way into the conversation she knew they had to have.

"I went by the house last night. The hurricane kind of beat her up, didn't it?"

"That old girl? She can take a lickin' and keep on tickin'." He smiled off into the distance. "They don't build them like that anymore."

Her mother and uncle's great-grandfather, Dr. David Lyman, had built the house at the turn of the previous century. The house and land—a narrow strip that ran a full block between 5th and 6th streets—had been left to her mother and uncle by their parents, but Uncle Lonnie had already been living in his current house and had insisted Callie's recently married parents move in to build their family.

Locals called their block the "Silk Stocking District" because all the homes were constructed by wealthy residents in the late 1800s and early 1900s. Unfortunately, her ancestors had lost most of the family's wealth in the stock market crash of 1929. But they'd managed to save the family home and pass it down from generation to generation. Until now.

"There's nothing you can't fix with a little duct tape and baling wire," her father and Uncle Lonnie used to joke as they patched leaky pipes and repaired the flickering, buzzing lights, which her mother was convinced would burn the whole house down.

Gripping her hands in her lap, fighting to keep tears at bay, Callie worked up her courage. "Uncle Lonnie, I'm so sorry you felt you had to sell the house. I know how much it means to you."

Uncle Lonnie's rocker stopped its rhythmic pattern, and she braced herself for his disappointment.

"Callie, darlin'," he said, "I'm a firm believer that things happen for a reason. We rarely know in the moment what that reason is, but you be patient and it'll show itself when the time is right. Maybe there's something even better in store for you than an old house that needs a bunch of work."

Callie stared at a section of the porch where the green paint was peeling back to reveal a lighter shade underneath, as a tear trickled down her cheek. "It's not just a house though."

"It is, sweetheart. It's just boards and nails and a little duct tape." He chuckled at the last bit. "It might be where you made the memories, but it's the people in the memories and how they made you feel that matter, and no one can take those from you."

Callie couldn't help but smile back at him through glassy eyes, wiping the stray tears from her cheek with the back of her hand. "It's just really hard."

"I know it is. But someone came along who cares about her like we do, and I'm certain she's in the right hands."

"Aren't they going to flip it though? Why would you think they care about it?"

"You haven't even been able to bring yourself to come back here in nine years, much less go inside that house," he said instead of answering her question. "You know I always do what's best for you, and I believe this is."

She looked at her feet, unable to continue meeting his gaze. She knew he was right, about her not being able to go back inside *and* about always looking out for her.

"I can't picture someone else living in our house." She sighed, relaxing into the rocking chair.

And then she tried. She saw a little girl with blonde pigtails running up the front porch stairs, jumping into the arms of a waiting mother, the smell of pot roast wafting through the screen door. And then she realized it might not be a family at all, it might be a young sailor stationed at the nearby base, transforming it into a bachelor pad. Her mind racing through the options, she began to feel the full weight of the decision Uncle Lonnie had made.

"You know what I love most about that house?" He looked over and she gave a slight shake of her head, not sure where he was going with this. "It's a livin', breathing thing, but it feeds off the people inside it. With no one there, the light has gone right out of her eyes. She needs to be filled with love."

Her mom and Uncle Lonnie had always referred to the house as a "she," and it really did feel like a member of the family. It had been witness to births, celebrations, heartaches, holidays, even deaths. It was the tie that bound all Lymans and the people they brought into it. That's why she couldn't understand how Lonnie could let it go so easily.

"I might move back someday." Even as she said it, she knew it probably wasn't true. There were no recording studios for hundreds of miles. Sure, Jacksonville was only an hour away, but it wasn't exactly a mecca for music.

"Your mom and dad wouldn't have wanted it to weigh you down. I think your dad and I did a pretty good job piecing that old girl together, but we weren't professionals." He chuckled to himself. "She needs someone who can patch her up and make her stand tall and proud again. She deserves that."

Callie thought about what her uncle was saying. If you loved something, you let it go when it was the right thing to do. It's what she had done for Jesse.

"Speaking of patching her up, I went by yesterday." She paused to gauge his reaction. When his face remained unchanged, she continued, "Jesse Thomas was there doing some work. What's that all about?"

"Oh, you know, just putting a little lipstick on the pig."

She couldn't help but smile. One time, she'd used that particular Southern phrase on Andrew, who was born and raised in New York City, and he'd looked at her like she was an alien from another planet.

"Yeah, but why fix it up now? Didn't you sell it 'as is'?"

"The buyer wanted us to shore up the windows and doors to protect the interior, and there are a few items I agreed to fix before closing," Lonnie explained, shifting his eyes from her face and out across the yard again.

She got the distinct feeling he wasn't telling her something. Her apprehension about someone else living in the house was quickly replaced with fear that the investor might have more dramatic plans. It was one thing for a new family to live in it, and for her to still be able to drive by and remember when it had been her home, but it was quite another thing if the house wasn't going to look like her house anymore.

"The buyer—what do you know about them?" Callie asked as casually as she could muster, trying not to panic.

"I know enough." He paused as if to decide how much he should reveal to her. "Enough to know it's all for the best." With that he closed his eyes and began to rhythmically rock back and forth, the heels of his cowboy boots clicking on the concrete porch with each repetition.

Uncle Lonnie had made his peace with it. Turning now to gaze down the street in the direction of her childhood home, Callie realized she still had not.

Chapter Four
Jesse

When Callie had shown up the day before, she obviously hadn't known Jesse was the one buying the house. He wondered how long Uncle Lonnie was going to wait to tell her. Jesse still wasn't sure why Uncle Lonnie was keeping it from her, but he'd promised to let her uncle break the news when the time was right. What was she going to think when she found out?

Jesse was unloading his truck the next morning so he could get back to work on the living-room window when he heard a car pull up on the street.

"Thomas." Austin Beckett's voice came from behind him. "How's it going?"

Turning, Jesse started walking down the drive toward where his friend had pulled up to the curb. "Honestly, it's a little overwhelming," he said as he approached.

Fen beat Jesse to the truck, wagging his tail as he sat outside the door.

"You know how you eat an elephant, right?" Austin teased.

"Yeah, yeah." Jesse rolled his eyes. Austin always had a cheesy cliché to fit any situation. "One bite at a time."

"You got it." Austin hopped out and reached down to pet Fen. Closing the truck door and leaning against it, he surveyed the house. "Sure beats working on those new monstrosities you're building down on the south end." He shot Jesse a knowing look.

For those born and raised on the island, the growing influx of tourists and second-home types was disturbing because it brought unwanted development to their quiet enclave. Debate had been raging on the island for decades: how could they balance enough outsiders to keep businesses open with the need to preserve the trees and historic buildings that gave Big Dune Island its appeal?

Jesse hated working on the modern builds and Austin knew it. "Gotta do it. Pays the bills."

"You're a saint, man." Austin shook his head. "Your dad's lucky to have you. I know you don't like what you're building these days, but I know it means a lot to your old man that you're keeping the family biz alive."

Thomas Construction had been run by three generations of Thomases. Jesse had wanted to become a civil engineer who specialized in restoring historic buildings so he could ensure the company played an active role in preserving Big Dune Island. His dad and granddad had been hardworking, honest men who'd built something the community trusted. Yes, his father was proud of him. But Jesse had planned for a more formal education that would allow him to turn it into something bigger. Something worthy of the future he'd planned with Callie.

He'd been on his way, scoring a partial scholarship to Vanderbilt. That was before they'd learned his father's accountant—who also happened to be Jesse's uncle—had been embezzling money from the business, and his family's world fell apart mere weeks ahead of him leaving for Nashville.

His parents couldn't afford his remaining tuition after what happened. Instead, he'd planned to simply go to Nashville and attend the cheaper junior college in town, get a job to set aside some money, and try to get grades that could land a full scholarship to Vanderbilt after a year or two—but Callie hadn't let him. She'd broken his heart, and he'd ended up staying on Big Dune Island helping his father save the business.

"What's it like being back in this house again?" Austin asked.

Although they didn't talk about it, Jesse knew Austin was aware he'd never completely gotten over Callie.

"It's like a time capsule," Jesse admitted. "I don't think Uncle Lonnie felt it was his place to clean it out, so he left it. Kinda eerie."

"Is she coming back to pack it up?" Austin raised an eyebrow.

"Apparently so. She's here now."

"In the house?" Austin's mouth was gaping open as he looked over Jesse's shoulder as if Callie might walk out the front door right on cue.

"No, she was here last night."

"Wow." Austin wiped off the sweat that was accumulating on his forehead in the morning sun. It wasn't even the beginning of summer according to the calendar, but it was already creeping into the eighties every day. "What was that like?"

"Awkward," Jesse said. "Lonnie hasn't told her I'm the one buying the house. She thinks he's hired me as some kind of handyman." Jesse laughed at the idea, but not at her expense. Why would she know what he did these days?

They hadn't spoken since the funeral nine years earlier, and even that had only been his strained attempt at offering condolences in front of his parents, while the music journalist she was dating stood at her side. All day, he'd fought back waves of jealousy and tried to focus on the loss of two of Big Dune Island's most beloved residents. He'd still been angry with her, but he would have forgotten it all if she'd shown up alone and turned to him for support. He'd hoped she'd need him in a time like that, but then she'd rolled into town with that slick hipster of a boyfriend in his slim-cut suit with pants so short you could tell he wasn't wearing socks with his dress shoes. What kind of guy didn't wear socks with dress shoes?

"How do you think she's going to take the news?" Austin's question brought Jesse back to the present.

"Hard to say. I can't imagine she'd ever want to live in it again when she can't even bring herself to go inside, but she did sound a little heartbroken about it being sold."

"Wait until she finds out you're the one who bought it."

Austin's tone was joking, but Jesse knew his friend was sympathetic to the situation. Jesse was in a bind with the company's investors—who had owned part of Thomas Construction since it nearly went belly-up—and buying the Lyman house was his last idea for keeping the company from becoming like all the other developers on the island who cared more about making money than preserving their little slice of paradise.

He'd always tried to keep the family drama with his uncle quiet because it was so embarrassing. Whose own flesh and blood steals from them? But Austin had been his best friend his entire life, and had always preferred hanging out with Jesse's dad over his own demanding father, so he'd been right there at the kitchen table the night the Thomases got the phone call that changed their lives.

"I don't envy you, man." Austin broke into Jesse's thoughts as he slapped him on the back. "I'm off to the salt mines." He opened the door to his truck and climbed back inside.

"Yeah, try not to sprain anything reaching for the mic today." Jesse laughed. Unlike him, Austin had been able to leave the island after high school. He'd come back following an injury that cut his professional baseball career short to host a sports radio show down in Jacksonville, a little less than an hour to their south. Next to Callie, he was the most famous person to have come out of Big Dune Island.

Tapping Austin's new-model black Ford a couple of times on the door as a goodbye, Jesse turned toward the house, calling for Fen to follow him as Austin drove away. As he looked at the house, he tried to picture adult Callie standing up on the front porch, greeting visitors. His head wasn't ready to admit he hoped she'd buy it when the renovation was complete, but it was pretty clear what his heart thought.

———

WHEN HE FINISHED THE LIVING ROOM WINDOW AND caulking the others that were still intact downstairs, Jesse grabbed some lumber from his truck and headed out back to trim it down into a new doorjamb. Rounding the corner of the house, he caught a glimpse of the old wooden swing that hung from the oak at the perimeter of the yard. The rope was frayed, one side down to mere threads. He was instantly struck by a memory, as he was most days at Callie's house. He'd walked her home from school when she was in kindergarten and he was the older second-grader. One day, she'd run to the backyard, throwing her backpack on the ground and leaping onto the swing. She lay on her stomach instead of sitting on it like a normal person.

"Sitting on the swing is boring, Jesse," she'd teased him,

her blonde curls blowing in the breeze and her blue eyes twinkling with excitement.

He hadn't been old enough to like girls in that way yet, but he remembered thinking she was something fragile, something he needed to protect. And she'd proved him right when she went flying face-first into the dirt. He'd run to her, but before he could get there she was already swiping at the blood on her arm and stifling tears to show how tough she was. But he'd seen the scared look in her eyes and knew she was only pretending. When he'd gotten home, his mom told him it was his job as the older one to watch after her and make sure she was safe. He'd taken that charge seriously and had been right there to pick her up every time she'd stumbled. Then one day she moved to Nashville and suddenly didn't need him anymore.

The day on the swing was his earliest memory of her, but it wasn't the first time they'd met. Their parents had all been high school friends and had introduced them when he was merely a toddler and she was a baby, fresh home from the hospital. They'd been inseparable from that day on.

Until Callie signed her record deal.

It all happened so suddenly it still didn't feel real, even thirteen years later. One day she was a rising junior on the makeshift stage built on Main Beach for the town's annual Beach Bash that welcomed in summer, singing for a crowd of a few hundred tourists and locals, then seemingly the next day she was being homeschooled on the road, opening for some of the biggest names in country music before releasing her first album and headlining her own tour.

He'd been there that day on the beach, like he'd been at every school, church, theater, and American Legion where she'd ever picked up a microphone. If he was honest, it was part of why he'd applied to Vanderbilt, so she could join him after she graduated the following year and pursue her music career.

It all changed the night of that year's Beach Bash though. He'd been in the front row cheering her on as she sang her five-song set. By the time she came off the stage, the record executive was already talking to her parents, and Jesse held her hand as they trudged through the sand to say hi to them afterward, Callie's blonde curls stuck to her forehead from the sweltering summer heat.

"Honey, come here," her mom gushed as she approached. "I want you to meet Mr. Wiseman."

"Well, hey there," Callie drawled, still breathless from her performance. "Nice to meet you."

Jesse's gut had sent out distress signals. It was a small town, the kind where everyone knew everyone, and you couldn't walk down Main Street without stopping a half-dozen times to talk about the weather or local politics. He'd never seen this man before in his life. And although the island was a popular destination for tourists this time of year, something about him seemed off. Mr. Wiseman's sweat-soaked body had his linen shirt sticking to his chest and stomach. He was wearing boat shoes, but they were clearly brand new and had never actually seen time on a boat or gotten wet. He was the only person on the beach with full-length pants, a belt, and closed-toe shoes. Beach Bash was more of a swimming trunks and flip-flops sort of thing.

"Jim Wiseman." The man extended his hand to Callie. "I'm the president of Big Blue Records."

At the same instant Callie's jaw visibly dropped, Jesse's heart did too.

CHAPTER FIVE
CALLIE

Callie decided to walk from Uncle Lonnie's to Gigi's office for lunch since it was only five blocks. Moments later, however, she found herself standing in front of her childhood home. She'd meant to avoid going by the house and risking another encounter with Jesse, but she'd been on autopilot, lost in thought over her conversation with Uncle Lonnie, walking a path from his house to hers the way she'd done hundreds of times as a kid.

Jesse's truck was in the driveway, and her initial reaction was to bolt in the opposite direction. They'd been civil—even friendly—the day before, but they'd kept everything surface level. She wasn't sure she was ready to confront the feelings that had been bubbling up ever since. Having to go back into the house without her parents again was stressful enough without having to face the second-biggest heartbreak of her life at the same time.

The sound of a saw cut through the thick, early summer air as she stood on the sidewalk. It sounded as if it was coming from the backyard, and she was so overcome with curiosity she couldn't help but try to sneak a peek. Staying close to the side of the house, she tiptoed toward the back, venturing a glance around an azalea bush at the corner of the house. Jesse was standing with his back to her, meticulously measuring out a piece of wood laid across the twin sawhorses. She could see Fen a few feet away from where Jesse was working, chewing on a tennis ball.

Jesse marked a spot on the 2x4, and then slipped the measuring tape into the back of his jeans pocket. She hadn't wanted him to catch her studying him on the deck the night before, but now she had time to look more closely. His dark blond hair had been highlighted by the sun over the years. It was cut much shorter now, not floppy like it had been when he was a teenager, and his face was more angular. He'd been a cute teenager, but he'd certainly become an even more handsome man; she'd worked hard not to let her heart flutter every time she'd caught him looking at her the previous night. As he pulled down the circular saw to make his cut, she caught sight of his bicep moving under the sleeve of his navy t-shirt and knew she had to leave before she had anymore thoughts about the man Jesse had become—even though she knew that sense of their old spark was just her body's automatic response to something familiar.

As she moved away from the bush back to the street, she tripped on a tree root snaking its way across the side yard from an old oak tree. She hoped no one heard the *oof* that had escaped her lips. Why couldn't Jesse have been sawing when she took her tumble? Retreating quickly, she heard Fen rustling in the brush behind her and Jesse calling for him to "knock it off." She'd almost reached the front of the house, where she could round the corner and be hidden again, when the dog spotted her and let out excited barks.

She made it to the front of the house and stopped, her pounding heart making it difficult to listen for Jesse's footsteps. Was he coming to investigate? There was nowhere to go from here that didn't leave her exposed, so she stood still against the garage doors, watching the corner of the house.

"Callie?" His voice came from behind her, causing her to jump and let out a surprised yelp.

He'd gone through the house and exited the front door, and was standing on the bottom step of the porch.

Turning slowly, she lowered her sunglasses. "Caught me." She forced a laugh to cover the nerves threatening to take over.

"Nice hat." He took a red rag out of his back pocket, looking down while he wiped his hands.

Her heart was pounding in her ears as she realized what he meant. It was a Boston Red Sox hat she'd stolen from him in high school. Over the years she'd told herself she kept it because it was big enough to allow her to pile her blonde curls underneath and remain incognito, but, if she was being honest, she'd held on to it because of the memories. Not just of Jesse; it was a reminder of the young girl she'd been with big dreams. She'd hesitated to put it on this morning knowing she might run into him, but a part of her had wanted him to see her in it, to prove she hadn't been "getting rid of the dead weight that might hold her back" as he'd accused her all those years ago.

"Hope you don't want it back." She reached up to straighten it on her head. "Gigi taught me all about adverse possession when she was fighting with old man Travis about her fence last winter. Pretty sure I have rights now after all these years."

"Nah, keep it." There was a smile tugging at the corner of his mouth. "Looks better on you."

Her cheeks warmed and she shifted her eyes away from his. He was looking at her the way he used to when they'd been teenagers kissing goodnight in this very spot, as her mother turned on the porch light to signal it was time to come in. He took a step forward and she resisted the urge to immediately move back. She'd made sure to keep distance between them the day before. But now he was standing so close she could see the small freckles that dotted his green eyes.

"You missed a piece." He reached up to gently tuck a curl back into the left side of her hat. His hand lingered there, and she inhaled the smell of sawdust and the Irish Spring soap he'd always used. She fought the part of her that wanted to press her face into the cup of his hand.

"Thanks." Her voice was quiet now as she stepped back and ran her hand under both sides of the hat to ensure her hair was safely beneath. "Can't be too careful." She cleared her throat. "You know how it is." No sooner were the words out of her mouth than she realized he had no idea what it was like to have people constantly taking your photo and splashing it across magazine covers and social media posts.

"I don't reckon I do." He stuffed his hands in his jeans pockets. "Want to go inside and get out of the limelight for a minute?" He nodded his head at the open front door.

Callie couldn't tell if he was teasing her or accusing her of being arrogant about her celebrity. As he turned and took a step toward the door, panic immediately rose in her throat. As long as she'd stayed away from the island, she'd been able to pretend her parents were still there, right behind the door. But as soon as she walked in that house, she'd have to face the emptiness. Her mother wouldn't be in the kitchen singing Dolly Parton and Reba McEntire. Her father wouldn't be on the couch reading the sports section of the paper.

"No, I can't stay," she stammered, retreating backward down the driveway. "I was just walking by and heard the sawing, that's all."

"It's still your family's house," Jesse said, as if the source of her discomfort was the sale.

"Oh, I know." She took another step back. "I'm meeting Gigi though. If I don't go over to her office she'll never lock up and leave, and she promised me she'd only work a half day." Giving an awkward wave, she turned and practically jogged to the sidewalk. She could feel his eyes on her, but she didn't dare turn back or slow down until she rounded the corner at the end of the block.

She wasn't ready to face any more time with Jesse, and she definitely wasn't prepared to face the house. She knew she'd have to go inside soon, but it didn't have to be today, and it definitely didn't have to be with her ex-boyfriend as an audience.

———

It was only a short walk through Big Dune Island's historic downtown to get from her childhood home to Gigi's office, where they were supposed to meet for lunch. This time of day the streets were still quiet, so Callie decided to chance walking down Main Street to see what had changed over the past decade. It was nearing the end of May and already hot outside, but the sticky summer weather that would necessitate an air-conditioned vehicle for even short distances hadn't settled in yet. That would change by next month, but Callie was only staying a couple of weeks.

She turned onto Main Street as the sun began to rise higher in the sky to the east, the stores now all open for the day. Shopkeepers were busy sweeping in front of their doors, several bringing out bowls filled to the brim with fresh water to entice passersby with dogs to stop and window shop while their furry companions lapped up a drink. It was quiet most days before lunch, but then the tourists would fill the shops and restaurants. The island's accommodations were a mile or more away on the east side, along the twelve miles of pristine beach that regularly graced multi-page spreads in glossy travel magazines, bestowing it with titles like "Happiest Seaside Town."

Not much had changed on Main Street since Callie was a teenager. Hurricane Eugenia had brought a rising river tide onto the street, but Uncle Lonnie told her only a few of the stores nearest to the river experienced any water intrusion. Most of the damage around town was from weak limbs in the old oak trees that had either fallen on roofs or been blown by the wind through plate-glass windows like the ones at her childhood home.

Callie had removed her sunglasses to get a closer look at beach-themed knickknacks on a bookshelf in the window of a decor store, searching for a gift Gigi might like, when she realized, too late, that someone had approached her on the sidewalk.

"Callie Jackson, is that you?"

Callie searched the woman's face for anything she recognized. Her brunette hair curled at the ends into a bob that fell under her ears. With her small nose and doll-like features, she was the definition of cute. Normal people stayed connected with high school classmates on Facebook these days, and would recognize each other from the photos, but Callie's lifestyle hadn't lent itself to staying in touch with childhood acquaintances.

"It's me," the woman said excitedly. "Chloe." She barely paused long enough for Callie to register the name. "Chloe Beckett, Austin's sister. I recognized you, even with that hat covering up those curls of yours." She smiled broadly, congratulating herself for being too smart to fool.

Jesse's best friend's kid sister? The one who had started all those rumors in high school? Gigi had told Callie that Chloe owned Island Coffee now, where every downtown resident got their morning brew. *Perfect, just perfect.* Word traveled fast in a small town, and it would only take running into someone like

Chloe for everyone to know Callie was back. She wasn't interested in their sympathy about her parents, or in signing autographs, or discussing her recent downfall, and those were sure to be the options for most conversations.

"Chloe." Callie mirrored Chloe's bubbly tone, faking enthusiasm the way any well-mannered Southern woman would do. "So nice to see you. How are you?" It was a perfunctory question expected in a place like Big Dune Island. As much as she wanted to get away from Chloe as quickly as possible, she thought of what her mother would say about the importance of being kind and making time for others.

"I'm great." Chloe's brunette bob bounced up and down as she gushed, "I read about what happened with your label, and I was so sorry. That's terrible. But you're basically the most talented person I know, so you'll totally be back on your feet in no time! Omigosh, I saw you on TV performing at the music awards last year. Holy smokes, I barely recognized you."

You and me both. Callie remembered looking in the mirror that night, feeling self-conscious in her leather boots and too-tight, too-short black sequined dress, and imagining what her parents would think if they could have seen her. Sure, switching from country to pop had made her more "mainstream," as Andrew had called it when he'd first broached the idea with her, but selling more albums and filling bigger stadiums hadn't made her happier. In fact, she'd felt even more isolated and alone than she had in the days following her parents' deaths. It was part of why she'd finally agreed to a real date with Andrew and let herself get carried away with him and all his big ideas about "going indie" and making their own records together. She didn't like her career as it was, so figured she might as well try something different.

Chloe was still looking at her expectantly, no doubt waiting for a morsel about how fabulous her life was in Nashville or even a tidbit or two about the failure of her record label.

"Yeah." Callie tried to laugh it off, sticking with a safe subject. "You never know what those stylists are going to dress you up in."

"It's totally amazing though, right?" Chloe was beaming at Callie like a teenage girl admiring a poster of a boy band. "Nashville and Los Angeles; it must all be so cool."

Callie told Chloe what she expected to hear while glancing over her shoulder, hoping no one else was around to overhear and recognize her. "It's definitely had its perks."

"I've got simple taste, I guess. I've got everything I ever wanted here. I love this town; don't you just love this town? It's so great you're back." Chloe was holding grocery bags in one hand, but used her free arm to reach over and grab Callie in an enthusiastic embrace.

Still trying to catch up with Chloe's level of enthusiasm, Callie hugged her back. She had to admit her walk downtown *was* reminding her how much she loved this place. Even if she didn't feel the same about the conversation she was being forced to have right now.

"Yeah, everything looks great." Callie glanced around again to make sure their reunion was still private. "Hasn't changed much, but I guess that's a good thing in a historic town."

"Well, there are developers who would salivate over getting their hands on some of these properties in the historic district." She leaned in before lowering her voice. "Speaking of building things, have you seen Jesse yet?"

That turned personal awfully fast. Funny how much small-town living was like being a celebrity; everyone thought they had a right to the details of your private life. Jesse was the last topic she wanted to discuss with Chloe.

Thankfully, a passing truck honked and diverted Chloe's

attention away from Callie, as its occupant—who looked to be Mr. Lawson, a former Big Dune Island mayor—asked Chloe what flavor muffins she had in stock this morning at the coffee shop. By the time Chloe turned back, Callie had a question locked and loaded to change the subject.

"Gigi told me you own Island Coffee now. That's awesome. Congratulations! I don't want to keep you from it, though—this must be a busy time of the day for you." Callie hoped she would take the hint and they could head their separate ways.

"Well, I own it with Austin." Chloe was sheepish now. "He's mostly a silent partner."

No doubt Austin bought the cafe for his kid sister with the money he'd made as a professional baseball player. It was sweet. Callie wished her family had let her do more for them over the years, but they never liked letting her pay for anything. Her parents had always flatly refused, and Uncle Lonnie had followed suit, even after their deaths. Their generation was too proud, she guessed. Good for Chloe for letting Austin spoil her a little. What was the point in making a lot of money if you couldn't use it to make the people you loved happy? Or was that the kind of thinking that had gotten Callie into trouble with Andrew?

"Speaking of the coffee shop, I better get back. I just ran out for more milk." Chloe held up the two full grocery bags as evidence. "The men's club should be there by now, solving the world's problems."

She was referring to the group of retired men who had gathered there every morning for as long as Callie could remember. It was nice to know some things stayed the same. The members of this "club" had changed over the years of her childhood as some passed on and other men took their place after retiring and being shooed out of the house by wives not used to having them home. But they'd always been at the cafe during the 9–10 a.m. hour, and could be overheard discussing everything from local politics to the nationwide avocado shortage.

"Can't solve the world's problems without coffee." Callie glanced around again. "Hey, do you think we could keep this between us? You seeing me? I'm not in town long and want to concentrate on spending some time with my uncle." The last thing she wanted was half the town stopping by offering to help her pack up or get rid of her parents' things.

Chloe's smile fell instantly, and Callie steeled herself for what she knew was coming next.

Her voice lowered, Chloe said, "Of course. I totally understand." She looked down at her feet, avoiding Callie's eyes.

Sympathy. Callie would have preferred being asked for an autograph.

After saying a quick goodbye and thanking Chloe for helping keep her secret, Callie crossed over 4th Street on the original cobblestones that had once paved all the local roads. Callie's mom and her friends at the historical society had fought to save the cobblestones for use in the crosswalks when the road had been resurfaced. Her mother had instilled in her a love of history, but particularly when it came to preserving Big Dune Island's heritage. Dubbed the Isle of Eight Flags for being the only place in America to be ruled under eight different nations, Callie had always loved walking downtown as a kid and imagining the days when real-life pirates had walked the same streets. Today, the only pirates were the mascot at the high school, and the costumed ones who took part in the "Pirate Invasion" tradition: running down Main Street from the marina to signal the start of Beach Bash, the town's annual summer festival.

Callie was comforted by the familiar signs for The Sailor's Wife, a used bookstore, and Henderson Hardware. Most of the shops had been passed down from one generation to the next by families whose ancestors had established the original commercial buildings in the late 1800s. Even the "newer" businesses had been around all of Callie's life.

As she continued down Main Street toward the river, she walked slowly to take in the creative window displays heralding the beginning of the summer season: the souvenir shops decorated with bold primary colors to attract the children who passed by, tempting them with sand pails and molds for sandcastles; and one of the home decor stores decked out its display in the soft-blue and green palette found in many of the homes on the island. But it was the neon-yellow flyer on the door of Lindy's, one of the local jewelers, that stopped Callie in her tracks.

SAVE THE BEACH BASH
Town Meeting
Wednesday, 7 p.m.
Historic Courthouse

SAVE THE BEACH BASH? SAVE IT FROM WHAT? Neither Gigi nor Uncle Lonnie had mentioned the festival was in danger. They both knew how much it meant to her; the festival was where she'd first been discovered by the record label, after all.

It was hard not to feel as if the universe was conspiring against her to take away everything.

CHAPTER SIX
JESSE

"Come on!" Jesse exclaimed to an empty backyard, holding up a new doorframe that was a full inch too short to fill the opening for the back door. Thankfully, there was no one around but Fen to witness his mistake. It was the second piece he'd cut wrong since Callie left, but he told himself the nervous stomach that had kept him from eating his tuna fish sandwich for lunch was about his afternoon meeting with Michael Russo, who ran the day-to-day for the group of investors.

Throwing in the towel for the day, he headed home to shower and change before heading to Island Coffee to go over the updated budget for the renovation. Although having the investor's money had been a blessing for Thomas Construction all those years ago, Jesse hated writing up these detailed budgets that accounted for every nut and bolt.

Settling into his usual seat, an aqua-colored booth that ran along the left side of the long, narrow shotgun-style interior of the cafe, Jesse checked his watch. He was fifteen minutes early. That gave him time to go over the numbers again. He shuffled and organized his pile of paper, making a neat stack on the table.

"Sweet tea?" Chloe called out to him as she walked by to deliver food to a tourist couple by the windows.

"Yeah, thanks." He read back over the amendments to the budget, reciting the justifications he'd come up with for each new expense. He mentally practiced his speech about how it was going to cost a little more than he'd originally projected, but he was positive they'd get their investment returned on the backside.

Chloe returned a few minutes later, plunking a delectable-looking treat in front of him. "One sweet tea and one slice of my key lime strawberry cheesecake."

"I didn't order cheesecake." He held up the small white plate adorned with tiny blue flowers along its edge. "Although this does look pretty good."

"Trying out a new flavor combo and need some honest feedback. Go ahead, try it."

Jesse took a bite and gave the appropriate oohs and ahhs to show he approved of her latest creation. It was delicious, but he still couldn't seem to work up an appetite. Chloe continued to hover over the table, as if waiting for him to say something more. "It's really good, Chloe. Thanks."

"Anything else you want to tell me?" She raised an eyebrow to make it clear she knew something she expected him to tell her.

"Michael's in town?" He tried to guess the right answer. "I know, that's who I'm meeting." Jesse knew she had a thing for Michael, but he could tell by her shocked expression that she'd been unaware it was so obvious.

"He is?" Her eyes darted to the door of the coffee shop. Smoothing down her hair with both hands, she glanced above Jesse at the mirrored wall extending from the booth to the ceiling, and tucked one side of her short brunette bob behind an ear.

"Yep, on his way now." Jesse pushed aside the dessert plate so he could concentrate on the budget documents.

The bell attached to the door rang, jerking Chloe's attention away from the mirror. She called out a rushed hello to Alice Barker, president of the garden club, before turning back to Jesse. "Well, I wasn't expecting him. But I did see someone else I was surprised to see in town today." Her eyes were still glued up front.

"Really?" He played dumb. "Who'd you see?"

Leaning in conspiratorially, she whispered, "Callie." When he continued to stare at her deadpan, she rolled her eyes and exclaimed a little more loudly, "Callie Jackson!"

He looked around to see if anyone had heard her. He was positive Callie didn't want all of Big Dune Island knowing she was back; that's why she'd been sneaking around in that old Red Sox hat of his. His stomach had flip-flopped at the sight of her in it after all these years, and he'd tried not to let himself think about what it meant. Especially not with this meeting looming. It had taken him years to convince the investors to allow him to renovate a historic property. Now wasn't the time to take his eye off the ball.

"Hey." He made a downward motion with one hand. "Take it down a notch. I don't think she wants everyone knowing she's here."

"So you do know," she said, her smile stretching from ear to ear, no longer making any attempt to whisper. "I knew she'd never come back to town and not see you."

"She did not come to see me, Chloe." He was stern with her now. "She's here to see Uncle Lonnie and Gigi."

Jesse's dad and Austin were the only people other than the investors and Callie's uncle who knew he was buying the Lyman house. As far as anyone else was concerned, Uncle Lonnie had simply hired him for some repairs. It would be public knowledge soon enough, but he was keeping it under wraps as long as possible. Jesse didn't need the whole town gossiping about him, wondering why he bought Callie Jackson's old house. Everyone knew they'd been an item in high school. It would only be worse if they found out Callie was here. And Chloe and her coffee shop were Grand Central Station for gossip on Big Dune Island.

"Does she know Uncle Lonnie's got you over there working on her house?" Chloe leaned in again, her big blue eyes searching his for clues. "Maybe that's why she came back. To, you know, supervise you a little more closely." She wiggled her eyebrows, the whole scene no doubt playing out in her mind.

"Yes, she's aware." He frowned at her to discourage this line of questioning. He figured keeping his answers short and simple was the way to go so he didn't have to outright lie to her.

The bell on the door jingled again, drawing Chloe's eyes away. Jesse wasn't sure he'd ever been so happy to see Michael.

A New Yorker from the Bronx, the investor stood out like a sore thumb on Big Dune Island. Dress attire on the island meant pants and close-toed shoes instead of shorts and flip-flops, but no matter how much time Michael spent in town he'd never converted. From his slicked-back black hair to his pinstripe suit, he looked like he belonged in a mob movie, though Jesse had worked with him long enough to know he was a teddy bear underneath.

It only took Michael a dozen steps to get across the small cafe to Jesse's table.

"Your usual?" Chloe asked him.

"You remember my order?" Michael was impressed.

"Sure I do." She winked. "Be right back." With that, she turned on a heel and scurried back behind the glass counter that displayed dozens of fresh-baked breads and pastries Chloe made herself each morning.

"Jesse, my man." Michael took the dining chair across the table from the booth-style bench along the wall, where Jesse sat. "Good to see you."

He reached out a fist, which Jesse proceeded to bump with his. Whatever happened to handshakes? Didn't they do those in New York anymore?

Palms suddenly sweaty, heart thumping in his ears, Jesse decided to warm up first. "How long you in town for?"

Michael was the only one of the investors who ever came to town, and he was usually in and out within a matter of hours. He was close to Jesse's age, and they'd fallen into a rhythm of working with one another over the years, although they often disagreed about what was "in the best interest of the business." Jesse reminded himself it had been Michael who'd convinced the rest of the investor group to restore the Lyman house. He hadn't had to do Jesse a favor.

"I fly out of Jacksonville tonight. Just looking at a couple more lots on the south end." He was referring to the more affluent part of the island where the investors cashed in by buying up undeveloped land and turning it into exclusive neighborhoods of custom-built homes. "Then it's back to the bright lights of the big city for me. I still haven't figured out what it is you do around here at night. Seriously, man, how do you meet women?"

Clearly, Michael hadn't noticed Chloe's flirting yet. As for Jesse, he didn't meet new women often. Sure, there were a few who'd flirted with him once they knew Callie was never coming back, but he hadn't been on more than a handful of dates with any of them over the years.

"I already know everyone here." Jesse laughed because it was true. He'd resided on Big Dune Island for nearly all his thirty-one years and could name the owner of every shop here on Main Street and tell you where they each lived.

"I don't know how you do it." Michael shook his head. "Better you than me."

As if on cue, Chloe appeared with Michael's drink, turning her back on Jesse as she presented it as if she was serving a king. "A soy latte with an extra shot of espresso." She extended the mug to the New Yorker.

"Thanks." He said it dismissively, not looking up or making any move to take the drink from her hand.

Chloe placed it on the table in front of him, her shoulders slumping as she retreated.

Michael picked up his mug and took a sip. "So whatta you got for me?" His New York accent had become more pronounced, as it always did when he talked business.

Jesse slid a duplicate copy of the budget across the table and walked him through the historic preservation tax credits he'd confirmed were available for the project from the state—a dollar-for-dollar credit the company could claim—and the ten-year tax abatement the house would qualify for under the local code. It was always best to lead with the good news.

"If something sounds too good to be true, it usually is. What's the downside? What are expenses looking like?"

Jesse took a deep breath. This was the part of the speech he'd rehearsed over and over. Michael hadn't flipped to the second page of the revised budget yet, but Jesse knew what the reaction would be when he did.

"Well, the house is over a hundred years old," Jesse started, pausing to clear his throat. "And it looks like it needs all new plumbing and electric. Basically, everything has to be brought up to code. The windows and doors all need to be replaced, and we'll have to source ones that fit the period in order to get approval from the Historic District Commission."

Michael held up a hand to stop him. "The Hysterical

District Commission?" he said, using his sarcastic nickname for the board. "Please tell me I don't have to go deal with the good old boys' club again."

Michael hadn't made any friends when he'd had to go before the commission on a previous project. There was a "good old boys' club," as Michael had put it, and they didn't like outsiders. Michael wouldn't have gotten the variance if his expensive New York attorney hadn't found a loophole in the city ordinance.

"Sorry, I know they're not your cup of tea."

"Jesse, I don't drink tea. And I'm not interested in getting involved in small-town politics again."

"I know," Jesse reassured him. "I have a plan. I just need you to approve the legal expense on the second page so I can hire a local attorney. Her name is Gigi Franklin, and I grew up with her. She's sharp, and she can charm the heck out of the commission."

Michael flipped the page while Jesse held his breath, prepared to further make the case for Gigi.

"This is what you need for legal?" Michael tapped his finger on the number.

"Well, it's an estimate." Jesse was afraid it was a little too much. "I spoke with a neighbor who used her for a similar matter and that's what he paid." He didn't want to tell Michael the real reason he hadn't gone to Gigi yet. She was the best land-use attorney in town, but she also happened to be Callie's best friend. He couldn't tell Gigi he was the one buying the house—at least not yet.

Michael leaned back in his chair and let out a hardy laugh. "Okay, I was wrong. I love this town."

Jesse stared back at him confused. "So... we can hire her when the time comes?"

"Yeah, sure," Michael said, casually drinking more of his latte. "If she can get it done at that number, ask if she can handle our next city commission meeting too."

"Umm, okay." He still wasn't quite clear.

"Do you know how much we spent on that last bout with the city?"

"No." Jesse started to get an idea of where this was going.

"Five times that." Michael tapped the figure on the page again. "That's the difference between a New York City attorney and one around here, I guess."

Jesse should have been relieved Michael approved the expense, but it only meant he was getting closer to Callie learning the truth. Would she be relieved the house was in good hands? Or would she feel betrayed by both him and Uncle Lonnie? Jesse knew Uncle Lonnie hoped coming back to town and facing the house would help shake Callie out of a funk she'd been in ever since her music career took a nosedive.

Jesse told himself he let Uncle Lonnie talk him into buying the house to renovate because it was a good deal, but feelings he thought he'd put to bed a long time ago had gotten stirred up just like the dust in the house when he first opened the front door. He still remembered walking in that first day and catching himself listening for her guitar or expecting to smell her favorite coconut lotion, as if he could still find her there.

"What about the rest of this?" Michael thumbed through the pages of the budget. "Can't we install new floors? It'll be cheaper."

"They're the original heart pine floors. You can't just rip them out. The historic commission would never go for that."

"You're telling me they get to tell us what we can do *inside* the house too?" Michael was incredulous.

"Yes. If we don't stick to the historic guidelines, no tax credits."

"Okay, Jesse." Michael closed his eyes and pinched his

forehead above his nose. "Please don't make me regret agreeing to this house."

"You're not going to regret it, I promise." Jesse hoped he sounded surer than he felt. The house was a bit rougher looking inside than he'd imagined when he made the deal with Uncle Lonnie.

"What about the niece? Has the old man told her yet?"

Jesse froze, his glass halfway to his mouth. Michael didn't know "the niece" was singer Callie Jackson. Jesse knew how Michael and his team operated; they'd exploit Callie's connection to the house, use it to drive up the price. What Michael did know was that Jesse was buying the house from a friend of the family, an older gentleman who was concerned about doing right by his niece. Jesse had earned the investors' trust over the years, so they had let him handle all the due diligence.

"No, she doesn't know yet." He looked down, concentrating on an ice cube floating in his tea instead of meeting Michael's eyes.

"Why'd he want the right of first refusal provision if he's keeping the sale such a big secret? You people fascinate me down here, it's like a soap opera." Michael shook his head.

Michael was referring to the right of first refusal Uncle Lonnie had insisted be part of the deal, which gave Callie the ability to buy the house herself at the end of the restoration at a reasonable price. Her uncle hadn't wanted to burden her with facing the house, and when Jesse mentioned he was looking for a historic property to renovate, Uncle Lonnie hatched a plan. He would give Callie the money from the sale of the house if she ultimately decided to buy it back, so she'd only need to pay for the renovations, which the house desperately needed before it deteriorated further. Uncle Lonnie wanted to restore the house before it was too damaged to save, but he was too proud to accept any of Callie's money, even for that. When he found out Jesse was waiting for a historic property to go up for sale so he could attempt a preservation project, Uncle Lonnie had hoped he could light a fire under Callie.

The plan was to sell Jesse the house slightly below market price, so he could show a good profit margin to the investors. Then she would have a choice as to whether she wanted to hold on to the house or let it go. Based on his past with her, Jesse thought Callie had no problem letting things go. But after seeing her reaction to the house, he wondered if it meant more to her than he had.

Jesse shrugged his shoulders. "You know how families are."

"Whatever." Michael pushed aside his now-empty coffee mug and stood to signify the meeting was over. "No skin off my teeth. It's a solid profit if she takes it, otherwise we'll put it on the market."

Jesse tried to imagine someone else living in the Lyman house, but all he could see was Callie on the front porch strumming her guitar and humming a tune. It had been a long time since he'd let himself picture her back on Big Dune Island, and now she was here. And despite everything that had happened, and the realization that he didn't really know her anymore, it was becoming obvious it would break his heart all over again when she inevitably left.

CHAPTER SEVEN
CALLIE

"Come on, Callie." Gigi held up her hands in prayer, begging. "I never get out now that I'm a lawyer. Help me live a little."

They'd finished eating dinner on the back deck of the cottage, the intoxicating sound of waves crashing mixing with the gulls calling overhead, when Gigi brought up the idea of going to Breakwaters, one of the only bars on the island.

"No way, someone might recognize me. I just want to stay safely tucked here on your couch in front of the TV in my sweats."

Gigi held up a finger, signaling for Callie to wait, then she darted back inside through the sliding glass doors. "Look what I got you," she said when she returned, reaching into a shopping bag to produce a short, auburn-colored wig with a blunt bob cut, and a matching one in platinum blonde. She lifted them up triumphantly.

Callie couldn't help but laugh. It looked like the first disguise she'd worn after she "made it big" and had a few days off to visit Gigi in law school. She'd brought Gigi a platinum-blonde wig with Bond-girl vibes and they'd gone out on the town one night. They'd both looked so ridiculous that they'd doubled over in laughter every time they'd seen themselves together in a mirror.

"I'll even let you wear cowboy boots," Gigi teased.

Callie had confided in her last year about an argument with Andrew over cowboy boots. She'd wanted to wear them out to dinner one night, and he'd pulled out his usual speech about how it wasn't "on brand" for her anymore. Apparently pop singers wouldn't be caught dead wearing cowboy boots in public.

Callie's resolve softened. It would feel deliciously good to do something Andrew wouldn't approve of.

"Tempting," Callie said, "but I didn't bring any."

"We're the same size; borrow mine." Gigi smiled, pouncing on the crack in Callie's argument. She was entering full attorney mode, ready to negotiate. "One hour, that's all I ask. It'll be like old times. And, seriously, look at this wig. How can you resist?"

Laughing, Callie rolled her eyes. "I'll make you a deal." She walked over to the kitchen and reached across the center island to grab the wig from Gigi's outstretched hand. "You figure out how to get me out of my recording contract, and I'll go with you for *one* hour."

"Deal," Gigi squealed. "A night out and detective work? Sign me up!"

———

GIGI WAS FAR MORE AMUSED THAN CALLIE TO LEARN it was open-mic night when they arrived at Breakwaters.

"Go on, get up there and show them how it's done." Gigi laughed, patting her on the butt like a coach encouraging a starting pitcher during a chat on the mound.

"Would you be quiet," she hissed, looking around the room to be sure no one recognized them. Luckily, the crowd looked to be barely old enough to be in the bar, so Callie didn't immediately see anyone she knew.

As they wedged themselves into a corner, a man in a cowboy hat that was a bit too big for his head finished his attempt at "Elvira," a tough one to cover because of its wide vocal range. A smattering of applause followed, and Callie relaxed and clapped along with them because she knew how difficult it was to get on a mic and let other people judge you.

Next up, the emcee said, was a young lady named Sienna Leighton. Callie watched as a girl in her late teens or early twenties climbed the three stairs at the edge of the stage, a guitar strapped around her. Sienna wore a long, flowing skirt with tiny purple flowers, the toes of her cowboy boots poking out from underneath.

Callie knew the song the instant the girl strummed the opening chords, "Me and You Someday." She had written it her first week in Nashville; a love letter to Jesse. It had also been her first No. 1 single. She hadn't heard the song in years, which had been for the best as far as she was concerned.

Gigi nudged Callie, her mouth open wide in surprise. She gave her a stern look, and Gigi turned her attention back to the stage.

As Sienna closed her eyes and sang, Callie recalled the real night that inspired the lyrics; her final night on the island. They'd driven onto the beach at sunset, let down the tailgate of Jesse's truck, and eaten the picnic she'd packed. They'd still been sitting there as the sun slipped behind them, darkness falling all around like a curtain call as he held her hand and she leaned her head against his shoulder. She remembered wishing she could hit pause and stay like that forever.

On the tailgate of your truck
Young love and a little luck

Sometimes we laugh, sometimes we play
It's gonna be me and you someday

As Sienna crooned, Callie glanced around the room, suddenly paranoid about sitting this close to someone singing her song. But everyone was captivated by the girl on the microphone. This time, the applause was deafening as the song ended, and Sienna humbly bowed her head appreciatively.

"That's our girl." The emcee clapped as Sienna descended the stairs. "Give it up for Sienna."

Smiling at one another, Callie and Gigi joined the rest of the room in applause. Sienna was fantastic. Good enough that someone outside of this little town should know about her. Callie's mind raced as she thought of how she could help the young woman. Maybe she could figure out how to get a demo from her and send it to the right people.

She knew what Andrew would say. She'd heard him say it the last time a young singer like Sienna had sent in a demo covering one of her old songs.

"That whole sweet, wholesome country girl thing isn't where the market is right now," he had said dismissively. "She should be playing songs off your new album, not that old stuff."

Although Callie knew her first album had come out a long time ago, and certainly the industry was always shifting, she hadn't liked how quickly he'd dismissed the young woman. Just because her original label thought moving into pop was right for Callie's career didn't mean country had ceased to exist as a genre. In fact, it was more popular than ever, which is why it mystified Callie that Andrew wouldn't even consider letting her put out a new country album to reconnect with the fans who had supported her from the very beginning.

Although their indie label had effectively gone belly-up after their business partner, Marco, misrepresented financials to the investors, both Andrew and Callie had been cleared of any knowledge or wrongdoing by the authorities. Unfortunately, it had tarnished their names just the same, and she blamed herself for letting the men keep her in the dark when it came to the business side of things. She'd trusted Andrew when he'd said they wanted to take all the business stuff off her plate so she could concentrate on her music, but now she wasn't convinced Andrew was as innocent as he claimed. It was a big reason why they were no longer together, even though he was still trying to change her mind.

His latest tactic was refusing to let her out of her contract, even though the label couldn't afford to produce a new record. Technically, he still had another six months to come up with the funding before he was in breach, so she could just wait him out. He still thought if he could pull out a win for her on the career front, she'd forgive him on the personal side. In the meantime, her professional life was at a standstill.

Thinking about the situation churned her stomach, so she forced herself to concentrate on the man on the microphone. Gigi was already tapping her foot in time to the next song, a Kenny Chesney cover from a guy in tight jeans, with long brown hair that kept falling over one of his eyes. He was totally Gigi's type, which meant they weren't getting out of here any time soon. So much for the one-drink promise.

Callie excused herself to go to the ladies' room, weaving her way across the sticky floor. She needed a moment alone. Those weren't something she got very often anymore.

Exiting the stall to wash her hands, she found Sienna already at the sink and waited patiently behind. Sienna's denim top fell slightly below where her skirt began, so the only skin showing was her shoulders holding up the spaghetti straps and her long, tan arms. Callie wished she still got to wear outfits like that on stage.

"I'm sorry." Sienna shifted to the side to grab a paper towel and make room for her.

"Nothing to be sorry about, I'm not in a hurry." Callie laid on the Southern drawl that had been trained out of her years ago in an effort to further disguise her identity. "By the way, you were great out there."

"Thanks." Sienna blushed. "It's one of my favorites."

"It's Callie Jackson, right?" She knew she was being a little brazen talking about herself, but one look in the mirror told her she was unlikely to be recognized. The auburn wig with the blunt cut and bangs couldn't look more different from her long blonde hair with its tight natural curls, but it complemented her blue eyes. To complete the look, Gigi had given her a deep-burgundy lipstick Callie wouldn't normally be caught dead in—because it made her look dead, the dark hue in sharp contrast to her pale skin. As luck would have it, she didn't have any real distinguishing features—no mole or dimples or out-of-the-ordinary nose or eyes—so it had always been easy to go incognito when she needed to.

"Yeah." Sienna smiled. "It was her first hit. I think she was about my age when she wrote it."

"Not one of those songs you hear very often." She wanted to keep the conversation going. Sienna felt like a lifeline to something Callie once had, and she wasn't ready to let go yet.

"No." Sienna shook her head, leaning against the wall next to the sink. "No one plays her country anymore. Her songs are really different now, but that's what sells I guess."

"Are you a fan of her newer stuff too?" Callie was curious to hear the opinion of what she thought was another talented artist.

"It's okay." The young woman shrugged. "I love that she writes all her own music, because I write most of mine too. But what she sings about now is nothing like what she did in the beginning. I mean, she still seems super nice and all, not like some of those artists who make it big and think they're such hot shots. But her lyrics just aren't the same."

Instead of feeling disappointed that Sienna didn't like her newer stuff, Callie felt gratified. She didn't like it either. She was contemplating how to respond when Sienna asked, "Are you a fan?"

"I know her music." Callie was cautious, stealing a glance at her disguise in the mirror again to calm her nerves. "And I agree it does feel a little different these days, doesn't it?"

"Yeah. I didn't even go see her on the last tour. It was the first time I hadn't gone to one of her concerts. I even saw her on her very first tour. My mom took me down to Tampa for it."

"Why didn't you go to the last one?" Callie felt genuinely curious. She knew the tickets sold out fast and the secondary market was pricing out many of her fans. She'd complained to the record company, but they saw it as a good thing. It was part of what Andrew had convinced her they could do differently if they had their own label.

"I guess I'd rather be here singing her old songs. I'm working on one of my own, but it isn't ready yet. Hopefully there are still people out there like me who want to hear a sappy ballad about falling in love on a hot summer night." She smiled, obviously thinking of someone in particular.

Callie understood. Most of her the songs on her first album had been about Jesse, some written before they broke up about young love and others after the breakup about love lost.

She suddenly felt it was time to go. Opening the door, the full volume of the guitar chords rushing into the bathroom, Callie turned back to Sienna. "It was nice to meet you. Good luck with that." She nodded toward the stage. "You were great up there."

Callie was already weaving through the crowd when she heard Sienna's voice behind her. "Hey, what's your name?"

Pretending not to hear, she expertly navigated back to Gigi and prayed Sienna didn't follow.

"Time's up," she said to Gigi, pointing at her watch. "The couch is waiting for me, let's go."

Gigi shrugged, staring disappointedly at the cute singer with the floppy hair and tight jeans, who was currently chatting up a curvy blonde by the stage. "Okay, you win. Couch it is."

Callie scooted around couples and groups on a girls' night out, gently nudging people aside as she worked her way to the front door. Her mood had turned sour, even though Gigi had agreed to leave.

Pushing the door open and stepping out into the warm air of early summer, she realized the feeling was jealousy. No one had asked Sienna to wear thigh-high black boots or fishnets yet to be more "edgy." They hadn't convinced her to abandon her country love ballads for songs more likely to make the pop charts. Sienna was just a girl with a dream and a guitar. She was what Callie used to be, back when things were simpler.

"Hey, wait up." Gigi exited the building several steps behind Callie, who was already making a beeline across the parking lot to Gigi's car.

She didn't see the man stepping out from between two of the parked trucks until they nearly ran into one another.

"Sorry." Callie didn't look at his face, reflexively reaching up to make sure her wig was still in place.

"No, my bad," came a voice so familiar it made her look up.

At the realization it was Austin Beckett she almost blurted out his name. By now, Gigi had caught up to them and was standing silently by her side as another dark figure emerged from between the row of cars. Callie knew who it had to be even before he stepped into the light from the lamp above them.

Jesse looked her up and down. "Callie? Is that you?" Then turning, "And Gigi?" He burst out in laughter at their getups.

Austin shot a confused glance at each, also looking them up and down. "Seriously? That's Gigi and Callie under all that?" He seemed skeptical.

"The charm bracelet." Jesse pointed at Callie's right arm. Her mother had gifted it to her for her twelfth birthday and added a charm every time they visited a new place or had a milestone to commemorate. When she moved to Nashville, there'd been a seashell to remind her of home. Then her mom had given her one shaped like a record to celebrate Callie's first album. But there'd been no more after that, because her mother wasn't alive to give them.

"Caught me." Callie tried to laugh away the flutter in her chest. She felt as if they were all back in high school, running into each other outside Mack's Diner after a football game. The four of them had been inseparable, although Austin and Gigi had never gotten past flirting disguised as fighting. Probably because Austin was too busy rotating through every other girl in their class. He had been sort of a ladies' man back then and likely still was. Callie could only imagine the women who flocked to a professional baseball player.

"Nice wigs." Jesse smirked.

"They're fun, right?" Gigi struck several Madonna-worthy Vogue poses.

"Open-mic night, huh?" Jesse turned his green eyes back to meet Callie's. "Interesting place for a singer who wants to hide out."

She squirmed under his gaze, uncomfortable with how it always seemed as if he could read her mind. "I didn't know it was open-mic night when I agreed to come." She glared at Gigi.

"Hey." Gigi held up both hands in front of her. "I didn't know either. It's not like I have time to spend a lot of nights out on the town."

"Too busy being Ms. Fancy Pants Lawyer, right?" Austin teased her.

"Why, yes, I do happen to own a very successful law firm." Gigi's hands were on her hips now, leveling a look at Austin. "It does take a little more time and preparation than sitting around chatting about baseball all day."

"Hey now," he said in mock defense, "I also have to talk about football and basketball sometimes too."

"Yeah, real rough life you have there, Beckett." Gigi laughed.

"We were heading home." Callie linked her arm through Gigi's and gave a tug in the direction of their car. "You two have a nice evening."

But Gigi wasn't budging, and Callie recognized the twinkle her friend got in her eyes when she was up to something.

"What's it been, like thirteen years since we've all been together? And you two might as well get over all this awkward first-time-we're-seeing-each-other nonsense." Gigi looked pointedly at Jesse and then Callie. "Let's go to Mack's and get cheeseburgers and milkshakes like old times." She was smiling again, clearly proud of herself for bringing the gang back together.

Arms still linked, Callie elbowed Gigi in the ribs and would have given her a death glare if she wasn't looking at the guys.

"We're fine," Callie said. "We've all seen each other. Now let's go home."

"I'm always hungry." Austin shrugged. "Let's do it."

"I'm game." Jesse stared directly at Callie. "Let's go."

She wanted to look away, but couldn't seem to make her

eyes do what her brain was telling them. She could swear he only did it because he could tell she was uncomfortable. She didn't know which was worse. Having to spill to Gigi in the car on the way to the diner, or enduring an entire meal feeling the pull of Jesse from across the table.

CHAPTER EIGHT
JESSE

As they drove to the diner, Jesse replayed the interaction in the parking lot. He got the distinct impression Gigi didn't know he and Callie had already seen each other. That was interesting. He assumed Callie told Gigi everything, like the old days. There'd never been any point in sharing something with one of them if you didn't want the other to know. The question was, why was it a secret? Was it because the encounter had been that inconsequential to Callie it hadn't merited telling her best friend?

They all piled into what had been their usual booth back in high school, only this time he and Callie sat across from one another instead of side by side.

"I get why you're wearing all this," Jesse said, trying to break the ice as he motioned toward Callie, "but what's your excuse?" he asked, turning to Gigi.

"Well, you know, I'm pretty in demand around here too." Gigi flipped back a lock of her icy-blonde wig. "I mean, I can hardly walk through the grocery store without some old man on an HOA board stopping to ask me if their rules allow him to insist his neighbor get rid of the bright-yellow patio furniture he hates on his balcony."

"I'm sorry." Jesse placed his hand over his heart in mock apology. "I didn't realize I was in the presence of not just two celebrities, but in fact three." He motioned around the table at the others.

"Who's the other celebrity? Beckett?" Gigi scoffed. "Puh-lease. He doesn't count. He's not even an athlete anymore."

"Hey now." Austin sounded slightly offended. "I played in the Major Leagues. I was kind of a big deal."

"*Was*," Gigi emphasized, dismissing him. "You can't play that card forever. Can you even hit a ball still?"

"Come with me to the batting cages," Austin dared her. "I'll show you a thing or two."

"Oh, yeah?" Gigi shot back, arching an eyebrow.

"Should we give you two some privacy?" Callie finally smiled and relaxed back into the worn red leather booth.

Sitting across from him, Callie had looked tense and on alert since they'd been seated at Mack's, her eyes darting around every time someone walked in the door or exited past them. Back in the day they had always snuggled into one side of the booth together, oblivious to anyone or anything else. Tonight, he was wrestling for leg room next to Austin.

"He wishes," Gigi said, winking in Austin's direction. "So I hear you two have already reconnected." She nudged Callie while looking pointedly at Jesse. "What are you up to over at the Lyman house?"

Her tone was teasing, but a tad accusatory. He imagined that was how she tricked people into incriminating themselves up on the witness stand in court. He knew she did land-use law, not criminal, but he'd also heard how she'd gotten people to admit all sorts of misdeeds with her disarming charm. He'd appreciated it last year when she'd nailed his biggest competitor—a developer from the mainland—for cutting down trees he knew local ordinances protected, resulting in a $300,000 fine. That company rarely took work on Big Dune Island anymore. But Jesse was nervous now that she was taking aim in his direction.

"Just fixing a few things for Uncle Lonnie." Jesse shrugged as if it were no big deal. "Doors that won't shut, windows that leak, that sort of thing."

Thankfully, they were interrupted by Mack himself—the owner of the diner—who had come over to take their order. An older gentleman with dark skin and deep brown eyes that were in stark contrast to his hair that had turned from black to white with age; he'd run the diner for thirty years.

"Hey there, boys." Mack slid a yellow pencil from behind his ear, poising it over his worn order pad. "Ladies first, what can I get y'all?"

Lucky for Callie and Gigi, Mack's eyesight wasn't what it used to be, so he probably thought Austin was bringing around more of his admirers. Austin might not have loved playing baseball, but he sure loved the attention that came with it.

The group ordered their burgers and milkshakes before Mack asked Austin how Chloe was doing with the coffee shop. The local business owners had always looked out for one another, sharing things when someone's supplier missed a delivery or recommending each other to the tourists who were looking for suggestions.

"She's great, Mack. Thanks for asking."

The older gentleman headed back to the kitchen to put in their order and Austin turned to Gigi. "Hey, G, speaking of the coffee shop, I've been meaning to come see you. I hear Mr. Barker might be starting to shop the building around quietly. Can you find out what he wants for it?"

"You want to buy the building?" Gigi sounded surprised.

"Maybe." Austin played with the sugar packets that sat

inside a black caddy on the table, not meeting Gigi's eyes. "It could be a good investment for me. It would give Chloe some security knowing she isn't going to get bumped out or have a big rent hike."

Gigi seemed at a loss for words as she processed the request. Jesse knew deep down Austin was one of the most unselfish and giving people around, but his friend liked to project a tougher image to the outside world. His dad had been relentless in his quest to make his only son a baseball superstar, pushing him to take private lessons and practice night and day from their T-ball days. His father had told him what his dream would be and then forced him to achieve it.

Unfortunately, Mr. Beckett's focus on his only son's baseball aspirations meant he largely ignored his daughter. Austin had always been protective of Chloe though, and Jesse sensed he felt guilty over the attention that had been on him through so much of their childhood. When Chloe put together a half-baked plan to buy Island Coffee a few years back when its owners were retiring, Austin had jumped at the chance to make it up to her by giving her the down payment and cosigning on the lease, despite Jesse's objections and reminders about the reality of being in business with family.

Gigi, however, was clearly impressed by Austin's generosity.

"Alright." She took a long swig of the strawberry milkshake Mack had put in front of her. "Not only will I help you, but I'll also take back everything negative I've ever said about you. Maybe you're not half bad, Beckett."

"It's okay, G." Austin smiled. "I've always known you have a thing for me."

"Never mind, I'm reinstating it all." Gigi rolled her eyes. "You're still a jerk."

"I saw Chloe today," Callie interjected. "She recognized me when I was walking down Main Street."

"In that?" Austin pointed at the wig.

"No, I just had my hair up in a hat." Callie stole a glance at Jesse, who remembered the pang he'd felt in his chest when he'd realized it was his old Red Sox cap she was wearing. "It was before lunch, and I thought I could get away with a cap and sunglasses."

"Good luck keeping it a secret you're back now." Austin shook his head. "I love my sister, but she's definitely the town gossip."

"I talked to her." Jesse looked down as he took a sip of his chocolate milkshake. "I told her you want to stay under the radar." He didn't look up to see Callie's reaction. He didn't want her to think he was coming to her rescue or anything. She didn't need him like that anymore.

"When was that?" There was concern in Callie's voice. No doubt she was trying to figure out how Jesse already knew Chloe had seen her.

"I had a meeting at the coffee shop this afternoon. She mentioned she'd run into you. I think only because she wanted to warn me you were back," he added, giving Chloe an excuse for sharing the information.

"A meeting?" Gigi leaned forward to place her chin in her hand, her eyes fixed on his. "What are you wanting to build now? A beachfront strip mall?"

Jesse winced at the insinuation that it was builders like him destroying the natural beauty of the island. Sure, he'd felt guilty clearing out lots on the south end to construct the homes the investors preferred, but he always tried to save the big trees, to incorporate them in his designs. He'd even taken an online class from the University of Florida last year about preserving trees in development projects. He'd wanted to learn how to preserve while still ensuring the profits that kept Thomas Construction alive.

"No, it's a go-cart track," Jesse deadpanned as he leaned down to drink more of his milkshake.

"Yeah, now that's something I'd love to see you bring before the commission." Gigi laughed. Then mimicking a male voice, she said, "But sirs, a go-cart track will attract more families to the island for vacation. It'll be good for the local businesses." She rolled her eyes in his direction.

Was that what Gigi thought of him? That he'd become a sellout and would do anything to make a buck? He wondered if that would make her more or less likely to help him with the historic district commission for the Lyman house. She had to know he would take care with the renovation given his personal connection to it, right? Or would she be angry that he and Uncle Lonnie went behind Callie's back to hatch this plan? Now definitely wasn't the time to broach that subject, which meant it was time to change it.

"We can't all be like you, swooping in to save the old post office and conserving the greenway." Jesse tipped an imaginary cap on his head in her direction. "Thank you for your service, ma'am."

Gigi blushed, smiling as she faked modesty and did her best impression of a bow while seated. Everyone at the table was laughing now. Flattery worked on Gigi every single time.

"Hey, what's going on with the Beach Bash?" Callie looked around the group. "I saw a sign at Lindy's today. Something about a meeting to save it?"

"You know how it goes." There was disappointment in Gigi's voice. "The Beach Bash doesn't bring in as much as it used to, so some people think it's time to retire it and try something new."

"If it's money they need, why didn't you tell me? I'd be happy to donate."

Of course Callie could afford to just stroke a check and save the Beach Bash. Their lives couldn't be more different.

"Why are you shaking your head like that?" Callie was staring Jesse down.

He hadn't even realized his head had moved. "No reason." He refused to meet her eyes.

"You have something to say, so say it."

"Money doesn't fix everything." He shrugged, looking at her now. "That's all."

"Well, what else do they need? I can't help if I don't know what to do."

"Don't worry about it." Jesse shook his head. "I'm sure the committee has it covered." It wasn't exactly true. His mother was the vice chair of the organization that put on the Beach Bash alongside Gigi's mother, Ms. Myrtle. His mom had been distraught for weeks over the city not renewing the contract beyond this year. If the Beach Bash wasn't a huge success, two new commissioners on the town council wanted to replace it with something "trendier."

"My mom's on the event committee," Gigi said. "Why don't we go see her tomorrow and see what they need. You know you can't show up here and not visit Ms. Myrtle." She elbowed Callie to cut the obvious tension growing as Jesse and Callie glared at each other across the table.

"Hey, I know," Austin interjected. "What if you sang at Beach Bash this year? That would sure draw a crowd."

Gigi turned to Callie. "That's actually not a bad idea."

Callie was shifting uncomfortably in the booth. "I don't know if I can. My agent and I are at a bit of an impasse."

"Don't you think helping save the small-town festival where you were discovered might be the positive publicity you need to get your career back on track?" Gigi argued.

"That's a good point." Callie toyed with the straw in her drink. "I'll talk to Andrew."

Andrew. Jesse felt his heart sink. So he was still around. Jesse knew he shouldn't care, but it was still hard to picture her with anyone else. When he had seen photos of them splashed on magazine covers, he'd told himself she was a different woman, not the girl he'd fallen in love with.

"Even if you only came along to Beach Bash, I'm sure that would be a big help," said Gigi.

"I wasn't planning to stay that long, but I'm sure I could manage a few more days," Callie said.

Jesse couldn't help it; his heart leaped at the mention of her staying longer, even if it was only a few more days. Rationally, he knew she would only be back long enough to pack up the house, but he had already started picturing what it might be like if she really did exercise the contract option to keep the house; what it would be like to see her more often.

Maybe Uncle Lonnie knew what he was doing after all.

CHAPTER NINE
CALLIE

Over breakfast the next morning, Callie and Gigi recapped what they knew about the sale of the house. Callie was really keen to learn more about the fate of her childhood home, and Uncle Lonnie didn't seem to be willing to share more details.

"Well, whoever bought it, they're not ready to show their hand," Gigi said as she got back in her car after running into City Hall on their way to visit Ms. Myrtle. Gigi thought some permits might have already been filed for Jesse's work on the house that might reveal the buyer, but she'd come up empty-handed.

"It was worth a try." Callie frowned as Gigi pulled her little red convertible away from the curb.

"Everything is just listed in Jesse's name since he's the one doing the work and the new buyer hasn't actually closed on the property."

"I don't understand what Uncle Lonnie's hiding." Callie crossed her arms over her chest.

"I'm sure he thought he was doing what was best for you."

Gigi began heading due east toward the beach. "You haven't been able to go back inside since—" She reached over to pat Callie on the arm. "Since you lost them. You haven't even been back on the island."

"That's what Jesse said. Actually, I think his exact words were that the house 'needs someone who cares about her.' A little harsh, don't you think?"

"Honestly, I think that's more about leaving him behind than the house." Gigi glanced in her direction, no doubt to judge her reaction.

Did that mean he still cared? Even if he was still angry with her, Callie couldn't help but want that link to still be there. To know what they had was real, even if they had just been kids.

"You know I did what I thought I had to at the time. Besides, look how great he's doing now. He found those investors, and they saved the company."

"The investors might have saved Thomas Construction, but the company isn't what it used to be."

"What do you mean?" Callie turned in her seat to face Gigi.

"I'm pretty sure it wasn't Jesse's dream to stay here and mow down trees on the south end to build McMansions for people who only spend a few days a year here." Gigi shifted gears as they slowed to a stop at the end of Main Street, facing the ocean.

Gigi's words made Callie pause. She'd seen the investors as white knights riding in to save the day. They would have had their own motives for saving Thomas Construction, but Callie had never thought about what those might be. She'd always assumed that things had turned around and Jesse had stayed in town because he was happy here. After all, even Austin and Gigi had returned after realizing the grass wasn't greener anywhere else.

As Gigi took a call from her assistant, Callie studied the landscape before her. Main Beach, the largest of the public beach accesses on the island, was directly in front of them on the other side of the intersection. All that was between their car and the water was a small parking lot that fit a couple dozen cars and the natural dunes that kept rising tides at bay. Sea oats danced in sync across the dunes as if an invisible conductor were directing a silent symphony. Sunlight made the ocean sparkle in the distance and, with the top down, Callie could hear the crash of the waves a hundred yards away from where they sat waiting for the light to turn.

Gigi's beach cottage was to the right a mile south, but Gigi turned left and headed toward North Beach where developers had been unsuccessful in buying up land. Instead, the streets were lined with two- and three-story houses raised on stilts to keep them above high tide during the occasional tropical storm or hurricane. Big Dune Island had never experienced a direct hit from a hurricane, and the recent storm had been a rare sideswipe that brought high water and damaging winds. Although the downtown area had some minor flooding from the high river tide, this side of the island was left relatively unscathed thanks to the dunes that created a fifty-yard barrier between the high-tide mark and the homes lining the island's twelve miles of beaches.

Unlike Callie and Jesse, who had grown up in the historic downtown district, Gigi spent her childhood at North Beach. It was only a little over a mile from Callie's childhood home to Gigi's, and by the time the girls were twelve, their parents let them ride their bikes between the houses with regularity.

Gigi pulled up in front of her family's house, which stood out a little among its neighbors. Most of the homes were on stilts that reminded Callie of bird legs: they were seemingly too skinny for what sat atop them. But not the Franklin house. Gigi's mother, Ms. Myrtle, was from Charleston, so she'd insisted on having a Lowcountry-style house when she married Dr. Franklin, and let him convince her to move to his hometown of Big Dune Island. She always said that if she had to leave her beloved Charleston at least she could live in a house that reminded her of home.

Although their house was raised like its neighbors, and similarly occupied the second and third stories of the structure, it didn't have the same open first story that others used as carports. Instead, the first floor was enclosed, with vented arches along the front. From the right side of the building, you could enter the garage space underneath. Facing the street, a double staircase led up to the front door on the second floor, which had a porch that ran the entire length of the home.

Everything was exactly as Callie remembered it, even though it had been more than a decade since she'd last climbed the stairs to the front door. The lawn was impeccable, with lush, bright-green grass that was no doubt the envy of everyone, even people whose yards backed up to one of the island's half-dozen golf courses. Callie resisted the urge to pull off her shoes and walk barefoot through it, which she knew would feel spongy and cool like it had in her childhood. When was the last time she'd walked barefoot through grass? She was rarely home long enough to spend any time in her own yard, and she was surprised by how sad that made her feel. She resolved to kick off her shoes when she got back home and walk around her front yard.

They climbed the porch stairs, decorated with flower boxes attached along the railing at perfect intervals, which Callie knew was no accident. As a child, she'd witnessed Ms. Myrtle measuring with a ruler to maintain their symmetry. Today, petunias in bright shades of pink and purple were spilling over the edges. Even the flowers seemed to have succumbed to Ms. Myrtle's perfectionism as they fell in elegant trails toward the first story, none too short or too long compared to the others.

"Georgia, darlin', you're late," Ms. Myrtle used Gigi's full first name as she opened the door to let them in. She virtually shoved Gigi inside as she turned her attention to Callie. "And Callie, my love," she said, embracing her in a hug, "let me get a good look at you."

Callie shifted her weight from one foot to the other as Ms. Myrtle held her at arm's length to appraise her. Callie had borrowed a sundress from Gigi after realizing she'd packed nothing that would meet with Ms. Myrtle's standards. Gigi's mother had been a debutante, raised by a wealthy doctor and his wife in a historic home on Charleston's famous Rainbow Row. She had always expected the girls to "dress like ladies," even when they were planning to play outside.

"You look lovely, my dear." Ms. Myrtle nodded approval, stepping back to motion Callie inside and into the foyer where Gigi stood, arms crossed.

"Last time I wore that dress, you told me it was the color of a wilted sunflower," Gigi deadpanned as she rolled her eyes.

"Yes, well, you don't have the right coloring to pull it off like Callie does." Ms. Myrtle was matter of fact. "And you were going on a date with that lovely Lucas Rushmore. I was just trying to make sure you got a second date."

Ms. Myrtle was known around town for her matchmaking skills, but it was no secret she considered it her biggest failure in life that she had yet to marry off her own daughter. Becoming a wife and mother was nowhere on Gigi's radar, however, much to her mother's disappointment. She'd been too focused on her career to settle down yet. Something Callie and Gigi had in common.

As Gigi entered her parents' formal living room she screeched to a halt, causing Callie to bump into her from behind. At the far-right side of the room a woman sat sipping a tall glass of iced tea. It took Callie a moment to place the woman because her once honey-gold locks were streaked with grey and her face was more rounded than it had been a decade earlier, but then it clicked. It was Betty Thomas, Jesse's mother.

Callie's pulse began to race. She hadn't known Mrs. Thomas would be here. She had seen the woman only once since she broke her only child's heart, and that had been at her parents' funeral where everyone had to feel sorry for her. Did Mrs. Thomas still see her as an orphan to be pitied? Or was she the girl who'd shattered her son's heart? Either way, Callie dreaded the reunion.

"Gigi, Callie, it's so lovely to see you girls together again." Mrs. Thomas set her tea on the table in front of her and rose to greet them.

"Mrs. Thomas, I didn't realize you'd be here." Gigi was obviously as shocked as Callie. Crossing the room to hug her, Gigi continued, "How nice to see you. How have you been?"

Still standing several steps behind Gigi, Callie marveled at how her friend transformed before her into a gracious Southern lady. It was like watching someone who was bilingual slip into another language as she listened to Gigi ask about Mr. Thomas and last week's bake sale to benefit sea turtle conservation.

Callie knew her turn would come, but she waited for Gigi to finish and step aside. She braced herself for whatever might come next.

"Callie, I'm just so happy you're here." Mrs. Thomas enveloped Callie in a bear hug.

Was it obligatory or was she really glad to see her?

Callie pulled away and tried not to look Mrs. Thomas in the eyes. "It's good to be back for a couple of weeks, and it's so nice to see you." Turning away awkwardly, she searched the room for somewhere else to go, something else to do.

Motioning for everyone to move toward the sitting area, Ms. Myrtle took her usual chair to the left of the couch. "Ladies, have a seat." Ms. Myrtle always had a way of holding court when others were in her presence. Callie stifled a laugh thinking how much Gigi reminded her of Ms. Myrtle these days. She couldn't dare say that to Gigi though—she'd be mortified.

"I think we all have a common goal here: to ensure the Beach Bash—one of our most treasured traditions—remains intact," Ms. Myrtle began.

Callie studied the older woman's face. She looked exactly the same as she had a decade earlier. Callie was certain she'd had some work done, but of course Ms. Myrtle would never admit that kind of thing openly. Her porcelain skin was identical to Gigi's, which she highlighted with a bold magenta lipstick that matched the flowers on her silk blouse. Her dark hair had no trace of grey and was expertly curled in perfect waves that barely shifted even when the rest of her body was animatedly moving to emphasize the points she was making about the importance of the Beach Bash to the community.

Turning her attention to Callie, she said, "Callie, Betty and I stepped in to chair the committee this year when we found out how dire the situation was, but I'm afraid it was a bit like stepping onto the *Titanic* after the ship had already struck the iceberg."

"If it's money you need, I would be more than happy to make a donation. Obviously, the Beach Bash means a lot to me. Just let me know how I can help."

"Yes, dear," Ms. Myrtle said, "while we would, of course, welcome a donation, the real issue is attendance. With only a couple of weeks to go until this year's event, all the marketing money in the world won't help us if we don't have a big reason for folks to attend."

"I'd love to perform—" Callie began before she was cut off by Ms. Myrtle.

"Splendid!" Ms. Myrtle clapped her hands together. "Wait until everyone hears we have the great Callie Jackson performing!"

Callie looked to Gigi, silently telegraphing her concern.

"Callie's contract requires her label to approve all performances," Gigi explained to her mother.

"Surely your label would understand you wanting to help save the very festival where you were discovered."

"It's..." Callie searched for the word. "Complicated." She recalled Andrew's speech last year when she wanted to sing onstage with her friend Kyra Miles, a country singer who'd opened for her before she began headlining her own tours. Andrew hadn't liked the venue, a small music amphitheater in Memphis. Kyra was doing a tour where she went "back to her roots" and played in smaller venues around the South. He thought it was a sign that Kyra could no longer sell out stadiums, that her star was falling. He had warned Callie against getting dragged down with her. She could already hear him telling her how playing the festival would make it look like she was desperate right now.

"I'm going to take a second look at her contract," Gigi said. "See if we can't find something that will help persuade Andrew to say yes."

Mrs. Thomas spoke softly. "I'm sure he'd support you if he knew what the Beach Bash meant to you—to your hometown and the people here."

"Of course he would," Ms. Myrtle interjected. "You just turn on some Southern charm and tell him this is something you simply must do."

Easy for Ms. Myrtle to say. Dr. Franklin would lasso the

moon and bring it down for her if she asked. Jesse had been like that, but they'd only been teenagers. That kind of infatuation probably would have worn off over the years. How would they have ever found the time for each other once their careers began?

Andrew always thought first and foremost about her career. About perception and PR. He was no match for Gigi though, and that gave Callie the confidence she needed to say yes. But, there was something else she wanted.

"Assuming Gigi can work her magic and get me out of my contract, I'm in," she said, which was immediately met with excited clapping from Ms. Myrtle. "But on one condition. I want this local singer we saw last night, Sienna, to open for me."

"Who's Sienna?" Ms. Myrtle pursed her lips.

"She's really good." Gigi nodded enthusiastically. "I think she's Graham Leighton's daughter."

"Well, I haven't heard of her," Ms. Myrtle said, "but if you're headlining for us, I don't care who opens."

The excitement bubbled up in Callie's chest, and she perched on the edge of her seat, ready to spring up and go grab a guitar so she could start practicing. Callie hadn't been sure she'd ever play again here in her hometown, but now that she had the opportunity, she was thrilled. She missed performing in more intimate venues where she could feel more connected to her audience.

She remembered the early days when she could linger after the show was over, meeting people and hearing how a particular song touched their heart. Then one day it all changed, and the only people who got near her were the ones who could afford VIP tickets. Andrew was always telling her she couldn't go back, that small venues were beneath her now. She couldn't imagine he'd think the festival was a good idea, but she was really tired of letting him and everyone else around her make all the decisions for her career.

A caterer ringing the doorbell ended their meeting. Ms. Myrtle had to start preparing the room for her weekly card club, so they were dismissed with their marching orders to "make it happen."

Callie couldn't remember the last time she'd felt so excited to perform.

CHAPTER TEN
JESSE

J esse found Uncle Lonnie as expected, in his rocking chair, creaking back and forth in an easy rhythm on his front porch. Although his feet were moving, everything else about the older gentleman was still, his eyes closed. His guitar was propped up against the house behind him, a nearly empty glass of tea at his side. Jesse didn't want to disturb his nap, but he had to talk to Uncle Lonnie about when he was planning to tell Callie the truth about the sale. If the night before was any indication, she and Gigi were hot on the trail.

Jesse cleared his throat as he began to ascend the porch stairs. "Uncle Lonnie."

The older man opened his eyes, never changing the rhythm of his old cowboy boots as he lifted the heels from the concrete in a steady beat to keep the rocker moving. "Jesse, come on up and take a load off," he said, motioning to the other rocking chair.

Jesse sat on the edge of the chair, leaning forward to put his elbows on his knees, clasping his hands together. "We need to talk. I saw Callie last night." He turned to gauge Uncle Lonnie's reaction, but his face was unflinching.

"Oh, you did, did you?" The corners of Uncle Lonnie's mouth began to turn up as he continued to gaze out across the front yard. "I reckon you two haven't seen each other in a coon's age, huh?"

Clearing his throat, Jesse admitted, "Actually, she came by the house a couple of days ago and found me in the backyard."

"Yes, I know." Uncle Lonnie looked at Jesse, his lips curling into a fuller smile. His grey eyes were twinkling.

So she'd told him already and he seemed to be taking some sort of pleasure in the charade of it all. Jesse was glad someone was having fun, because he wasn't sure he was. He looked down at the scuffed, chipped green paint on the porch floor. Uncle Lonnie used to repaint it every spring, but it didn't look like he'd gotten around to it this year. Jesse made a mental note to come paint it for him one day. He'd have to do it while Uncle Lonnie was at the American Legion, otherwise he'd only protest that he could do it himself. But the older man wasn't moving as well lately, and Jesse figured it was something small he could do to repay his generosity in selling him the Lyman house.

"Did she also tell you she thought I was a handyman you'd hired to do a little work before the sale?"

"She did." Uncle Lonnie chuckled now. "She'll understand it all when we're done."

Jesse shook his head. "You're not going to tell her now? You're going to wait?"

"Well." He leaned his head back against the chair as he rocked. "I don't think it's quite time yet."

Jesse wished Uncle Lonnie would be more specific. Was he going to tell Callie while she was still in town, or was he hoping to send her back home with assurances he had everything handled and tell her after the sale was complete?

"Did she go inside?" Uncle Lonnie asked.

Jesse couldn't see Uncle Lonnie's eyes because they were still fixed on the yard, so he wasn't sure if the older man already knew the answer.

"No." Jesse stared at his hands. "She sat on the back deck, but that's as close as she got."

Jesse had watched Callie's face when she looked up at the bedroom that had been hers, but he hadn't been able to read her expression. What had she been thinking? That she'd come a long way since she sat in her window seat up there writing songs? Her life back on Big Dune Island must seem so small now. He winced as he realized she was probably glad she left him behind and didn't have anything from her past holding her back.

"Hmm." Uncle Lonnie continued his slow, methodical rocking. "Well, I guess she'll go in when she gets good and ready."

"She has to go in soon to pack up, right? We close in less than a month."

Uncle Lonnie nodded. "Yes, I imagine she'll have to face what's inside before too long."

Jesse's throat tightened. He knew that *inside* meant more than just what was in the interior of the house. Callie still hadn't fully faced losing her parents.

"Maybe I can help her." The words were out of Jesse's mouth before he could stop them. His first instinct was still to come to her aid. He shook his head, feeling stupid. Callie was a big girl who didn't want his assistance anymore.

"I think that would be nice," Uncle Lonnie said, the smile returning to his lips. "Let me know how it goes."

Clearly, he felt like their business was complete.

Jesse hadn't meant to volunteer to be the one who got Callie to pack up the house. She'd never once even reached out to ask how his dad's company was doing after he stayed behind to help save it. First, he'd been hurt, then he'd been mad. Eventually, he thought he no longer cared, but as soon as he laid eyes on her that first night she was back in town, the wound had reopened.

He wanted to protest and tell Uncle Lonnie he shouldn't be the one to help her, but Lonnie had already grabbed his guitar and started strumming a slow, steady tune. Jesse leaned back to rock his chair to the rhythm of the chords as he thought about what he'd agreed to. Maybe it wouldn't be so bad. The house did need to be cleaned out. It was becoming more and more difficult to find work he could start on that didn't disturb any of the contents. Maybe he wasn't looking at this the right way. This wasn't just about helping Callie; it was the next practical step in his project.

Jesse said goodbye and made his way back down the street to the Lyman house, the sound of Uncle Lonnie's playing growing fainter.

This had been a good visit; he felt better already. It was Uncle Lonnie's decision when to tell Callie the truth. Jesse would help her clean out the house, like any old friend would, then he'd be closer to making this renovation a reality.

CHAPTER ELEVEN
CALLIE

"How's it coming? Are you making good progress at the house?" Impatience permeated Andrew's words. She'd told him she'd be gone for a couple of weeks, but he hadn't understood why she couldn't just hire someone to clean out the house.

"There's more to do than I thought, but I'm feeling inspired to write here." It was a little white lie she knew would appease him. The truth was, she'd underestimated how difficult it would be to go back inside the house. Between that and learning about the struggles with the Beach Bash, time was getting away from her quickly. She was definitely going to be here longer than two weeks.

Even if she didn't really have the time for it, Callie wished she had the inspiration to write here. She hadn't gone such a long spell without writing a song since she first picked up a pad and pencil and scribbled down lyrics at ten years old. She knew what the problem was though. She wanted to go back to her country roots, but Andrew was still convinced she should stick with pop—that the last album had only flopped because the label had lacked vision.

"Really?" He perked up at the mention of new music.

She knew he still thought the rights he held to her next album would save his career and land them both at another record company. He was nothing if not predictable. Always the producer and label exec first.

She bit her lip, not wanting to perpetuate the lie any further.

"Anything I can hear?"

"Umm—not yet," she said, quickly. "But soon, I promise."

"We both need this," he reminded her. "Marco didn't just mess with your career, he messed with mine too."

Yeah, but who brought him into their lives? She wanted to remind him that it was his fault they were in this position, but she knew it was pointless. What was done was done.

"I know. I'll let you know when I have something ready for you to hear."

"Good. I'll let you get back to packing up everything so you can focus on writing us some more hits."

She'd never confided in Andrew about why she hadn't returned to Big Dune Island after the funeral. He wasn't very perceptive about anything outside of their work. She was sure he just thought she'd been too busy to go back. So, of course, he'd assume it was no big deal to go back in the house and start packing.

"Right. Well, I'm still sort of assessing the situation and figuring out what to keep and what to donate." It was the second lie she'd told him. She hated lying, but it was easier than trying to make him understand the truth.

"Maybe I should have come to help you. I still can. I've got a meeting at Epic tomorrow," he said, referencing one of the labels he was hoping would buy out Callie's contract and offer him a producer job. "I can hop in the car after that."

He still thought he could make things up to her and win

her back, but she didn't want to give him false hope. She still wasn't sure what role he'd played in the downfall of the label. Initially, she'd given him the benefit of the doubt because she'd known him so long. Andrew had been on her team since the very beginning, so part of her wanted to believe he was as invested in her career as she was. Six years her senior, he'd been an assistant at the record company when she'd first signed her contract. He was fresh out of college, and every bit as green as her, and his star had risen right alongside hers as they worked side by side on all six of her records.

They were constantly together due to the nature of their working relationship, so it was only natural that it eventually became something more than that. When the label talked her into the transition album from country to pop a few years prior, she and Andrew had spent even more time together than usual on rebranding, song selection, and recording. Callie had been uncertain about the change in direction, but Andrew backed her up in meetings when she'd fought for things she believed in the most—such as not cursing or talking about sex in her lyrics—and had been patient with her when she'd struggled with the new sound.

After a particularly rough few days in the studio trying to bring the right emotion to a song about being reckless in love —something she had absolutely no experience with herself— Andrew had canceled their recording session and taken her to the Nashville Superspeedway to teach her how to drive a race-car. It had certainly felt reckless, not only to take the day off when they were already on a tight deadline, but also to go speeding around a racetrack at speeds that topped 120 mph.

Her adrenaline had been pumping so hard by the time they exited the racetrack, she'd thrown her arms around Andrew and kissed him on the cheek. When she pulled back, she'd seen the look in his eyes and the way he glanced down at her lips, and she'd thrown caution to the wind and kissed him square on the mouth right then and there.

"How's that for reckless?" she'd asked him after he kissed her back.

"I'd say you're ready. Why don't we call the boys into the studio tonight and get that track recorded?"

They'd laid down the track that night, and Andrew asked her to dinner the next. By then, he'd become her friend and her protector at work, and it was easy to let that bleed into her personal life. He'd always understood who she was and what her career demanded. Until he got blinded by the shiny objects Marco waved in front of him, that is.

"It shouldn't be too much longer," Callie said to him on the phone. "I think I just needed a change in scenery to get my creative juices flowing again."

The truth was, she had a severe case of writer's block, which was only compounded by the fact that she hadn't even packed her guitar. She'd never imagined she'd be gone long enough to need it, especially considering she hadn't really played in the last few months.

The hopelessness she felt about her career had pushed her to come home and pack up the house herself, instead of letting Gigi arrange for someone else to do it, as she'd kindly offered. As much as it hurt her to face her family home, it was preferable to facing the truth about her career.

———

FROM WHERE CALLIE STOOD ON THE STREET, UNCLE Lonnie appeared to be napping in his chair on the porch. His head was tilted ever so slightly to the left and forward, enough to be an unusual position for someone who was awake, and the rocker was still. She watched him for a minute, debating whether to wake him.

She let her attention wander from Uncle Lonnie's porch to the hydrangeas that reminded her of Aunt Doris. That woman had been a force of nature, much like Ms. Myrtle. Uncle Lonnie would do anything to make her smile. He got up early to make her coffee so when she woke there was always a steamy mug on her nightstand. And the blue flowers, the only ones that color on the whole island, were a lasting testament to his devotion for her.

Callie couldn't imagine Andrew bringing her coffee in bed or adjusting the acidity in the soil to produce her favorite flowers. But he was fiercely protective of her career. When her parents died, he'd been the one who'd made tough decisions and ensured everything was taken care of, from the funeral to helping her get back on tour and back on the stage, the only place she could find happiness after that.

She might be able to get inspired here if she gave it a try. After all, the songs on her first album were mostly about Big Dune Island and the people here. Okay, maybe only one person here.

"You gonna stand out in the road all day?" Uncle Lonnie's voice cut through the thick midday air.

Smiling as she crossed the lawn in his direction, she relished the feel of the spongy earth beneath her, blades of grass tickling her feet as her flip-flops slapped with each step. How many times had she run barefoot through the grass as a kid, leaping over a sprinkler as it rotated back and forth across the yard? Her heart swelled as she pictured her parents, Aunt Doris, and Uncle Lonnie all piled on the front porch, passing around a pitcher of sweet tea and laughing as she and Jesse and the other neighborhood kids chased each other in the yard.

She was brought back to earth by the empty rocker next to Uncle Lonnie's. A porch that was once filled with so much life had been quieted over time, whittled down to a single inhabitant. As she climbed the stairs, the crushing weight on her chest underscored why she hadn't come back to Big Dune Island before now. It only reminded her of the things she didn't have.

That's why she needed to get Uncle Lonnie's guitar and work on some songs tonight. Marco, Andrew, the label... they'd taken a lot from her, but they couldn't take away her talent. It was the one thing she still had.

"Why so glum, chum?" Uncle Lonnie asked, an eyebrow raising above his glasses as Callie lowered into Aunt Doris's rocking chair.

"Oh, nothing, I was just lost in thought." She forced a smile in his direction. "You looked like you were asleep, so I didn't want to wake you."

"Nah." He guffawed, waving her off. "I was only restin' my eyes for a spell."

"Sure, Uncle Lonnie." She laughed. "Whatever you want to call it."

"Besides, my niece only comes to town once every decade or so." He smiled as he settled his head back against the rocker. "Can't miss any chance I have to catch up with her."

"Yeah, yeah. I know, I'm an easy target around here. Everyone has to tell me how long it's been since they've seen me. I was on the cover of *Us Weekly* a few months ago," she joked, referencing the article that broke the story of her failed label. "You'd think they'd have seen plenty of me standing in line at the grocery-store checkout."

"True enough, and any day now you'll be on the cover again, telling your comeback story. Everyone loves a comeback."

Callie smiled as she relaxed into the rocker. Uncle Lonnie still believed in her, and that was enough right now.

"Well, speaking of my music, I've come to ask a favor." She turned to look at him. "Can I borrow your guitar? I need to see if I can get inspired to write something new while I'm here and I didn't bring mine."

"I thought you were only here to pack things up." Uncle Lonnie's eyes followed two cardinals chasing one another in the crepe myrtle tree at the edge of the yard.

"Yeah, that was my plan. But then I heard about the Beach Bash, and I want to help."

"It's a shame about the Beach Bash." Uncle Lonnie shook his head. "Attendance has been down the past few years, and the island needs that event to attract new people and keep the local businesses afloat."

He was right. In the past, the festival had brought thousands of people from all over the region who stayed in the local hotels, and bed and breakfasts, ate in the restaurants, and purchased goods from the merchants who set up tents all down the beach during the festival.

"Ms. Myrtle wants me to sing. You know, to draw a crowd. I know if I ask Andrew, he won't let me do it." She took a deep breath. "But Gigi thinks she can get me out of my contract."

"Let you?" Uncle Lonnie abruptly stopped his rhythmic rocking and sat up on the edge of his chair, turning to meet her eyes. "That's the second time in as many days I've heard you talkin' about what someone else will or won't let you do. You're a grown woman, Callie, and a successful one at that. Why are *you* letting anyone *let* you do anything? Don't you own part of that label too? What's left of it anyway."

Callie had ceased rocking now too, frozen as his grey eyes penetrated hers. She was more than a little taken aback. Uncle Lonnie was always so even-keeled; he never got upset. She swallowed hard, unable to find the words to respond.

"Now I know you got yanked into this world before you were old enough to understand what was even happening, and I know you lost your mother and your father." He barely paused to draw in a breath. "But you're still your own person and it's time you start making your own decisions. What does Callie Jackson want to do? What makes you happy? Do you even know anymore?"

She stared back at him, still speechless. She couldn't remember the last time anyone asked her what she wanted. She hadn't even picked out what she ate or wore most days for the past decade. She was always at the studio or out on tour with someone else making decisions for her.

An exasperated sigh escaped his lips, and Uncle Lonnie threw up his hands as he leaned back into his chair and resumed his gentle rocking. "I don't have my guitar. I loaned it to Fred. He's teaching his grandson to play."

"That's okay." Her voice was quiet as she folded her hands in her lap, her mind still reeling from his questions. "I think I still have one at the house."

In fact, she knew there was. Her parents had bought her a brand-new guitar when she signed her record deal, so the old banged-up one she'd played as a teenager stayed behind when she moved to Nashville. It was probably still propped up in the corner of her bedroom where she'd left it. At least that's where it had been nine years ago when she'd last been inside.

CHAPTER TWELVE
JESSE

"Sure, Ms. Myrtle. I'll meet you there in the morning to go over the new plans."

Ms. Myrtle had called to tell Jesse she wanted to adjust the building plans for the temporary stage and seating at the Beach Bash in a couple of weeks' time. He'd gotten so wrapped up in the Lyman house project he'd almost forgotten he needed to start work on the stage and tents the following week. He didn't have the time right now, but he'd helped with the festival since he was a little boy, wearing a toy tool belt and construction helmet, and trailing behind his dad. Thomas Construction had been building the temporary structures for the Beach Bash since its inception when his dad was about the age Jesse was now. Plus, it was one of the few things the investors approved of doing that counted as community involvement—mostly because it was free advertising for their company. Not one of the investors had ever actually attended the festival.

Jesse exchanged pleasantries with Ms. Myrtle before ending the call and heading back out to the truck. He needed to grab more wood to replace the rotted windowsills upstairs.

He stopped in his tracks at the site of Callie standing at the top of the driveway. He could see her through the narrow windows on either side of the front door, but she was staring at the second story, oblivious to his presence. Obviously, she knew he was there from his truck in the drive. Had she come to see him?

Furrowing his brows, he batted the thought away. Why would she be there to see him? She'd had no interest in him, or how he was doing, for the past nine years. He couldn't let himself even imagine the possibility she might care now. That would only lead to heartbreak when she inevitably left again.

She seemed to be studying something upstairs, her head tilted up slightly so he could just make out the curve of her face under the brim of her cap. There was a sinking feeling in his chest as he realized it wasn't his navy-blue Red Sox hat that day, but instead something in pale pink. He got the message. She didn't want him to confuse a hat with how she felt about him.

Opening the door and stepping out onto the front porch, he cleared his throat loudly in case she hadn't heard him coming out. Whatever spell the house had on her seemed to be over, because she jammed her hands in the pockets of her cutoff shorts and began walking his way. He had to keep reminding himself to stop looking at her long, lean legs as she approached, but he didn't want to look her in the eye either.

When she'd locked eyes with him on the back deck the other day, and then again for a moment at the diner the night before, he'd felt his heart pound in his ears. His body wouldn't seem to listen to his brain, so he'd have to avoid contact with her as much as possible. She'd have to get back to Nashville soon, to her boyfriend and her career.

"Hey." Her head was down as she lightly bumped the front edge of her flip-flop on the bottom stair. "Whatcha working on today?" She looked up at him then, squinting her eyes against the afternoon sun as her tipped-up ball cap revealed eyes that looked puffy and red.

Fen had woken up from his nap inside, drawn to the sound of their voices. He bounded down the stairs to greet her, but Jesse stayed at the top, keeping his distance. As she bent over to pet the dog with one hand, she swiped her other hand across her eye. Had she been crying? Was the mere sight of the house still that upsetting to her? It wasn't as if she'd been back to visit much, even before her parents died.

"Just repairing some of the windowsills on the second floor." He pointed up. "After the windows blew out in the storm, water got in and pooled on top. It's no big deal, though. I was heading out to grab some more wood from the truck."

Her brows knitted together as she leveled a questioning look at him, temporarily forgetting her sadness, it seemed. "You're out here putting in all this time and effort when it's already been sold. Don't they know what they bought?"

He had to think fast. Uncle Lonnie said handling Callie and her questions was his domain.

"I'm doing the work for them." It wasn't a lie. He *did* work for the entity that bought the house. He also happened to be part owner, alongside Michael and a couple of other investors.

Instead of looking her in the eye, Jesse focused his full attention on screwing a loose finial back on top of a porch light on the side of the house. This was Uncle Lonnie's discussion. Besides, she wasn't his to protect anymore.

With both the house and the festival on his plate, he had to focus on getting back to work. As he brushed past her at the bottom of the stairs on the way to his truck, his arm glanced hers and set off an electric spark that rushed through his body. Having her here was nothing but a distraction, and he didn't have time for distractions. He already had a tight schedule, and now he was going to have to take time away from the house to get things ready for Beach Bash. Last he'd heard, the festival was surviving on fumes. Maybe that meant Ms. Myrtle's change in plans was to downsize everything. It was a shame, but that would get him back to the house project faster. As would volunteering to help her clean out the house. The faster she went inside and packed it up, the faster he could finish his renovation.

He picked up a long piece of wood he could cut down to fix both upstairs windowsills and turned back to the house, where Callie now sat on the second stair of the porch, Fen at her side. The same way Coop used to always sit next to her in the stands at Jesse's baseball games in high school. The memories came flooding back so quickly he could almost hear the crack of the bat and the smell of fresh-cut grass.

He was brought back to the present when he heard her sniffle, tears glistening in her eyes once more. He fought the urge to go to her, wrap his arm around her shoulders and tell her everything would be okay.

"Did you need something?" He shifted the wood off his shoulder to rest one end on the sidewalk. He stood in front of her now, looking down at her hunched on the step like a small child who'd been sent outside to play against her will.

She peered up at him then with those big blue eyes rimmed with tears. Something in his heart tugged at him, telling him to reach down and wipe them away, but he stood firmly where he was planted.

"My guitar." Her voice was a near whisper. "I came to get my guitar. But, umm..." She paused, biting her lip. "I haven't been in the house since..." Her voice trailed off as a single tear fell down her cheek.

Fen snuggled into her even closer, before looking at Jesse as if to say, *Help her, you fool.*

"Oh." He was surprised at her sudden display of vulnerability. "Want me to get it for you?" He chastised himself for sounding so overly eager. He'd jumped to her aid so quickly, but old habits die hard.

"Would you?" She looked up at him again with hopeful eyes. "I need it to write a little. I didn't bring mine with me, and Lonnie loaned his out."

Uncle Lonnie had been playing his guitar when Jesse was there that morning. Had he really loaned it out to someone in the span of a few hours? Or was this his way of nudging Callie to go inside the house and Jesse had ruined it by volunteering to come to her rescue? Oh, well, it was too late now.

"Sure," he said as nonchalantly as he could. "I'll get it."

As he climbed the stairs toward the little back bedroom, Jesse realized Callie wasn't the only one who'd been avoiding the house. At least this part of it. The door to her bedroom had been closed when he first got the keys from Uncle Lonnie and had come over to survey the state of disrepair. He'd left it that way, telling himself the broken windows were the first priority.

Turning the knob now, he opened the door to a time capsule. It looked as if Callie simply walked out of her room thirteen years ago and closed the door, and time had stood still waiting for her to return. Rays of light streamed through the window at the back of the room, cutting through the stirring dust, as he disturbed what had to be years of containment. The bedspread, once bearing bright-yellow stripes and bold bouquets of flowers, was faded, its matching curtains pulled back from the window.

Callie's parents had never let them be unsupervised in her room, so he hadn't spent a lot of time here. On more than a few occasions, he'd snuck down the street late at night and stood below her window, watching her for a few minutes before she noticed he was there. One minute her brows would be furrowed as she tried chords that didn't work, quickly crossing out lines on her notepad, but then her face would light up when she hit the right note or found the perfect words.

He could stand there and watch her for what seemed like hours. Then she'd glance down and see him, waving furiously, a broad smile taking over her other tiny features. The stairs creaked too much to allow her to sneak down, but she could lift her window, and they'd whisper back and forth to one another in the moonlight.

Forcing his concentration back to the present, Jesse spotted her guitar leaning in the corner to the right of the window seat. The instrument was covered in an inch of dust, cobwebs stretching up its neck, extending toward the wall like roots looking to plant themselves. Picking it up, Jesse sneezed as he disturbed the remnants of time that had settled on it. He took a rag out of his back pocket and attempted to brush off what he could. The guitar was going to need a good clean and tuning before it could make music again.

Jesse closed the door on his way out, trying to disturb as little as possible. He felt he'd invaded Callie's privacy, stepping inside after the years had made them practically strangers. He'd leave it like it was until he could convince her to face it and clean it out.

After all, he'd eventually need to get in there and strip the wallpaper border he'd spotted peeling around the top of the walls. It'd need a fresh coat of paint, and he'd refinish the hardwood floors when he did the rest of the house. Or—and he knew this was crazy—could he turn her room into a small recording studio if Callie decided to keep the house? Maybe she could spend her downtime here instead of Nashville. It was the most outlandish thing he'd let himself imagine in a very long time. But it couldn't hurt just to check out what that would require, right? He shook his head as if to loosen the idea before it took hold.

Exiting the house, he found Callie waiting for him. "Here you go." He handed the guitar to her.

She was standing just outside the front door, but at an angle where she couldn't see through to anything inside. She looked like Alice in Wonderland, afraid to get too close to the mirror for fear of falling into another dimension. She took the guitar from him so gingerly it was as if she thought it might bite. Once again, he had to fight back the urge to wrap his arms around her and tell her it would all be okay.

"Do you remember that time we went into Jacksonville to get new strings?" She smiled at him. "You'd just gotten your license, and we couldn't wait to get out of here and go somewhere. We told our parents that the music store over the bridge was out of strings so we could drive further."

What he remembered was how he couldn't keep his eyes on the road because he was so distracted by her sitting next to him in the truck. At sixteen and fourteen, they'd been best friends. But that was the spring he'd started seeing her as something more than the girl down the street. All he could think about were her long legs and big blue eyes. His body lit up every time she was nearby, and he'd wondered if she could tell how his feelings about her were shifting.

"Yeah, we had to drive all the backroads because my mom wouldn't let me go on the interstate yet." He smiled at the memory. "But we didn't mind because it meant the drive took even longer."

"Yeah." She laughed. "Back then it felt like a real road trip, like we could take a turn and go anywhere. Our own big adventure."

"Little did you know just how many adventures the future had in store for you." He leaned against the doorjamb and crossed his arms. He was reminded once again that while his greatest adventures had all been with her, hers had not included him.

"Trust me, that old truck of yours beats a tour bus any day." She looked down at the guitar, picking a cobweb from between the strings.

As she lifted her head, their eyes locked and his heart thumped against his ribcage. She seemed to be pleading with him. But to do what? The moment passed before he could decide how to ask her what was wrong.

"Thanks." She looked down at the guitar as she turned it over in her hands to examine it. "I told Andrew—my, uh, producer"—she caught herself—"I'd write some new music while I'm down here."

Jesse knew who Andrew was. He'd seen them on the cover of *Us Weekly* last fall. "*Callie Jackson and Producer Andrew Walker Get Cozy at Titans Game.*" They'd been in a luxury suite at a Tennessee Titans football game, his arm around her, pulling her close. That's who comforted her now, not Jesse.

Jaw tightening, Jesse merely nodded at her.

She started down the porch stairs, and he thought their conversation was over, but then she looked back in his direction. "This is how I used to get all my inspiration. Maybe the magic will be there again." A small smile played on her lips as she looked wistfully around the porch, her eyes settling on his for one heart-stopping moment. "See ya around."

Turning again, she was down the stairs and across the yard in seconds, the guitar strapped across her back, like the town troubadour off to find another street corner to play.

Had she been saying it was him that inspired her? The house? Big Dune Island? He cursed himself under his breath for wanting to know the answer. He pulled out his phone and looked up that little music store in Jacksonville, in the hopes they'd know what he'd need to build a miniature recording studio if Callie did decide—against all odds—to stay.

CHAPTER THIRTEEN
CALLIE

E very time she saw Jesse, it was like flipping through the pages of a scrapbook. His old pickup truck, their road trip to buy guitar strings, how he used to stand on her front porch and look into her eyes as if he could read her thoughts. They'd locked eyes like that after he'd gotten her guitar for her earlier, but then she'd mentioned Andrew and she'd seen his expression change in an instant.

It was clear he was aware Andrew hadn't been just her producer. But did he know they weren't together anymore? Probably not. They'd managed to keep that out of the press so far, not wanting to give the media even more fodder for stories. No one needed to know her personal life was wrecked alongside her professional one, but she'd wanted to tell Jesse in that moment. Even after all these years, she wanted him to know that she'd never felt about anyone the way she'd felt about him.

Forcing herself to focus on the task at hand, Callie shut herself up in the guest bedroom with the guitar and a notepad and settled in to work. After a long tuning, the guitar was as good as new.

She'd always been inspired by the sights and sounds of Big Dune Island, and Gigi's house gave her a perfect vantage point from which to work. Located at the back of the house, the guest-bedroom window faced south, but if she angled herself next to it, facing east, she could see down the long stretch of beach. Strict development codes kept developers from building right on the sand, so fifty yards or more of dunes stood between the beach and each home. Some were tiny cottages like the one Gigi bought, built in the 1940s and 1950s, they had passed down from generation to generation. Over the years, more had been sold as tear-downs and were replaced by larger two- and three-story homes. The code kept builders from going to a fourth story, but many pushed the limits with widows walks or rooftop decks that skirted around the rules.

Jesse had become one of those builders, according to Gigi. Callie had a hard time picturing it though. Jesse had always wanted to be a civil engineer, but not because he wanted to develop every square inch of their pristine island. He'd wanted to restore historic buildings, preserve downtown Big Dune Island and all the other little towns up and down the coast. Although Callie was still emotional about saying goodbye to her childhood home, it did provide some comfort that Jesse was doing the restoration. She knew he'd take good care of it.

Pushing thoughts of Jesse out of her mind, Callie forced her fingers to find their familiar home on the guitar. She'd search for a rhythm and find a few chords she liked first, hoping the lyrics would make their way to her as they had in the past. The last album had been the most difficult to write. She used to bring dozens of ideas to Andrew and the others in the early years. It had seemed as if inspiration for songs came to her around every corner, and she'd scribble them out on the tour bus or backstage in the green room.

Pop music had been much more difficult for her. The

songs had to be "edgy." She could hear Andrew's voice in her head, coaching her to become more like this or that. At some point, being herself wasn't good enough anymore. Or at least that's what they all told her.

Callie thought back to the talented young singer she'd met at the bar. Sienna had liked the old Callie. And she'd sounded great singing Callie's song. Gigi said she'd help Callie get in touch with Sienna so she could talk to her about Beach Bash. The girl had talent, she just needed her big break, the way Callie had gotten hers at the festival all those years ago. Sure, there probably wouldn't be a record label president in the audience, but every public performance got you one step closer to being discovered. She needed to check in with Gigi to see if she'd found Sienna's contact information.

Callie was so consumed with thoughts of Sienna and the Beach Bash she hadn't even realized her fingers had started to move across the strings, her foot tapping in rhythm. It was a mish mash of chords, but the pace was soothing. Callie focused her attention on the ocean waves crashing against the empty stretch of sand outside. It wasn't long before she had pieces of a melody, and then the words started coming.

The sun rises over the sea
As I'm finding pieces of who I used to be
Feel that Southern breeze blow by and
Realize that I've been crying

She alternated quickly between scribbling on her notepad and toying around with the chords, piecing them together until a song began to emerge.

I was chasing dreams that ran away with me
And now I'm right back where I started

———

WHEN SHE AWOKE THE NEXT MORNING, CALLIE grabbed the notepad off the nightstand to check she'd written a song last night or only imagined it. To her relief, it was there. She read through the lyrics again, singing them softly to the tune still reverberating in her head.

"Wow, Cal." Gigi's voice surprised Callie as she made a small change to a line in her notebook. "Did you just write that?"

Callie hadn't heard Gigi open the door. Heat rose to her cheeks like it always did when she played a song for someone for the first time. "Yeah, last night. What do you think?"

"I think you haven't lost your gift for looking inside people's souls and showing them what they can't put into words." Gigi smiled, crossing the room to sit beside Callie on the bed. "That's how I felt when I came back. Like I'd found myself."

Callie considered what Gigi was saying. "Don't you think everyone feels that way about their hometown though?" She sat the notebook on the nightstand and looked out the window at the morning sun glinting off the sparkling blue water.

Gigi shrugged. "Maybe read back through those lyrics and think about what you're trying to say." Smiling at Callie, she patted her hand before standing. "I've gotta get to court. I'll see you tonight."

After Gigi left, Callie read over what she'd written. She really liked it, but she knew Andrew wouldn't. It was too much like her old music and didn't have the kind of "attitude" he preferred in her pop music.

She'd worry about him later. Right now she had to get dressed and get herself down to Main Beach to meet Ms. Myrtle, who was moving full steam ahead with plans to unveil Callie as the headliner of the festival.

Checking her watch, Callie decided she had time to walk

to Main Beach from Gigi's house instead of driving the short mile south. She threw on shorts and a tank top, grabbed the only hat she could find, slid on her flip-flops, and took the boardwalk down to the beach.

As soon as she got to the end of the boardwalk, she took off her flip-flops so she could walk in the sand. It felt cool underneath her feet, even though it was already warming up outside. She'd forgotten how good it felt to have sand between her toes. There was nothing like it, and she'd experienced enough of the world to know that for certain. Closing her eyes, she lifted her face so she could feel the light wind tickle the tendrils around her cheeks. Glancing around to make sure no one was near her, she took off the hat and freed her hair, letting the wind blow her curls back. She closed her eyes for a moment as she walked and tried to concentrate on the sound of the waves crashing on the sand to her left.

It was low tide, so there was a wide swath of beach between the dunes and the water. This time of the morning, the only other people on the beach would be a walker or two with a dog or a cup of morning coffee. She saw one woman up ahead of her, 200 yards away, throwing a tennis ball into the surf for her golden retriever to fetch. No one was behind her that she could spot. She truly had the beach to herself.

The walk did more for her than the last decade of therapy had. This was what cured the soul—the sound of the waves rhythmically crashing, the salt in the air, the sand under your feet, and the sun beating down on your face. People thought money could buy anything, but it couldn't buy this.

By the time she arrived at Main Beach, her hair safely tucked back under her hat and wearing big shades, she'd jotted down lyrics for another song on her phone as she'd walked. It was amazing how this place could inspire her.

Thankfully, Ms. Myrtle had agreed to an 8 a.m. meeting: early enough—Callie hoped—that they wouldn't run into many people at Main Beach. It was one of the few beach entries on the island with a large parking lot, meaning it mostly attracted visitors, not residents. With it not being quite peak season, the lot was empty.

As Callie approached, she realized Ms. Myrtle was animatedly talking to someone Callie couldn't see between the cars. As Ms. Myrtle spotted Callie and turned to wave, the person between the cars stepped out. Callie's breath caught in her throat as she realized it was Jesse. The jolt of electricity that coursed through her body was unnerving, as it had been every other time she'd seen him since she arrived. Could she not go anywhere on this island without running into him?

"Callie, dear." Ms. Myrtle opened her arms to welcome Callie as she crossed the sand to the edge of the parking lot. "I was just telling Jesse about how you've agreed to help out our little festival this year." Ms. Myrtle kissed her on each cheek, squeezing Callie's now tense shoulders.

"I didn't think you'd have time for anything other than packing up the house." He rubbed the back of his neck and frowned.

His mother obviously hadn't told him about the meeting at Ms. Myrtle's house, and he certainly didn't sound happy at the prospect of Callie's involvement.

"She's going to be our headliner." Ms. Myrtle stood proud as a peacock. "That's why I asked you to meet us here, Jesse. We're going to need a much bigger stage and more seating. We're going to need more of everything," she gushed, her arms sweeping around to emphasize how much bigger everything would be. "People are going to be lined up halfway across the island to get in to see Callie Jackson."

Callie could feel her cheeks flushing. It still felt weird to come back home and have her fame acknowledged.

"So the label or whatever is going to let you perform?"

Jesse asked. By his tone it was clear he hadn't believed she'd get a yes when Austin suggested it.

"Something like that."

She still felt uncomfortable going behind Andrew's back, even though Gigi seemed certain she could get Callie out of the contract. She slipped her hands into her pockets and focused her attention on a gull that had landed nearby and was preening its feathers. Why was he so eager to avoid her? Was he still that mad at her after all these years? When she'd broken up with him, she'd always thought there would be some time in the future when she'd be able to explain to him why she'd done it, and he would say she'd made the right decision. But in the blink of an eye, it was thirteen years later, and she'd never had that chance. Maybe staying for the festival would give her the opportunity to finally set things right.

Jesse turned to Ms. Myrtle. "Do you think it's smart to have Callie play the Beach Bash? We don't have the security for that kind of thing."

Ms. Myrtle waved him off, turning back to Callie. "It's a publicity dream. Picture it: *Callie Jackson returns home to save the festival where she was discovered*," Ms. Myrtle said, moving her hand across the sky from left to right as if she was unveiling a headline.

"I know the Beach Bash is a little underfunded right now." Jesse ran a hand over his short-cropped hair. "But there has to be another solution. Callie doesn't want to come back to sing in front of a few hundred people at a beach party, right?" He turned to her. "Couldn't it also look bad for you if it's a small event?"

She wasn't sure if Jesse was showing genuine concern for her career or if he was just trying to get her out of town. She couldn't read his eyes because they were hidden behind sunglasses. His body language wasn't promising though: all stiff and closed off with his arms crossed over his chest.

"Underfunded," Ms. Myrtle huffed. "This goes beyond a little underfunding. If it was only money, I'd take up Callie on her offer to make a donation. This is about making a splash." She threw her hands into the air like a water fountain exploding from the ground. "Now, Jesse, it's going to be all hands on deck." She began steering him back toward the parking lot. "Let's go talk about the stage and all the extra bleachers and tents we're going to need. You leave security up to me; I'll call Sheriff Johnson this afternoon." Her voice trailed off as they walked away.

Jesse's protests against Callie performing at the Beach Bash only made her want to do it more. She needed to prove to him that she still cared about the event and about Big Dune Island. Maybe she could even convince him that she'd ended things all those years ago because she cared about him too.

———

THE WHOLE TIME CALLIE HAD BEEN MEETING WITH Ms. Myrtle to go over logistics, she'd watched Jesse hauling materials and tools from his truck to the beach. From the strides he took, to small mannerisms, like the way he wiped the sweat off his forehead, she could have picked him out of a crowd, even from a distance. He was more muscular now than he'd been as a teen, and his baby face had given way to sharper angles along his jawline, but if it was possible she found him even more handsome now.

"Callie, did you hear me?"

She focused her eyes back on Ms. Myrtle. She had no idea what Gigi's mother had been saying. "I'm sorry—"

Ms. Myrtle cut in before she could continue. "He hasn't dated anyone seriously, you know. Not since you." She pursed her lips and raised an eyebrow.

"Jesse?" she asked, as if Ms. Myrtle could be talking about

anyone else. Callie had asked Gigi not to tell her anything about who Jesse did or didn't date after she'd first moved to Nashville, and she'd held up that deal ever since. Not that Callie hadn't ever wondered; she just didn't think she could take hearing about how he was madly in love with someone new.

Ms. Myrtle put an arm around Callie's shoulder, steering her to walk down the sand toward the water. "My first love's name was Howard Tynsdale. I'm sure he's old and paunchy now, but back in high school all the girls swooned over Howard. He was the cat's meow, as we said back then." She smiled at Callie.

"Now, don't get me wrong, Dr. Franklin is absolutely the love of my life, but no love is ever the same as that first one. It's a novelty the first time you truly love someone. When every look, every touch, is the very first you've ever experienced. It's thrilling and terrifying all at the same time. If you could capture that electricity, you could get rich selling it by the bottle like a drug. Some people spend the rest of their lives trying to find that high again. And, sure, most of us find someone else who produces a different kind of electricity we enjoy in an entirely different way. But I think sometimes you're only set for one frequency. Do you know what I mean?"

"Maybe?" Callie said it more like a question than an answer. Ms. Myrtle was right. No one had ever made her feel like Jesse had, and she sensed the light inside her flickering, waiting to be turned on, every time she was around him now.

Ms. Myrtle turned them back toward Jesse and stopped, her hands firmly on Callie's shoulders. "You can't escape destiny, no matter how far you run. The universe has a way of guiding us back to the people and the places that truly matter. But it's up to you to decide what you do with that."

Callie was still thinking about Ms. Myrtle's words as she

made her way back to Gigi's house. She knew Ms. Myrtle had a penchant for matchmaking—at least five couples she could name on the island met because Ms. Myrtle invited them to a dinner party and sat them next to each other—but was she really suggesting that the universe had brought her back Big Dune Island to give her another chance with Jesse?

It made no sense. She lived in Nashville, and her career was a landmine she still had to figure out how to navigate. Jesse's life and career were here. What did they even have in common anymore, other than their shared childhood? High school sweethearts reuniting might work in the movies, but it wasn't real life. Hers was a mess, and right now she had to focus on writing some new music, saving Beach Bash, and then resuscitating her career.

CHAPTER FOURTEEN
JESSE

Images of Callie in his Red Sox hat, walking barefoot in the sand that morning brought back memories—afternoons splashing in the waves, Callie on a striped beach towel strumming a guitar, summer nights walking along the shoreline as the moon reflected off the water to light the way. They were memories Jesse was still trying to beat back when he returned to the Lyman house to work on the front porch railing that was hanging at a precarious angle.

Why had she worn that stupid hat again? Was she trying to send him a message? And if she was, what was it?

He nearly fell over the porch and into the overgrown flower bed below it as he took out his aggression on the edge of the railing, rocking it back and forth until it finally gave way and disengaged on the one end that was still attached to the porch column, tumbling to the ground below. Fen had run back inside the open front door, fearing for his safety.

Jesse pulled a rag out of his back pocket and wiped it across his sweaty brow. Callie was staying in town until Beach Bash. That was nearly two weeks away. He wasn't going to be able to hide his involvement with the house that long, they'd be ready to close by then.

He debated going back to see Uncle Lonnie, but he couldn't spare the time. With Ms. Myrtle and Callie cooking up this new plan for Beach Bash, he'd have to get started on the stage and bleachers over the weekend.

"You look like you're having a rough day, man." Austin's voice surprised Jesse as he came around the corner of the porch. "What's up?"

Hands on his hips, Jesse let out an exasperated sigh, debating how much to tell Austin. These were his problems to solve.

"Nothing, just trying to figure out whether I can sand down these balusters and slap on a layer of paint and call it day, or if I'm going to have to build all new ones."

"Did you uh"—Austin leaned over the edge of the porch to view the railing lying on top of the shrubs below—"mean for the railing to end up down there?" Turning back to Jesse, Austin laughed a little in an attempt to lighten the mood.

"Sure." Jesse stuffed the rag he'd been using to mop his face in his back pocket. "It had to go somewhere." He shrugged. "I'm gonna grab a water from inside, you want one?"

"Thanks." Austin followed Jesse around the porch to the front door.

They grabbed cold bottles of water from the fridge in the kitchen. The air-conditioning was a welcome respite, so they opted to stay inside at the small table and chairs that filled the breakfast nook. Jesse had dusted and cleared it off weeks ago to have a place to lay out the original floor plans. He folded the plans back in half so they had a little room at the table.

"How's it going?" Austin relaxed in his chair and took in the long galley kitchen that extended from the breakfast nook down the back side of the house. "Staying on track?"

"Well, I was." Jesse took a big swig from the water bottle before continuing. "But Beach Bash will probably put me behind. I've gotta build the stage and get all the bleachers and tents out next week. That'll set me back a little."

"Then let me help you. I can swing a hammer. And I look darn good in a tool belt, I might add." Austin's perfectly white teeth gleamed in the sunlight filtering in through the windows behind him.

"Nah, can't have you showing me up." Jesse laughed, hoping Austin would back off. It was nice of him to offer, but this was Jesse's responsibility.

"He who is too proud to ask is too good to receive."

Jesse stared at Austin blankly. "What?"

"Read it on a bottle cap this morning." Austin grinned.

Jesse responded by picking up the top from his water bottle and throwing it at Austin, which he batted down before it hit him square in the forehead.

"Man, why can't you accept a little help?" Austin's expression was serious now. "You don't have to do everything yourself. There's nothing wrong with letting someone help you. I'm your best friend, that's what best friends do."

Jesse sighed, staring out the window behind Austin's head, not meeting his eyes. "I'll think about it, okay?"

"I'll take it." Austin was all smiles again as he lifted the water bottle back to his lips.

"I learned something, umm"—Jesse searched for the right word—"interesting. I met Ms. Myrtle at Main Beach this morning. She said she wanted to adjust the plans for Beach Bash. And, you know, they're having all these financial issues, so I thought she meant making things smaller." Leaning back in his chair and looking up at the ceiling, he sighed again before continuing. "But it sounds like Callie is going to headline the thing."

Austin let out a long whistle as he put his feet up on the

chair next to him. "I mean, I know it was my idea and all the other night, but I didn't think she'd actually be able to do it."

"Well, it seemed like it was a done deal now."

"Wait." Austin removed his feet from the chair, sitting up to face Jesse. "Callie was there too?"

"Yeah." Jesse rolled his eyes. "Seems she's everywhere these days." It was a fact he both loved and hated. He had to admit he still felt the same pangs of excitement at seeing her as he had all those years ago, but he couldn't afford for her to get in the way of restoring the house. This time, it was his turn to be selfish and go after his dreams.

"Man, I feel for ya. You go a decade without seeing her and suddenly she's back." Austin shook his head.

"Yeah, and now her and Gigi keep asking questions about who bought this place." Jesse motioned around the room.

"She wouldn't be doing that if she knew what you were doing here." Austin raised an eyebrow in Jesse's direction. "Wouldn't you wonder if your uncle had sold away your childhood home without asking you about it?"

"What can I say? Uncles can't be trusted." Jesse thought of his and how he'd nearly ruined their family.

"You know as well as I do that Lonnie is looking out for her, but someone's going to have to tell her if she's sticking around and digging into things with Gigi. Dude, Gigi is way scary these days. I wouldn't mess with her." Austin laughed.

"You didn't look very scared of her the other night at the diner." Jesse smiled at Austin.

Austin winked. "That's because she can't resist the Beckett charm."

"Great, then you go distract her with your charm and keep her away from this house."

"I do need to go see her about the building downtown." Austin changed the subject. "I'd really like to buy it for the cafe."

Jesse wasn't sure how to respond. He wanted to warn his friend against doing business with family, but it was one of Austin's most endearing qualities, the way he took care of his sister. But Jesse couldn't help it, family and business didn't mix.

"Are you sure? I know you helped her get things up and running, but how deep do you want to be in this thing?"

Austin frowned. "She's my sister, dude. I'm all in. I know your family has a history of—well, you know." He waved off the rest of his thought. "But the coffee shop is a good investment. *Chloe* is a good investment."

"Okay." Jesse held up his hands. "Fair enough." There was no point in trying to change Austin's mind once it was set.

Jesse only hoped he wasn't the one who was in too deep. Accepting Uncle Lonnie's offer had seemed like a good idea at the time, but things were getting a lot messier now Callie was back in town. The last thing he needed was to be caught up in someone else's family drama. The house was business, not personal. At least, that's what he kept telling himself.

CHAPTER FIFTEEN
CALLIE

That afternoon, Callie called her publicist, Piper Presley, to tell her about Beach Bash, the new song, and Gigi's plans to find a way out of her contract. Piper had been part of Callie's team for years, and she'd been working overtime to keep Callie's image intact after the news of the failed label broke. Callie paid her directly, so Piper had no loyalty to Andrew or the label. In fact, she'd been putting together plans for how to help Callie reinvent her career as soon as the final year on her contract was up.

"Hey, I've got an idea," Piper said. "I don't know if Andrew would go for it, but what if you could debut that song you wrote down there at the festival? A brand-new song at the festival where you were discovered? I can sell that story all day, and he's in no position to turn down good press coverage on you."

"Do you really think you could convince him?"

"You leave it to me. I can see the headlines already. Heck, maybe I'll even mock up a front-page feature to show him. *Callie Jackson Plays Hometown Hero, Saves Festival with New*

Single. Something like that." She mumbled other ideas with the words moved around here and there.

"It's worth a try." Although Callie trusted Gigi to find a solution with her contract, it would be easier if Andrew could simply be convinced to go along with her playing Beach Bash.

Piper was a natural flirt, and even Andrew wasn't immune to her charm. If she persuaded him this would make Callie—and thereby, Andrew—more marketable, he might go for it. She hoped he wouldn't ask to hear the song. That would likely blow the whole thing, because it definitely wasn't a song he'd approve of. Too sweet, not enough sexy.

Callie hung up with Piper and turned back to the lyrics and notes she'd scribbled down the night before. If she was going to stay and headline the Beach Bash, the song was going to need a little more work. She could move it into a different key, punch up a few notes to give it that upbeat quality they loved in pop music. It needed a stronger chorus too. Scrunching her nose at the lyrics, she wondered if they were too—what was that word Andrew used all the time?—*pedestrian*. What did that even mean? The lead on her pencil broke as she crossed out another word.

Laying the guitar on the bed, she rummaged around in her makeup bag for a pencil sharpener. It was made for eye pencils, but it would have to do. She didn't want to hunt around in Gigi's home office and get distracted. The melody was still repeating itself in her head; she was too in the zone to quit now.

While she sharpened the pencil, Callie stood in front of the window in the guest bedroom and angled herself east, watching the sea oats bending in the ocean breeze, blue water extending to the horizon in an unbroken line beyond the dunes. Her fingers stilled as the song's name came to her. "Saltwater Revival." Yes, it was perfect!

Tossing the sharpener back in the direction of her

overnight bag, which had clothes exploding out of it in every direction, she raced back to the notepad to write down the words before she lost them.

Oh, this place has always been my bible
I'm at home with the waves
Saltwater revival

She was strumming the guitar, tweaking a line that contained too many syllables for the chords she'd found for the bridge, when her cell phone interrupted her. She'd forgotten to put it on silent when she started working. Flipping it over on the blanket, her stomach dropped when she saw Andrew's name on the screen. She knew it was too soon after her talk with Piper to be good.

"You want to headline a little beach party on Big Dune Island?" He didn't even bother to say hello when she answered.

"It's a festival, not a party."

"It's a terrible idea." He made it sound like an open-and-shut case.

"Is it? The Beach Bash is where I was discovered, remember?" Andrew hadn't been there, but everyone knew her story. The record label had loved having her tell it back when she was first starting out. "They're struggling with it this year. Money is tight and interest is down. It's the biggest event of the whole year for this town. The businesses here count on the visitors it brings in."

"I understand how you must feel about it." His voice was gentler now. "But can't you just make a donation? Superstars don't play small-town festivals. We don't want people to think you're struggling."

Callie wanted to point out she *was* struggling, but she bit her tongue. "I did offer to make a donation, but Ms. Myrtle said it wasn't enough. She said they needed someone who could draw a crowd, and it's too late to find someone else on such short notice."

"Ms. Myrtle? Who is Ms. Myrtle?" He didn't pause to wait for an answer. "Sounds like something you'd name a pet turtle." He laughed. "Let me see who I can find. I heard this singer-songwriter at a showcase last week, but she was too country for my taste. Perfect for your little festival though."

"Is it really that big of a deal for me to sing here?" she asked as nonchalantly as she could. "It would be fun. I've been darting around town wearing a big hat and sunglasses, Gigi even got us wigs, so I can fly under the radar here. It'd be nice to be myself for a few days. I could surprise everyone and debut my new song. Did Piper tell you how much publicity she could get me? We both know I could use some good publicity."

"So there's a song?" Excitement rose in his voice. "You got some new writing done?"

"Yes." She jumped on a glimmer of hope that the conversation was steering in a better direction. "Jesse got my old guitar for me, and I was up late last night writing." She looked at the scratched-out lines on the notepad in her lap. "It only needs a few more tweaks. Then I'll send it to you, I promise."

"Jesse? Your high school sweetheart?"

Callie couldn't quite read his tone, but Andrew wasn't the jealous type. "Yeah, he's working on the house. I didn't bring my guitar because I didn't think I'd be here that long, but he grabbed my old one for me."

She heard Andrew acknowledge someone who'd walked into his office before he came back to her. "Send that song over when you get it finished."

"And you'll think about Beach Bash?" She tried not to sound too excited at the prospect.

A man's voice murmured something in the background before Andrew said, "I've got to run, Callie. Look forward to hearing that song though." He ended the call before she could respond.

No answer was better than a no, right? And she and Gigi still had their backup plan.

Gigi had texted over Sienna's information earlier, and Ms. Myrtle had given Callie the go-ahead to invite Sienna to open for her, so Callie decided to call. If she got in deep enough, it would be impossible for Andrew to say no. It would look even worse to hit the news for bailing on Beach Bash than whatever Andrew was imagining would happen if she actually headlined the thing.

"Hello," Sienna answered on the second ring.

"Is this Sienna?"

"Yes, can I help you?"

"Actually, it might be you who can help me. I know this is a little unusual, but I met you at Breakwaters a couple of nights ago in the bathroom. We talked about Callie Jackson?"

"Oh, sure. Hi! I don't think you told me your name though."

"You're right. I didn't." Callie paused, feeling a little overly dramatic, but even she recognized what she was about to say would be a shock. "I know this is going to sound crazy, but I'm Callie. I'm home taking care of some family business, and my best friend dragged me out for the night in disguise."

There was a long pause before Sienna answered. "You're kidding me, right? Is this Ainsley? Are you pranking me?"

Callie laughed. "I swear I'm not. I could name all my No. 1 hits in order. Or maybe sing a few bars?" She sang a couple of lines from one of her songs.

"Omigosh, you're serious. I can't believe I met Callie Jackson and didn't even know it." She suddenly gasped. "Omigosh, I told you I didn't like your new music. I totally insulted you, and you didn't say a thing. That's so terrible. I'm so sorry!" Sienna was speaking faster now, the excitement in her voice clear.

"Please, there's no need to apologize. I happen to agree with you. I can't even listen to my last album, I hate it so much."

"It's not that bad," Sienna insisted. "I'm such an idiot. I can't believe I said those things to you. You have to know I absolutely love you. I want to be you when I grow up!"

"That's sort of why I'm calling. You actually do remind me a lot of myself at your age, which is why I'm hoping you'll agree to open for me at Beach Bash."

After Sienna asked her a half-dozen times if she was serious and gushed about how it was the best day of her life, Callie made plans with her to meet up over the weekend to talk more about the upcoming festival.

"I can't believe I get to meet Callie Jackson," Sienna squealed before they ended the call. "I can't believe I'm *opening* for Callie Jackson!"

When they finally said their goodbyes, Callie's cheeks hurt from smiling so much. There was no doubt now. She was singing at Beach Bash, and there was nothing Andrew could say to stop her. He'd have to come down and drag her off the stage.

CHAPTER SIXTEEN
JESSE

"D on't you have music to write?" Jesse asked Callie the next morning. She'd snuck up behind him as he was hauling wood out of his truck to drag down to the beach for the stage.

Or a house to pack up? he thought but didn't ask.

The sun had begun its slow climb from the horizon. It was a ball of orange reflected in the still waters of a low tide, lapping at the shore more like a lake than the crashing ocean waves that would come later in the day with high tide.

"It's nice to see you too, Thomas."

He winced at the sound of her calling him by his last name. She'd always been the only person besides his parents to call him by his first name.

She stepped up beside him to peer into the bed of his truck. "Can I help you grab something? Ms. Myrtle sent me over to help reconfigure the stage."

He knew why Ms. Myrtle sent her over, and it had nothing to do with the stage. She was trying to play matchmaker. Everyone on the island knew it was one of her favorite pastimes. He'd figured that out after Callie left the beach the day before and Ms. Myrtle kept asking him how it was to see Callie again. She didn't know about the house, so he couldn't expect her to understand why Callie's presence made him uneasy. Besides, it was Callie who'd left him, not the other way around. What was he supposed to do about it now?

"And risk a splinter in your finger so you can't play your guitar?" He kept his tone light, teasing her as he took more wood from the truck. "No thanks, I'm good. What are you doing here anyway?" Austin had been right; she'd gone from nonexistent for a decade to constantly either in his thoughts or standing right in front of him.

"Geez, sick of me already? I've only been in town a few days." She tucked an errant curl back under her hat.

Jesse was relieved to see she wasn't wearing his Red Sox hat today. He needed to concentrate, and that was nearly impossible with her around, even worse when she was dredging up old memories. Every time he saw her in that hat it was as if someone had yanked open a file drawer that had been locked, stirring up the dusty contents in his mind. He had to get the supports for the stage built out today so he could return to the Lyman house to put a second coat of paint on the porch railing before it got too dark to work outside.

"Guess you'll be here longer now, huh?" He grunted as he stacked one more piece of wood on his pile, struggling to balance it as he swung around from the back of the truck to head down to the beach.

"Looks like it." She bit her lip. "Still waiting to get the official okay."

He could feel her nipping at his heels as he carried his load down to the sand, like a little dog you couldn't shake. One of those cute white ones with curly hair that filled the covers of calendars and Valentine's cards. The kind that were so cute it hurt.

Dropping the 2x4s in the sand, he shook the image from

his head. What the heck was he even thinking? She wasn't cute, she was a distraction. He had work to do.

"There's this girl that sings at Breakwaters," Jesse said, taking off his work gloves to pull the stage plans out of his back pocket. "Sienna is her name, I think. Sounds uncannily like you, even sings some of your old songs—"

"Yeah," Callie broke in, bouncing around in the sand until she was standing directly in front of him, "She sang—" She stopped suddenly as if she'd caught herself about to say the wrong thing. "One of my songs the night we were there. Do you know her?"

"No, but I've heard her sing. I was just thinking maybe *she* could headline Beach Bash. You know, since it's not your kind of thing anymore." Although he had to admit having Callie headline the Beach Bash would be huge for the town, he couldn't risk having her there trying to unravel his deal with Uncle Lonnie.

"Not my kind of thing?" Her hands were on her slender hips now. "What is that supposed to mean?"

"That you're a superstar now." He refused to meet her eyes as he fought against the wind to hold the plans up where he could read them, effectively creating a barrier between himself and Callie. "I get why your—" He couldn't make himself say the word "boyfriend." "*Andrew* wouldn't want you playing some festival here in Mayberry." The locals sometimes disparagingly called the island "Mayberry by the Sea."

"Stop."

She was inches from him now, and even though he couldn't see through her sunglasses, he knew her eyes were squinting into that look she got when she was angry. He'd always hated it and had spent years doing everything in his power to keep her trademark thousand-watt smile on her face. He'd only meant to tease her, not upset her.

"I hate when you call it that. What's wrong with Mayberry

anyway? And, besides, Mayberry or not, this is my hometown. It meant a lot to my parents, and it means a lot to me."

Her voice got quieter as she finished, and he hoped she wasn't going to cry. He'd be powerless if he saw her cry again. He swallowed hard, unsure what to say next. Clearing his voice and giving the plans a shake with both hands, he erected the makeshift wall between them once more, turning away from her to try to work with the wind instead of against it. He could feel her trying to peer over his shoulder, but the top of her head barely reached that high.

Then she ducked under his outstretched left arm, dipping under it so that it was practically around her as she moved to get a closer look at the plans. "This is why I'm here." She jabbed a finger at a line running from east to west, drawn to represent the front of the stage, which would be perpendicular to the water line. "The stage is all wrong."

Releasing the large sheet of paper from his left hand, he lifted his arm up and over her to close her out as he examined the plan again, trying to calculate where the footings for the stage should start on the beach. He needed to account for the shifting tide, which could move the water line thirty or forty yards closer to the dunes. They never left any permanent structure intact after the festival, meaning he had to remeasure and rebuild each year. That was because prime season for sea turtle nesting was around the corner, and any impediment the mothers encountered while coming ashore to build a nest might make them turn around and head back to the water without depositing their eggs.

"I know you do the same thing every year, but hear me out. May I?" She had her hand outstretched, reaching for the plan.

"Sure, go right ahead." He shook his head. The sooner he heard her out, the sooner he could get her out of here and start the footings.

He handed the plans to her, but he let go before she had a good grip, and the paper was suddenly flying across the sand, tossing and somersaulting like a tumbleweed down the beach a few feet away. She was already chasing after it, her laughter lifting over the sound of the waves, creating a melody he recognized from so many sunny afternoons spent on this very beach.

As she caught up to the paper, pinning down an edge with her toe, the wind swept up under the bill of her hat, sending it rolling across the sand to her right. With a few quick strides he caught up to it and bent down to snag it before the wind continued its charades. Dusting the sand off as he rose up, he realized she was in front of him now. Her curly blonde hair whipped across her face, free from its imprisonment in the hat. The sun glinted off it, giving it the quality of spun gold.

It was like glimpsing back across time, and he felt the same warm glow he'd always felt in her presence. When he saw her on the cover of magazines, her hair was always unnaturally straight, and he could barely make out anything he remembered of her beneath the layers of makeup—she was all cat eyes and red lipstick. But the woman before him with a clean face and curly hair was simply an older version of the girl he'd laid next to on a beach towel all those years ago.

Giggling, she interrupted his trip down memory lane. "Trade you." She passed the plan to him in one hand while reaching out to take her hat from the other. Grabbing her hair in her other hand, she twisted it up until she could push the hat down on top of it, reaching around the rim to stuff all her hair up underneath. She tightened it an extra notch in the back. "Good as new," she declared. "Okay, let me see the plans again, I promise I'll take better care." She was smiling up at him now.

"They go like this." He reached over to turn the plans ninety degrees so they'd be right-side up.

She jerked back before he could grab them. "No, that's what I was trying to tell you. I think it should be like this."

He stepped behind her so he could see over her shoulder. Now he was close enough to smell her shampoo, the scent wafting on the breeze as if it was beckoning him. It smelled of coconuts, as it had when she was a teenager. He resisted the urge to close his eyes and take a deep breath.

"See," she was saying, "what if the back of the stage was parallel with the water, that way when people were watching the act on the stage, they could see the ocean beyond it. I mean, that's why people want to be on the beach, right? And this time of year, the sea breeze always blows off the water, so it would help carry and amplify the sound."

He looked up from the plans to the water and back down again. She was right, it would set a better scene. In the past, festivalgoers were looking at the side of the stage as they entered from the parking lot, with the front facing north, up the beach. Turning it this way would mean they could see everything happening on the stage as soon as they entered the parking lot, and never lose sight of the water while they watched the acts on stage. Why had no one ever thought to do it that way before? They'd all just been doing things the same way they'd always done them. That was Big Dune Island's M.O.

"I like it." Although it pained him to admit it. He backed away so he could disconnect from the smell of her. He inhaled deeply so the salt air could fill his lungs and flush out the memories. "Thanks. I'll talk to Ms. Myrtle."

"No need." She waved a hand. "When she called this morning, she said she trusted the two of us to make whatever adjustments were necessary. I guess we still make quite the team."

She was smiling at him now, pushing the sunglasses sliding down her petite nose back up. He hated the way his heart had leaped into his throat when she'd called them a team. They weren't a team anymore.

He ignored her comment. "I've gotta go back for more." He nodded his head in the direction of his truck.

"It's pretty cool you still do this every year." She followed him to the parking lot. "I remember when you used to help your dad. How is he?"

"He's good." Jesse hefted his toolbox out of the rear of the truck. "He can't work like he used to; rheumatoid arthritis. But he still likes to come visit the worksites." He pulled metal sand anchors out of the bed one at a time, tossing them on the pavement in a series of loud clangs.

"That's nice he's still able to check in on things. I'm sure that makes him feel useful." Callie grunted to pick up the toolbox. "I can carry this."

"You sure?" The toolbox had to weigh close to fifty pounds. There was little chance she could carry it all the way from the parking lot to the beach, but he knew she'd be too stubborn to admit it.

"Yeah, I got it." She strained to get each word out, nearly toppling over as the tools shifted within when she let go of the handle and attempted to move her other hand underneath.

Carrying as many of the anchors as he could grab, he followed behind her. He tried not to chuckle too loudly as he watched her zig-zag across the parking lot ahead of him, legs wide as she lumbered under the weight of it.

"Shut it, Thomas. I got this."

"I'm not saying a word." He stayed behind her so she couldn't see him smiling.

This was the Callie he remembered. Scrappy and stubborn and someone who never took no for an answer. It made him wonder why she looked so nervous earlier when she mentioned not yet having the go-ahead to headline the Beach Bash. He knew Andrew had some measure of control over her—over her career—but didn't she own part of the label too?

Miraculously, Callie made it to the edge of the sand before she dropped the toolbox onto it, her chest heaving, gasping for air as if she'd crossed the finish line at a marathon.

"Power Pilates for the win!" She pumped her fist in the air before doubling over to put her hands on her knees, still catching her breath.

"Impressive," Jesse admitted. "Leave it there, I'll get it." He walked past her to deposit the anchors next to his wood pile.

She staggered over and let herself collapse into the sand a couple of feet from the anchors. "Okay, I'm going to let you do that." She held up one hand to gesture OK as she let her head slump forward toward her knees.

He returned to the parking lot to grab the remaining anchors, but he let himself stop and observe her from behind for a few seconds on the way back. She'd lifted her head up now and was staring out toward the water. The sun had climbed higher in the air, turning from orange to yellow as the first few beachcombers began to pick through the shells left behind by the low tide further down the beach.

The morning had felt like old times. He'd almost forgotten she was a Grammy award-winning artist who traveled the world, gracing the covers of magazines that lined the checkouts at the local Publix supermarket. In her cutoff shorts, tank top, and hat, her tiny frame curled into a ball as she hugged her legs to her body, she looked like the Callie he remembered. The Callie that had once been his.

CHAPTER SEVENTEEN
CALLIE

As she sat and watched Jesse twist the large metal anchors into the sand, she realized she might not know anything about him anymore. She'd asked Gigi how his family's company was doing a few times that first year—mostly to assure herself she'd made the right decision—but she'd asked Gigi not to tell her anything about Jesse specifically unless her friend really thought she needed to know.

It hurt too much to be reminded of Jesse in those days. All she could see when she thought of him was the hopeful gleam in his green eyes when he'd stood in her driveway and said, "See you soon," on their final night together. Thankfully, she hadn't been forced to confront the hurt in his eyes when she'd told him weeks later that he couldn't join her, but she'd heard it in his voice. The sound of him spitting out his final good-bye, "Enjoy Nashville, I hope it's everything *we* always dreamed," was tattooed on her heart, a permanent scar.

She'd tried to ask him earlier about his dad and Thomas Construction, but then she'd carried that stupid toolbox—what was in that thing, anvils?—and it had taken what felt like five minutes to get her breathing back to normal. What kind of life had she left him behind to live?

One time, after she'd been gone about a year, her mother said he was taking classes online, but it wasn't long after that her parents were gone and her lifeline to the island was virtually severed. Gigi had been off at college and then law school, and Callie's calls with Uncle Lonnie had been far too infrequent.

"So what kind of work do you do these days when you're not moonlighting as a handyman for my uncle or building festival stages?"

"We do a lot of the new builds on the island." Jesse reached up his gloved hand to wipe the sweat from his tan forehead. She thought she could see his jaw tighten as he continued. "The investors bought up a bunch of the land around the greenway and down on the south end. Mostly second home kind of stuff."

That much she'd already known. She realized what she really wanted—*needed*—to know was how he felt about it. She needed to know his life had turned out okay. That, looking back, he could see how important it was for him to stay on Big Dune Island and help his dad with Thomas Construction.

"How's business?" She shielded her eyes with one hand as she squinted into the sun to watch him.

"It's good." His face was etched with concentration as he screwed the next anchor into the sand.

It was like pulling teeth to get any real details out of him, but she continued to push, determined to get more. After all the years of feeling guilty, she wanted proof she had made the right decision.

"I saw your mom at Ms. Myrtle's. It was nice to see her again."

"Yeah," he grunted, stabbing down another anchor to form the third corner of the rectangular shape he was mapping out across the sand, "she didn't mention seeing you. I guess she figured how I'd feel about you being back."

"And how's that?" She was scared she wouldn't like the answer. Her heart pounded in her ears as she waited for his reply, racing faster with each silent second that passed.

He stopped, straightening up to put his hands on his hips and face her. The sun rising above the water silhouetted him from behind, tracing the shape of his arms. She'd noticed them the first day she'd run into him in the backyard. He'd always been in good shape, even as a lanky teenager, but now his muscles rippled from beneath his shirt sleeves, defined over years of manual labor. They were taut, his body rigid as he looked off in the distance beyond her, considering his answer to her question.

"I just wasn't expecting you to come back." His body relaxed again as he stuffed one hand in the pocket of his jeans and let the other drop to his side. "Caught me off guard."

"Yeah, I was a little surprised to find you in my backyard too." She smiled in an attempt to lighten the mood. They'd once been inseparable. They'd shared everything. Nothing had happened in her life that she hadn't run to tell him first, and vice versa. That had all come to an abrupt end, but now they were adults surely they could find some common ground and be friends again.

His mouth opened to answer her, but then it seemed he thought better of it.

"What? I'm sure you must know more about it than I do. What's the deal?"

"Like I told you before, you'll have to take that up with Uncle Lonnie."

There'd once been a time when he told her everything, when there were no secrets between them. The realization that he no longer considered her a confidant cut deeply.

"So how much of that do you get to do these days?

Restoring old houses, I mean. I remember you always wanted to do that."

"Not much." He looked down as he dug the toe of his work boot into the sand. "You can make more money on the new ones."

"Seems like Thomas Construction is doing pretty well these days though." She wanted to tell him how proud she was of what he'd done to help his dad. Gigi hated new developments, but she was impressed with how careful Jesse was about saving the trees on his lots and working them into the design.

"Yeah, at least my dad has been able to mostly retire. He deserves it after all those years out on job sites." A small smile played on his lips.

Callie could tell he was proud he'd been able to take things over so his dad could slow down. Her heart swelled with pride too, knowing everything he'd sacrificed to stay back and do the right thing. Everything she'd sacrificed too, so that he could do it. Even if he hadn't seen it that way back then, he must see it now.

"So you don't regret not coming to Nashville?" She bit her lip. The question had tumbled out before she'd thought it through. She hadn't realized how badly she needed to know the answer.

She noticed a ticking in his jaw as he studied a young couple, twenty yards to their right, loaded down with beach chairs, umbrellas, and bags overflowing with sand toys and towels. They were struggling to get everything from the parking lot down to the beach, two small boys running ahead of them toward the water.

"Well, that wasn't really my choice, now was it?" He turned back to face her and looked her directly in the eyes. Even with sunglasses blocking them from sight, she could feel the electric current as their gazes locked. "But, yeah, it was the right thing. My dad needed me. You didn't."

"It wasn't that I didn't need you—" she started.

But he held up a hand. "Cal, it's fine. It was another life ago." He turned from her and back to the anchor he'd left lying in the sand.

"But it wasn't like that." She scrambled to her feet as he turned away from her and squatted down to turn the anchor into the sand. "There was nothing I wanted more than for you to come be with me in Nashville, but I knew you'd regret it." She was standing in front of him, looking down on the back of his head as he silently worked on the anchor. "Your family needed you," she pleaded, "and you would have resented me if you'd come."

He stood up so fast she almost lost her balance as she stepped back.

"You didn't even ask me how I felt about it." He was gesturing in her direction with both hands, suddenly animated. "We could have had a conversation about it. Instead, you just made the decision for me. Told me to stay home."

Her eyes welled up with tears behind her sunglasses. She hadn't expected him to still be so mad all these years later. "I was sixteen." It was a weak attempt to defend her actions. "I was being asked to make a lot of decisions about the rest of my life really fast. I'm sorry if I didn't make all the right ones." She couldn't hold back the tears any longer, and they began streaming down her face. Covering her face with both hands, she sobbed lightly.

His arms were around her in an instant, and she let herself lean into his chest. It was firm, and his strong arms encircled her easily. She instantly felt safe. For the first time since she set foot on Big Dune Island, she felt she was home.

"Hey." His voice was soft, his mouth so close to her ear she could feel the warmth of it even as it sent chill bumps down her arms. "It was a long time ago. It all turned out okay. You became a big superstar, and I'm right where I belong. I never would've fit in to your world there anyway."

A wave of sadness washed over her that he thought she'd been better off without him there. She wondered what the experience would have been like with him by her side. Would he have distracted her from what she'd gone there to do? Maybe she'd be like her friend Kyra, back singing in small-town amphitheaters and bars. But would that be so bad? Maybe then she'd still be wearing what she wanted and—more importantly—singing what she wanted. Sure, there'd be less money and smaller crowds, but maybe she'd be happier.

It was a pointless mental exercise. That's not how things had played out.

Leaning back, she took off her sunglasses so she could look him in the eye. They were mere inches from each other. She could see the freckles in his green eyes, the tender way he looked at her like he had all those years ago.

"Jesse, I'm sorry." She said it so quietly she wasn't sure he heard her over the sound of the surf crashing behind them. Her breath caught in her throat as his eyes searched hers, and she felt the warmth of a tear that escaped and began tracing its way down her cheek. "Can you forgive me?"

When he didn't answer immediately, she almost repeated her question. But then he reached up to wipe the tear, his thumb igniting a spark as it touched her skin. "Yeah," he whispered, "I forgive you, Callie."

She began to cry again, burying her head in his chest so he couldn't see her tear-streaked face that she was sure was a mess. They weren't sad tears though. They were happy tears. She hadn't realized how much she needed to hear those words until he'd said them.

CHAPTER EIGHTEEN
JESSE

J esse was still reeling from his and Callie's encounter at the beach when he pulled up to the Lyman house that afternoon. He'd never given a lot of thought to forgiving her. He assumed it had just sort of happened little by little over the years, the way that you don't realize someone you see every day has started looking older. He'd gone about his life, and one day he no longer asked himself how many days, weeks, months, or years it had been since she'd left. Sure, he still thought about her plenty—it was hard not to when she was all over the covers of magazines, her familiar voice filling his truck speakers as he surfed through the channels—but he hadn't thought about her like *that* in a long time. Not until she'd come home.

But when he'd told her that morning he forgave her, he'd felt as if a weight had lifted off his shoulders. A weight he hadn't known he was carrying around all those years. She'd said her goodbyes quickly afterward, saying she had to get out of there before Main Beach got more crowded and someone recognized her. She seemed embarrassed by her outward display of emotion, but it had been nice to see a crack in her tough exterior.

He'd stopped by his house first to get Fen, who brought him back to the present, whining to get out of the truck. Opening the door, Jesse grabbed a yellow tennis ball from the cup holder, chucking it across the front yard as he got out. Fen scrambled out behind him, galloping happily across the green grass until he reached the ball. Grabbing it in his mouth, he pranced around the yard in a circle, showing off his prize.

"Come on, Fen. Inside, let's go."

Jesse unlocked the front door with the key Uncle Lonnie had given him, and Fen followed him in, ball in mouth, settling into a corner of the living room to chew on it. The heart pine floors that extended from the hallway into the living room were original to the house, and Jesse knew he could breathe more life into them if he sanded them down and stained them, but he hadn't wanted to move any furniture yet. Instead, he had started his work on the doors and windows to prevent further damage from wind or water and then had moved to porch repair.

Until Callie came to pack up, he was afraid to do too much inside. It didn't feel right to touch their things. The more time he spent around her, the guiltier he felt for not letting her in on the secret.

Following Fen into the living room, Jesse paused to look at the framed photographs on the mantel above the fireplace. Callie smiled back at him from each of them, her blue eyes lighting up even behind the years of dust. In the first one he picked up she looked about five. She was sitting on her dad's lap, an arm slung around his shoulder, the camera catching her in the middle of a laugh. Placing it back on the mantel, he picked up the next one. She was younger, barely old enough to walk, one parent on each side of her holding a hand. The three of them had their backs to the camera and were walking toward the ocean. That's how he remembered them—as a family.

The three of them had always been close, even when Callie was a teenager. She hadn't been the kind of teenage girl who picked fights with her parents or who snuck out after curfew. They were "thick as thieves" as she liked to say. Her mom hadn't hesitated to drop everything and move to Nashville with her so she could sign with the label, and her dad was up there every chance he got in those first couple of years.

They'd died on their way to see her concert in Atlanta. He'd never understood why they were driving so late at night instead of flying. They'd been struck by a drunk driver who crossed over the grassy interstate median and hit them head-on. The entire town was devastated by the loss of two of their own. His parents had wept at the news.

His first instinct had been to call her. He knew she'd be shattered. He would have driven all night himself if he could have gotten to her then and held her in his arms. But she'd long since changed her number, and he didn't know it. Then she'd shown up to the funeral with some other guy by her side.

His trip down memory lane was cut short by a knock on the door. His heart leaped into his throat as he wondered if it was Callie on the other side. Would she knock on the door of her own house? As he placed the photograph carefully back in its place on the mantel, Fen trotted into the hall, ready to inspect their visitor. Jesse opened the door to reveal it wasn't Callie, but instead his father, Bob Thomas.

"Hey, son." His dad shuffled in the door and patted him on the shoulder before leaning over to stroke Fen's head.

"Hey, Pop." Jesse closed the door behind them.

His father let out a whistle as he took a few steps into the living room to the left of the front door. "Wow, it's like a time capsule."

"Yeah, it's a little eerie. Everyone just walked out one day and never came back." Realizing the weight of his words, Jesse's heart ached again for Callie and everything she'd been through.

"Lonnie told me she hadn't been home, but I didn't realize it was like this." His dad walked around the room, pausing at the same photographs Jesse had been studying. "Your mother says she's back now." He turned to Jesse with a curious look.

"Yeah, she's come by a few times. She hasn't come in yet though. Apparently, she hasn't been in the house since the funeral."

"I can only imagine." His dad shook his head as he picked up the photo of the Jacksons on the beach, their backs turned toward the camera. "There must be a lot of memories for her here."

He couldn't see his dad's eyes, but Jesse knew he was talking about more than just the house.

"I think she's struggling. I wish I knew how to help her. Eventually she's going to have to come inside."

"I know you've got deadlines to hit, but don't push her too hard, son." His dad turned back to him with a serious look. "There's plenty for you to do around here. Work around things as long as you can. Give her time to process everything she must be feeling."

"I know, Pop. I'm not heartless. Uncle Lonnie actually asked me to help her when she's ready to come inside. It can wait a few more days though. I've fixed the windows and doors that were leaking, and I have a lot of work to do on the front porch before I move indoors."

"You're not trying to do this all alone, are you?"

"It's a one-man job for now, Pop. I can't have the whole town knowing what I'm doing here."

His dad let out another long whistle as he looked around the room. "This is one heck of a job for one man. I know you don't want the whole crew here, but I can still pound a nail or sand a floor."

"No, Pop. The doctor said no more manual labor for you. I want you to just enjoy your retirement. You and Uncle Lonnie should go fishing or something."

"Fine." His dad held up a hand. "At least let me do your supply runs. I'll even let Hal load it in my truck," he said, referring to the owner of the hardware store in town.

Jesse knew it was important for his dad to still feel needed and useful, so he relented. "Sure, you can pick up some things." Then he thought of the porch railing outside with its intricate design he desperately needed to salvage. "Hey, come look at this porch railing for a minute. I could use your advice."

They went out together and squatted down to inspect the balusters. Weather and bugs had eaten away at some of the sections, but Jesse hoped some wood filler and a patch here and there would do the job. His dad confirmed it was best to try to repair what was there instead of attempting to shape new ones by hand, and then he noticed the side porch railing still lying in the overgrown bushes.

"Having some trouble over there?" He rounded the corner of the wraparound porch for a closer look.

"It was hanging by a thread." Jesse failed to mention he'd been the one to sever that final thread, sending the railing overboard.

"Come on, I'll help you get it back up." His dad started toward the stairs.

"No, Pop. No manual labor. I can get it."

"It's a fifteen-foot section of railing, Jesse. I assure you, son, this part is not a one-person job. It'll take us two seconds."

"You want to tell Mom you're lifting a fifteen-foot section of porch railing? Or should I?" Jesse knew his father was far more afraid of his wife chastising him than his doctor.

His dad guffawed. "You wouldn't."

"Oh, yes I would." Jesse smiled at his father who'd stopped dead in his tracks at the foot of the porch stairs.

"Then get Austin over here. He could stand a hard day's work. I can't believe they pay that boy to talk on the radio all day." He was shaking his head, lowering himself onto the porch stairs to sit as Fen bounded down the stairs next to him, bringing him the ball to throw. His dad launched it across the yard and Fen took off across the grass.

"I'm fine, Pop. Stop worrying. I'll get it all done."

"Come here." His dad patted the spot next to him on the stairs. "Let me tell you something."

Jesse complied, coming down from the porch to sit on the stairs next to his father. Front porch stairs were his father's favorite place to dole out life lessons. They'd sat on their porch stairs more times than Jesse could remember talking about everything from being honest, even when it hurt someone, to the value of a job well done.

"Jesse, there's nothing wrong with asking for help and accepting it."

"Pop—"

"No." His father put a hand on Jesse's shoulder. "Don't interrupt me, son. I have something important to say."

Jesse quieted, looking down to study the laces on his work boots. He felt as if he was a teenager again, being scolded for sneaking out to stand below Callie's window late at night. His dad had caught him once, and had waited for him on the porch stairs when he returned home. He talked to him about rules and the value in following them, how they exist for a reason.

"Ever since your uncle—" His dad paused, collecting himself. "Did what he did to the company, it's been you and me against the world. In the beginning, we were all we had. Then one day we had to open ourselves up to help from the investors. We did what we had to do to save the legacy your grandfather built." He paused again, looking down at his clasped hands. "I know it hasn't always been perfect, and things certainly aren't the same. But I'm so proud of the man you've become. A man who's worthy of taking this business into the future. Lord knows I wouldn't have heeded the advice to slow down if I hadn't believed it was time for me to step back, to let you lead this company."

Surprised by his father's uncharacteristic display of emotion, Jesse snuck a look at him. His eyes were glassy, but they didn't meet Jesse's. Bob Thomas was usually a man of few words. Although Jesse had always known his dad loved him, it wasn't something they said out loud all that often. It didn't require words.

"Thanks, Pop," he said quietly, at a loss for what more he could say.

"This is the future of our company." His dad looked back at the house. "You've wanted to save these old houses since you were a little kid. And no matter what happened—how much your life plans changed—you never gave up." His dad looked him in the eyes now. "You made this opportunity for yourself, and that's admirable. But don't screw it up because you're too stubborn to admit you can't do it alone."

"You know why I have to do it alone, Pop." Jesse got defensive. "I can't trust anyone—"

"That's it." His dad gestured toward him. "You can't trust anyone. That's your problem. And, believe me, I understand why. What your uncle did changed our lives forever. But you can't run a company alone. At some point you have to rely on other people. You'll learn that soon enough. But all I'm asking right now is that you learn to ask for help. Call Austin and let him help you. You can fail all on your own for being stubborn just as easy as you can fail because someone else screws it up for you."

As much as Jesse didn't want to admit it, he did need help. Austin was his only real option, since he was the only one who knew about the deal other than Uncle Lonnie. Besides, Austin was the person he trusted most in the world after his parents.

"Okay, Pop." He reached an arm around his dad to pat him on the back. "You win. I'll ask for help."

They said their goodbyes, and he watched his father walk gingerly back down the drive to his truck, parked behind Jesse's. Waving as he left, Jesse took out his phone and punched the first few numbers until Austin's name popped up on the screen. He should've been back from his radio gig in Jacksonville by now.

"What's up?" Austin asked when he answered after a couple of rings.

"Grab your tool belt. We've got some porch railings to repair."

CHAPTER NINETEEN
CALLIE

"Whoa," Gigi said, when Callie finished recounting her conversation with Jesse that morning. "I knew you'd have to have that talk sometime, but I figured you'd both been avoiding it."

They were lounging under an umbrella in twin Adirondack chairs on Gigi's back deck, which offered an expansive view of the beach before them. They'd eaten lunch outside, and Callie was relishing the opportunity to just relax and catch up with her best friend. Was this what normal people did on the weekends?

"Yeah, it just kind of happened. One minute I was asking him about the construction company, and the next I was bawling like a baby in his arms. I feel kind of stupid now." She didn't admit it out loud, but it had felt good to be in his arms again.

Gigi lowered her sunglasses to look Callie in the eye. "You are *not* stupid. You're human, like the rest of us." She pushed her sunglasses back up with a finger, even though they were hardly needed this time of the day. "Even if you are a big-time superstar." She was grinning now.

"Haven't you ever seen those 'Just like us' sections in *Us Weekly*? Celebs are people too." Callie laughed.

"Seriously, Cal. I think it's good you two got it all out. It needed to be said. Now you can move on. Maybe even *together*." Gigi wiggled her eyebrows.

"Oh, for heaven's sake, Gigi. That's not happening. I'm still going back to Nashville to hopefully salvage my career, and he's got a whole company to run here."

"And he'd drop that company like a hot potato if he thought you'd let him come back to Nashville with you."

"He would not, and I wouldn't ask him to." At least she didn't think he would. Not after all he'd done to save his family's company for all these years. He couldn't walk away from it now. What was she even thinking? She wasn't asking him to come back to Nashville. They hardly even knew each other anymore.

"Mmmhmm." Gigi sipped her wine, returning her attention to the gulls circling over the beach. "Did I mention that I once caught him buying a magazine with you on the cover down at the Publix?"

She blushed at the thought of Jesse buying a magazine with her face on it. First Ms. Myrtle and now Gigi. Why did everyone insist on stirring up her feelings about Jesse? She focused on the ocean in the distance. Nothing put her more at ease than watching the waves crash, their frothy spray dancing in the air, the sound rhythmically soothing her soul.

But the thought of Jesse still wanting to come to Nashville was gnawing at her mind. It was such a ridiculous idea. Sure, he'd forgiven her for what she'd done all those years ago, but it wasn't like he was trying to win her back. Quite the contrary. He'd seemed ready for her to get her business done in town and head off.

He had gotten her the guitar though. That was something, right?

"Whatcha thinking over there?" Gigi pulled her sunglasses onto the top of her head, narrowing her eyes in Callie's direction.

"Me? Nothing. Just enjoying the sound of the ocean." She wasn't ready to discuss this any further with Gigi, at least not until she'd sorted out her feelings. She focused on watching each wave roll in, one after the other like an assembly line.

"Suuuure," Gigi drawled. "Maybe you're thinking about how much better Jesse looks in his jeans than that hipster fraud Andrew."

Callie had to admit Gigi was right. Jesse filled out a pair of jeans much better than Andrew ever could. She couldn't even imagine Jesse wearing the black skinny jeans Andrew preferred.

She didn't realize she'd laughed out loud until Gigi said, "See, you know I'm right."

Callie was dissolving in hysterics now. "I'm trying to picture Jesse in those skinny black jeans Andrew always wears."

"Don't forget the black leather jacket and the shades too." Gigi was laughing so hard her face was turning red. "A little gel in his hair to complete the look."

They had a good long laugh at Andrew's expense, and it felt cathartic. Callie had let Andrew tell her what to wear for far too long, it was only fair she critique his wardrobe too.

"Honestly, I have no idea what you ever saw in that guy," Gigi said, leaning back in her chair. "You had nothing in common but work."

"Geez, G, there's nothing in my life that isn't about work. This isn't a nine-to-five where I get to go home at the end of the day and scroll through a dating app looking for someone to take me to dinner. I'm either in the studio, writing music, or on the road. Work *is* my life."

"Maybe that's the problem." Gigi raised an eyebrow before taking another sip of her wine.

"What's that supposed to mean?" Callie shot back, turning to look at Gigi.

"I think it's pretty obvious," Gigi said coolly.

"Please, do enlighten me, Counselor." Callie swept an arm in front of her dramatically.

"You bury yourself in work, Cal. Ever since your parents died—" She paused and her voice softened. "You don't let anything into your life that isn't work-related. Heck, even when you see me it's only because I come to one of your concerts. Which, don't get me wrong—I love seeing you perform—but you haven't been home in almost ten years. You never see Uncle Lonnie; you don't keep in touch with anyone else but me. All you've surrounded yourself with are these superficial relationships with the people you worked with, all of whom virtually disappeared the instant you got a little bad publicity."

The words stung and Callie fought back the tears now threatening to spill over her bottom lashes. But she knew they hurt because they were true.

"Hey, I didn't mean to make you cry." Gigi leaned over the arm of her chair toward Callie to embrace her in a hug. "I'm sorry. I shouldn't have said all that."

Callie sniffled. "No, you're right, G. My work is my whole life. That's why I feel so lost right now. Andrew is guarding my contract like it's his lifeline—which, it kind of is—and my manager keeps telling me to be patient and let everything die down. I'm out here treading water all alone, waiting to see if someone is going to throw me a lifesaver."

"The contract! Did you find a copy yet?"

There'd been so much going on, Callie hadn't had time to look through her old emails for a copy. "I'll go through my email tonight. It's in there somewhere. My manager has already looked through it though. He says the best thing to do is wait. Either Andrew will find a new label to buy it out or it'll lapse and then we can go talk to labels ourselves."

"Seriously, Cal, why is this guy not trying to find a way out? Is he Andrew's manager or something too?"

"Worse," Callie admitted. "They're poker buddies. He's convinced Andrew had nothing to do with the downfall of the label and that we're both going to get snapped up as soon as this all blows over."

"Of course they're poker buddies." Gigi sighed. "The good old boys' club is still alive and well, I see. You know I love taking on entitled white men." Gigi jumped up from her chair and turned to extend a hand toward Callie to help her out of hers. "Go find me that contract."

———

AFTER SCROLLING THROUGH WHAT FELT LIKE hundreds of emails, Callie found the contract and forwarded it to Gigi, then sat down with her guitar again to work on the chorus for the new song before Sienna came over to meet her. She sang the words she had, humming in the spaces between, willing the rest of the words to come.

Instead, she kept replaying that morning with Jesse. She could still smell the Irish Spring, feel the warmth radiating off his chest as he held her close, his strong arms encircling her. She thought back to him getting the guitar for her, how he didn't judge her for not being ready to go back in the house yet. Images of the rooms floated through her mind in time to the chords she was still strumming, like a flashback reel from a movie. And then words finally started coming to her.

I was chasing dreams that ran away with me
And now I'm right back where I started
Oh, I should have known I couldn't build a home

145

So far away from where my heart is
There's a difference between living and survival
Oh, how I miss this
Saltwater revival

The sound of clapping behind her made Callie turn. Gigi and Sienna were standing in the bedroom doorway, giving a miniature standing ovation.

Sienna blushed when Callie's eyes met hers.

"You've already met Sienna," Gigi said, motioning toward the young woman with both arms outstretched like she was showing off a new car. "But it's time for Sienna to meet you. The *real* you."

Callie put down the guitar and rose from where she'd been sitting on the bed to walk toward them. Sienna held out a hand as she got closer, but Callie held out her arms. "I'm a hugger."

After a quick embrace, Callie stepped back. "I'm just playing around with a new song. Let's go sit in the living room."

As they followed Gigi back down the hall toward the living room, Sienna turned to Callie. "I really liked what I heard. It sounds more like your country music."

Callie nodded. "I guess it does. I found some chords I liked last night and have been playing around with them. Finally started to get some words to go with them."

"Does that mean you're doing another country album?"

Callie and Sienna sat in two of the armchairs in Gigi's living room, and Gigi excused herself to do some work she'd brought home.

"Between you and me, I'm not really sure what I'm doing." She laughed. "As I'm sure you've probably seen, my new label is sort of a mess right now. Gigi is trying to help me sort through that, but I'm going to leave the business stuff to her and just focus on the music while I'm here."

"Well, I think you're on the right track," Sienna said. "'Saltwater revival.' I liked that line. Is that the title?"

"I never write the title until I'm done with the whole song, but you're right. That does have a nice ring to it. 'Saltwater Revival' it is. Now I just have to figure out the bridge before Beach Bash."

"Oh, wow, you're going to play it at Beach Bash?"

Callie shrugged. "Might as well try it out. I thought it might be fun to sing something new."

"People are going to go crazy when they find out you're playing Beach Bash. When are you going to announce it?"

Callie ran through Ms. Myrtle's current plans, which included looping in Callie's publicist Piper. She told Sienna how many songs she'd need to prepare for the opening, and then asked what song she'd like to do together.

Sienna clapped a hand over her mouth, her eyes going wide. "We're going to sing a song together?"

"I always sing a song with the opener when I come on stage," Callie said, as if it was no big deal. Of course, she knew it was probably a big deal for Sienna, the same way it had been for Callie when she'd opened for Miranda Lambert ahead of the release of her debut album.

Sienna's eyes were full of tears now. "I just can't believe it. You're making all my dreams come true."

Callie smiled. "Hopefully not *all* your dreams. I have a feeling this is just the beginning for you."

After they talked through logistics for the show, they agreed to meet up and practice later in the week. There was another big hug on the way out the door, and Callie was so buoyed by Sienna's enthusiasm that she went straight back to her room to finish the bridge.

A few hours later, she'd finished her new song: "Saltwater Revival." It was an ode to Big Dune Island, the only real home she'd ever known, and the people here. Sure, she'd lived in

Nashville a similar number of years, but it wasn't home. No, home was where you felt loved. There were people in Nashville who cared about her career, but as Gigi had so aptly pointed out, they weren't people who cared about *her*. With that realization, she had been able to finish off the lyrics. The second verse still needed a little work, but there was enough of a song to send it off to Andrew for a first pass. She knew from fan mail and social media conversations it would be something her audience could relate to. She sent a recording on her phone off to Andrew and fell exhausted into bed.

———

WHEN SHE AWOKE THE NEXT MORNING, SNIPPETS from a dream she'd had were still running through her head. She'd been inside the house, and her parents had been there too. They showed up in her dreams every few months, but it usually left her feeling sad and empty when she awoke. It was different this morning. They'd all been so happy. She felt as if she'd been able to steal a few extra moments with them and the feeling left a glow that was still radiating through her body.

Unlocking her phone, she swiped down to read through her notifications. Nothing from Andrew yet. He wouldn't be up this early, but since he was a night owl, she'd figured he'd still been awake last night when she sent the song.

Today was the day. He was either going to love the song or he wasn't, and she wasn't sure she even cared what he thought anymore. She loved it, and that was what mattered.

CHAPTER TWENTY
JESSE

"I'm surprised to see you, Thomas," Gigi said, taking off her reading glasses as she looked up from a stack of papers on her desk. "To what do I owe the pleasure?"

Jesse stood awkwardly in the doorway to her office. It was time to show his hand. He knew he was about to put her in a bad position, but he didn't have much choice. "It seems we're in need of a lawyer." He shifted his weight from one foot to the other.

"Well, quit trying to hold up my doorway and have a seat." She motioned to the two brown leather wingback chairs that sat opposite her.

He sat on the edge, running his hands over his knees. "The investors have given me the authority to hire you for a new project."

Gigi raised an eyebrow in his direction, setting her glasses down before clasping her hands on top of the desk. "Well, you're just full of surprises today." She smirked. "Why on earth would a developer like you hire an environmental freak like me?"

"This is a..." He searched for the right words. "A *different* kind of project for us."

"Okay, I'm listening."

"The thing is." He cleared his throat. "I need to know what I tell you is covered by attorney-client privilege." He shifted on the edge of the chair, and it creaked beneath his weight.

"Now I really am intrigued. Sure, all my client consultations are attorney-client privileged. Spill."

"I mean it, Gigi." He looked her in the eye for the first time since he'd sat. "What I'm about to tell you cannot go beyond the four walls of this office."

"Scout's honor." She held up her hand in a Boy Scout salute, then leaned back in her chair, ready to listen. Jesse knew she couldn't possibly be prepared for what he was about to tell her. He decided to get it over quickly, like ripping off a bandage. "Gigi, I'm the one who bought the house from Uncle Lonnie."

Her mouth fell open, her eyes wide. "You what?" she said, leaping to the edge of her chair and stretching across the desk. "You're the buyer?"

He held up his hand. "Please, Gigi. Let me explain." He told her about how he'd been trying to find the right project for years. He shared how he'd convinced the investors to let him try it, and then he told her about Uncle Lonnie's plan to help Callie finally face her childhood home—and the right of first refusal clause.

She let out a long breath, leaning back in her chair again and raising a hand to her temple. "I can't believe you're telling me this, Thomas. When are you going to tell her? How am I supposed to keep this from her?"

"Uncle Lonnie said he's taking care of it. I don't want to get in the middle of all that."

"Don't want to get in the middle?" Her voice rose. "How

much more in the middle could you be? You bought her *house*."

"Yeah, well she can buy it back." He slumped in the chair, crossing his arms over his chest.

"This is a mess, Thomas—a mess." She shook her head. "I can't believe you attorney-client privileged me and want me to actively *lie* to my best friend. You realize I don't actually have to take you on as a client, right? It's a giant conflict of interest."

His face fell. He hadn't considered she might not take on the job. He knew he was putting her in a tough position, but he figured after he explained it all and assured her Callie could have the house back, she'd be on his side, even if it was reluctantly.

"Is it time for lunch yet?" She checked her watch. "I need some air. I've gotta figure out how to get us out of this disaster without destroying *both* of our relationships with her."

He wasn't sure if that meant she would help him or not, but he was too afraid to ask. They walked in silence over to Island Coffee together to grab a sandwich. He passed his usual table to sit in the very back corner, positioning them as far away from other people as he could so they would have some privacy while they talked.

"So that's why you already started work?" Gigi hissed across the table at him. "You're not just the contractor, you're the investor."

"Well, technically, no. The investors are still the investors, I'm just the labor. Forget that it's her house for a minute, Gigi." He leaned forward. "This is a *good* thing. If I can come in at budget on this, I can prove to them that restoring houses is as profitable as building new houses. I can shift our entire model, save more buildings in town."

She rolled her eyes. "If you think they're going to suddenly stop buying up every square inch of land on this island to painstakingly restore houses downtown, you're delusional, Thomas."

"Fine, be a cynic." He threw his hands up in the air. "But what if you're wrong? What if this is my shot at changing things?"

Her look softened. "Okay, okay." She held up her hands. "I get it. I just wish there had been some other way to get this done."

"So you'll help me? And you'll let Uncle Lonnie tell her what's going on?"

"On one condition." She raised an eyebrow. "You let me see this contract. I want to make sure she really can get the house back if she decides she wants it. No loopholes. And you sign a waiver allowing me to represent Callie *against* you if I see any funny business in that contract."

"That's two conditions." He tried to lighten the mood, but the stern look on her face told him she meant business. "Okay, fair. It's a deal." He extended a hand across the table, which after a few tension-filled moments she finally reached out to shake.

He exhaled deeply, easing back into his wicker chair as Chloe approached their table.

"Fancy seeing you two here." Chloe winked. "Brought back together by a common acquaintance, I imagine."

"She knows?" Gigi jerked her head away from Chloe and back to Jesse.

"Yes." Jesse leveled a look in Gigi's direction. "She knows Callie is in town. Remember? They ran into each other downtown the other day." He hoped Gigi would catch the hint and realize she only knew about Callie being back in town, not that he bought the house.

"Oh, yeah." Gigi met his eyes with understanding, before turning to smile at Chloe. "She mentioned how lovely it was to see you."

"Don't worry." Chloe placed a finger over her glossy lips. "My lips are sealed."

"Thank you, Chloe. I know she appreciates it," Gigi said.

"But hey." Chloe lowered her voice to a whisper. "Can you tell her someone was here yesterday asking a bunch of questions about her? Wouldn't tell me her name."

"A tourist?" Gigi asked. "Someone wanting to know more about where she grew up? That kind of thing?"

"No." Chloe's brown bob bounced as she shook her head. "It was different than usual. She was asking if I knew the last time she'd been home. She wanted directions to her house. Lots of people ask stuff like that, but she was dressed up kind of fancy to be your run-of-the-mill tourist."

"Paparazzi maybe?" Gigi asked. "If they figured out she wasn't in Nashville, maybe they came looking for her here?"

"Seriously?" Jesse asked. "They just track you down wherever you go?"

"Oh, sweet, naive, Jesse." Gigi shook her head. "Yes, when you're a multi-platinum recording artist who was recently splashed on the front of every gossip rag on the newsstand, people want to know where you are and what you're doing at all times."

Jesse hadn't considered how much Callie was under a microscope. Sure, he saw her on TV and in magazines, but most of that was at public appearances. Would someone follow her all the way back home? He'd seen movies where paparazzi dug through a celebrity's trash or climbed over a fence to get a photo, but did that really happen? He'd have to be more careful about locking up the house from now on. In a town like Big Dune Island, you didn't always bother with such formalities.

"I dunno," Chloe said, glancing toward the front door at the sound of the bell. "She looked too prim and proper to be paparazzi, but then I guess I don't know what one looks like.

Don't worry, I didn't tell her anything. But she did have Callie's address. I told her it had been sold though, so maybe she won't go poking around over there."

"What did she look like?" Gigi asked.

"Tall," Chloe said, holding a hand up way over her head, "like taller than normal for a woman. She was older, maybe my mom's age. Perfectly pressed linen suit—which is pretty impressive because linen wrinkles, like, the second you put it on." Chloe looked off into the distance as she tried to remember more details. "Short, straight black hair that fell to her shoulders. She was attractive."

"Thanks, Chloe," Gigi said. "Let us know if you see her again."

"You bet." Chloe excused herself to take orders, promising to bring them both sweet tea upon her return.

"I'll text her and give her a heads up." Gigi pulled her phone from her purse. "Good thing she's staying at my house, I guess. Hopefully no one will know to look for her there. We should probably tell Uncle Lonnie too, just in case."

"I can swing by later and let him know," Jesse said.

"Why don't you also let him know that it's time to let his niece in on this plan of his?" She was staring him down now. Austin was right, she was a little scary these days.

"I'll be sure to mention it," he promised.

Gigi picked up her bread plate from the table, examining the pattern of pink and blue flowers, before putting it down and glancing at the plate in front of Jesse that was adorned with gold lattice work around the edge. "You know why these don't match, right?"

"Some sort of quirky charm thing?" Jesse guessed.

"It's actually kind of sweet," Gigi said, tracing a ribbon that ran between the bouquets with a finger. "You know about china patterns?" She paused, waiting for him to nod that he understood. "When you get married, you choose an everyday pattern and a formal pattern—fine china they call it. I'm sure your mom has them. Every good Southern woman does."

"Sure," he said. "She has the plates she uses all the time and then there's a fancy set in the china cabinet in the dining room that only comes out on holidays like Easter and Thanksgiving."

"Well, china patterns are very personal. It's a woman's way of expressing herself. And when a woman looks at her china, she remembers the Easter when little Johnny was only two and couldn't sit still at the table long enough to eat because he wanted to go hunt eggs in the yard, or the Thanksgiving when her husband insisted on frying a turkey and burned it to a crisp."

He nodded, still not understanding where this was going.

"So." She sighed. "Then she gets older and wants to pass down her china and her ungrateful children don't want it. Her son's wife wants to choose her own or her daughter is a digital nomad and can't have *stuff* tying her down. And women have this emotional connection to their china because they have so many memories tied to it. So Chloe found a way to preserve it for every woman in this town."

Jesse looked down at the plate in front of him again, tilting it up so the light caught the gold trim and reflected it back at him. "It's a nice touch." Maybe he'd tell Callie about it when she got around to going through her mother's china cabinet as a way to ensure a piece of her mother stayed on Big Dune Island.

As they ate, Gigi gave him some good intel on what the Historic Commission would—and would not—approve. He was going to need to apply soon, because he couldn't replace any of the glass in the windows without permission first. He'd patched up what he could to keep the wind and water from intruding any further, but much of the glass needed replacing and he wanted to change out the back door for something more weatherproof.

He headed back to the house after lunch to start cataloging all the things Gigi said they'd need to take before the commission for approval. As he turned the corner at 5th, he spotted Callie's car across the street and his pulse quickened. Had Gigi called her the second they'd parted at the cafe?

He pulled into the drive, but didn't spot her anywhere. Had she finally gone inside? He was pretty sure he'd left the front door unlocked, but of course she probably still had a key. He called out her name when he entered the front foyer and listened for a reply or footsteps inside. Hearing none, he walked through to the kitchen at the back of the house and spotted her in the backyard staring up at her bedroom window.

"Hey." He exited the rear door onto the deck. "Whatcha doing out here?" He held his breath, hoping Gigi hadn't gone back on her word.

Callie startled at the sound of his voice, as if she had been lost in her thoughts. "Oh, hey." She glanced back at the window. "I was just thinking about how many songs I wrote up there."

"It still looks the same." He walked down the few steps to the yard to stand next to her. "I hadn't gone inside your room yet, but then when I got your guitar..." He paused, looking for the right words. "... it was like going back in time. Everything is exactly how you left it."

"I didn't even sleep here when I came back for the funeral." Tears glistened in her eyes. "I just couldn't."

"That's understandable." He tapped the toe of his boot into the grass, not meeting her gaze. "I think anyone would have felt that way." He wondered what it meant that she was making a habit of being so vulnerable with him. It felt like old times, back when they told each other everything. He had to remind himself not to drop his guard, because he was still keeping a giant secret from her. One that was becoming increasingly difficult to justify.

"Hey," she said, turning away from the window to face him. "I'm sorry about the other day at the beach. I didn't mean to get so emotional."

He kept his eyes on the little lump of grass he was flattening out with the toe of his boot. "No need to apologize. It's water under the bridge." He almost told her how nice it was to see a glimpse of who she used to be, but he was afraid she'd take it the wrong way. He didn't want to backtrack with her now they were connecting again. He knew it was crazy. What did it matter anymore? But he found himself wanting that connection with her anyway.

"It helped though; I think." Her voice was lighter now. "I finished the song I was working on when I got back to Gigi's."

"That's great." He met her eyes for the first time. "I'm happy for you."

She'd been inspired here. That had to count for something, right?

"I had a dream about them too." She glanced back at the house. "About my parents."

"Oh?" He had no idea whether that was a good or bad thing.

"I think I'm ready to go inside." She stuffed her hands in the pockets of her shorts. "But maybe you could go with me?"

His heart pounded. She needed him. He'd never said yes to anything so easily in his life.

CHAPTER TWENTY-ONE
CALLIE

S he was sure she'd chicken out if she tried to go inside the house alone. At first, she'd planned to ask Uncle Lonnie, but she was sure it was tough for him as well. After all, he'd stayed out of it all these years and made the decision to sell the house.

Something about going in the front door felt overwhelming. As if, no matter how many years passed, she'd still always expect her parents to greet her there. The back door though, that felt safe. Maybe if she snuck in through there the memories wouldn't catch up to her as fast.

"After you," Jesse said, pushing the back door open and stepping aside to let her enter first. "Whenever you're ready."

From where she stood on the deck, she could make out the kitchen table inside the door. It was covered in giant sheets of paper that looked like floor plans. She felt a pang in her chest as she remembered that Jesse had already been in the house, working. Had he needed to move things around already?

Her feet were as heavy as lead as she lifted one foot over the threshold and then the other. She hadn't realized she was holding her breath until she let it out in a big rush of air.

Looking to her right, she gazed down the expanse of the galley kitchen that ran the length of the back of the house. Sunlight filtered through the window over the sink, illuminating the dust-covered surfaces. It all looked like she remembered, but there were no traces of her family here. Although in desperate need of a rag and some 409, the counters were empty with the exception of an old coffee pot that sat unplugged like a lone soldier guarding his post. Her dad had liked to leave his coffee mug sitting right next to the pot so it was ready for him the next morning, but its absence was another reminder that he was no longer there.

Leaving the safety of the doorway, she took slow, measured steps around the kitchen table and down the hallway that led to the front door, the formal living room to the right of the entry foyer, and dining room to the left. She gasped, her hand flying to her mouth.

"What?" Jesse immediately appeared at her side. "What is it?"

She pointed. "The floors, they're ruined."

Jesse let out a long breath. "They're okay, Cal. Uncle Lonnie and my dad got the windows boarded up the day after the hurricane came through. They had humidifiers and fans brought in. They saved them. They just need to be refinished. They'll shine up good as new, promise."

She crossed to the fireplace, running her hands over the hand-carved golden oak mantel her great-grandfather had commissioned from a local woodworker. Her mother always said it was the perfect mantel for Christmas, with enough room for all three of their stockings to hang, and deep enough to accommodate the enormous fresh garland she brought in and decorated with magnolia leaves and pinecones. Callie closed her eyes and imagined the smell of fresh garland mixed with the giant fresh Frasier fir her mom would place in the corner to the left of the fireplace. Next to salt air, it was her favorite smell in the world. Callie couldn't even remember the last time she'd put up her fake tree in Nashville, and she resolved to put up a real one this Christmas.

When she opened her eyes, she was drawn to a photo on the mantel. She was between her parents, each of her hands holding one of theirs. They had their backs to the camera, but she knew they were all smiling; happiness radiated from the image. Picking up the frame, tears threatened to spill over and stream down her face. Using the bottom of her shirt, she wiped dust from the glass. The colors were brighter now, as if she'd brought the scene back to life, and that made her smile. Placing it back on the mantel, she reached for another photo. As she moved to wipe it with her shirt, Jesse stepped up beside her.

"Here, you'll get your shirt all dirty," he said, pulling a rag from his back pocket and reaching for the frame.

"Thanks." She sniffed back tears.

They worked like that as a pair, moving through all five frames on the mantel. She'd hand him one, he'd clean it off, then she'd take it back and let the memories wash over her, smoothing out all the edges of her soul that felt broken and jagged.

She circled the rest of the room, running a hand along the back of the navy-blue couch. The room was dimly lit thanks to the boarded-up window, and dust caught the light from the other window as it floated around the room like snowflakes in a snow globe, shaken from its slumber by their presence. Being inside the house, surrounded by her memories, she'd expected the ache in her chest to deepen, but it had the opposite effect. It was like being in a warm embrace. She was overwhelmed, not by a feeling of sadness, but by a swell of love.

Stepping back into the foyer, she stopped at the bottom of the stairs, running her hand over the newel post at the end of the banister. Like the mantel, it had been hand-carved when the house was built. Glancing up, she remembered her attempts to slide down it as a child, the way people always did in movies. She never could get her balance quite right for more than a short stretch though, and as she tumbled onto the stairs the sound would always draw a shout from her mother wherever she was. "Callie Jackson, get off that banister! It's more than a hundred years old for heaven's sake."

Once, after a failed attempt, her father had tiptoed to the top of the stairs, a finger over his lips, winking down at Callie before he hopped on the banister and slid nearly the whole length before being tossed off three-quarters of the way down.

"Joe, that better not be you coming down those stairs!" her mother had yelled as she ran to the bottom of the stairs to find him standing next to Callie, the two of them doubled over in laughter.

"You two want to see how it's really done?" her mother had asked.

Before they even realized what was happening, she was at the top of the stairs, propping one hip up on the railing before taking off down it in one elegant ride straight to the bottom. She had popped off the end to land in the foyer on her heels like a gymnast executing a perfect dismount. "Now, that's how you slide down a staircase," she'd said, dusting off her hands before bending to take a bow.

Callie realized Jesse was standing next to her, probably wondering why she had a goofy grin on her face when moments before she'd been teary-eyed looking through photographs. She shared the story, smiling again at the memory.

"I can remember us trying to master that when I was about ten and you were eight." His crooked grin widened.

The feeling of warmth grew around her as memories of her parents mixed with those of her and Jesse. She'd had a wonderful life here. It had felt like someone else's life for a time, but being back on Big Dune Island was reminding her that maybe it was her choice. Maybe she could simply *choose* to be who she used to be. She just wasn't sure what that looked like. Uncle Lonnie's words echoed in her head. *You're a grown woman, Callie, and a successful one at that. Why are* you *letting anyone let you do anything?*

Climbing the stairs, she made her way to the little bedroom that had been hers. When she opened the door, sunlight flooded into the dark hallway, and she stepped forward into what felt like a time capsule. Everything was how she remembered it, right down to the wallpaper border that matched her bedspread. She crossed to the window seat, lowering herself onto it and sliding her back against the right side of the bay window. She brought her legs up, crossing one over the other, and looked out the window at the oaks in the backyard, Spanish moss dripping off the branches and dancing in tune to the wind.

She remembered how she used to write music that way, by imagining what melody would match the swaying of the Spanish moss. Wondering if it still worked, she focused her attention on an oak on the far-left boundary of the yard. The breeze lifted the strands of moss delicately before it fell again and swung from side to side. The longer she watched, the more she felt in sync with the rhythm. And, suddenly, there it was. A little melody repeating itself in her head as she watched the wind do its magic. As a feeling of warmth began to envelop her, her fingers began to itch to write it down before she lost it. Maybe the one song she'd written here hadn't been a fluke.

"Hey, is there a pad and pencil over there?" She pointed toward the small white wooden desk to the right of the doorway where Jesse stood. She had to write this down before she lost it.

One side of his lips curved into a smile before he broke

their gaze to rummage through the top drawer of the desk. "Got it." He held up a notepad and pencil before walking them over to her. "Do you want me to leave you here?"

"No." She was already scribbling notes on the pad. "You can stay. I just need to write this down before I forget it."

He sat on the edge of her bed silently until she laid the pad and pencil in her lap and let out a contented sigh.

"The moss? Does it still speak to you?" he asked.

She turned to smile at him. "Apparently it does."

"So how do you write in Nashville? Last time I checked, they don't get much Spanish moss up there. No ocean waves to inspire you either." He was leaning forward now, elbows on his knees.

Callie was a little surprised he wanted to hear about Nashville and about her life there. "Well, I do most of my writing on the road these days. Sometimes it's someone I meet backstage or a beautiful view from my hotel room. You never know where inspiration will hit you." She shrugged. "Although, to be honest, it hasn't been hitting me much at all lately. At least not until I got back here."

"Do you still love it?"

"Writing songs? Yeah, it's my favorite part. I only tour because it's what you have to do to make money. I mean, sure, it was fun the first couple of tours when I was getting to see parts of the country I'd only ever dreamed about or taking my first trip to Paris or London. But it's like any other job, it's still work. Someone plans my entire schedule and tells me where to be and when, and I show up and do what I'm asked."

The first trip to Paris with her mother had been incredible. They'd snuck away at dawn the morning after her concert and grabbed croissants to eat at the foot of the Eiffel Tower before their plane left. Eventually, though, she'd visited all the places she'd wanted to, and she was usually too rushed or too tired to sightsee. Life on the road had become a grind, but her manager told her it was the only way to stay relevant and generate any significant revenue.

"Seems like you might have earned a little say-so now and then," Jesse said.

It was the same thing Uncle Lonnie had said to her days before, but somehow it sounded different this time. She'd been surprised when Uncle Lonnie had pointed out how much she'd lost of herself, but now she'd had time to think about it, she knew he was right.

She wasn't the same girl who'd left Big Dune Island all those years ago in pursuit of her dreams. Sure, being a working musician was an entirely different life, but that didn't mean she had to change the core of who she was. Except now she was back, with the people who knew her best, she knew that was exactly what had happened. She'd just kept chasing the next award or the next milestone, desperate to prove that all the things she'd lost—her parents, Jesse—had been worth it.

"Yeah, I guess I didn't realize how off course I'd gotten until I came back home. I'm not the same girl who used to sit in this room writing songs just for the love of it, but maybe I could be again."

"I think you may be on to something." He winked before standing up. "Stay up here awhile. Maybe you'll get inspired to write another song."

Callie felt a warmth spreading through her body as she watched him walk toward the door. It was the first time she'd felt listened to—really heard—in a long time. It was a conversation she could have never had with Andrew. He was even more obsessed with success than she'd become.

"I think I might go back to Gigi's and grab my guitar," she said, wanting to accept his invitation to stay at the house longer. "Is that okay? I know you need to work. I'll stay out of your way. I just want to sit here for a while and see what happens."

He waved her off. "Of course, you're not a bother. I don't need to do anything up here right now anyway. The door will be open. Come and go as you please. It is still your house after all."

On her way out, she went into the living room and grabbed the photo at the beach, the one with their backs to the camera. She liked seeing them like that, as if they were heading off on their next big adventure together. It was exactly how she wanted to remember them.

———

GLANCING AT HER PHONE AS SHE SLID INTO THE driver's seat of her car, she saw three missed calls from Andrew. The warm aftereffects of her trip inside the house were suddenly replaced by knots in her stomach. Was he calling to say he liked the song... or that he didn't? It had been thirty-six hours since she sent it, which seemed like a bad sign.

Not wanting to ruin her mood, or the melody playing on repeat in her head, she decided to call him back later. She made the quick two-mile drive to Gigi's house, humming the new tune over and over again, trying out lyrics as they came to her. Gigi was at work, so Callie could grab her guitar and go straight back to the house before she lost her flow.

But as she slowed down to turn into Gigi's driveway, she saw a black Maserati was parked there. No one around here drove that kind of car, but she knew who did. It couldn't be, could it? Her breath caught in her throat as she turned into the drive and saw the car had Tennessee plates. Pulling up beside it, she realized Andrew was sitting inside, cell phone to his ear, talking animatedly to someone. He spotted her car out of his peripheral vision, said something else into the phone, and then opened his door.

Callie took her time putting the car in park. Finally, she

turned off the engine and collected her purse from the passenger seat. Her mind was racing. Why would he have driven all the way down here? And how did he know where Gigi lived?

He opened her car door and stepped back so she could get out.

"Andrew, you're here." She stepped out of the car awkwardly, wondering if he was going to try to embrace her. "I can't believe it. How did you know where to find me?"

He patted her on the shoulder quickly before taking a step back. "Gigi's address is listed," he said flatly. "She should consider making that more private. What if she had a client who was mad at her or something?"

Clearly Andrew didn't understand how small towns worked. Every single one of Gigi's clients knew where she lived, and it wasn't because she was listed in a directory.

"We need to talk," he said. "Can we go inside?"

Callie's heart sank at the ominous tone of his voice. He was here to deliver bad news.

CHAPTER TWENTY-TWO
JESSE

Austin had shown up minutes after Callie left, and Jesse was glad he hadn't interrupted their time inside together. It had been so different than he imagined. Callie hadn't broken down. Instead, it had been like watching her come back to life. The light had returned to her eyes, even behind the tears.

And she'd written something again. It had only taken a minute or two once she relaxed back into her window seat and focused on the world outside. He'd seen the instant she could hear the melody in her head. She'd squinted her eyes, her brow furrowing, and then a smile had started playing ever so slightly at the corners of her mouth. He remembered that look from when they'd been teenagers. It could appear out of nowhere when they were at the beach or riding around the island in his old truck. Something would come to her, and she'd dig around in her bag for a pad and pencil to write it down before it was gone.

He'd forgotten what it was like to watch her at work, doing something she loved so much. It was nice to see she hadn't lost that, even if her songs didn't sound like something she'd write anymore. He'd once felt jealous that she'd gone off to chase her dream while he'd had to abandon his, but he didn't feel that way anymore. She'd done what she thought was right, which as it turned out was pretty insightful for a sixteen-year-old. Seeing the pride on his father's face the day before had been all the proof he'd needed.

"Okay, what's first?" Austin clapped his hands together as he joined Jesse on the porch.

The railing was still lying in the bushes where it had landed. Jesse could have muscled it out on his own, but he had to admit it was an easier job for two.

"Let's hoist the railing over there back up onto the porch." He motioned for Austin to follow him down the stairs.

"See, I knew you didn't mean for it to end up down there," Austin said, grinning in Jesse's direction.

"Shut up. You're here to work not run your mouth." Jesse turned his back on Austin so he wouldn't see him smile in return as they headed around the side of the porch.

"Yes, sir." Austin gave a salute. "So what'd you decide?" He gestured at the railing resting on the tangled branches of the overgrown shrubs. "Sand and repaint it?"

"Yeah, I think so," Jesse said, grabbing one end of the railing and directing Austin to grab the other. "It'll be a lot faster than trying to make a new one to match the rest. I think I can salvage most of it, maybe just a little patchwork on a few of the balusters."

As they hefted the railing up onto the porch, sliding it on its side so it was lying flat, out of the corner of his eye, Jesse saw a person slowing on the sidewalk in front of the house. Austin was already hoisting himself up onto the porch, but Jesse kept watching the woman. There were lots of walkers downtown, a mixture of residents and tourists. He didn't recognize her, but it occurred to him that she fit Chloe's description of the woman who'd been asking questions about

Callie in the cafe. She was tall and thin, her dark hair pulled back, but it was the suit that separated her from the usual tourists that might linger to get a look at the house where the great Callie Jackson was raised.

She'd already started moving down the sidewalk again. She hadn't made an attempt to speak to Austin or Jesse, and she hadn't whipped out her cell to take photos like the tourists either. There was no camera Jesse could see, so maybe not a paparazzi either. But something about her wasn't right.

Jesse made a mental note to lock the doors tonight and check the security of the boarded-up living room window. The woman was too nicely dressed to be a thief and, besides, Big Dune Island wasn't the kind of place that experienced break-ins. It was probably nothing. Just a nosy, overdressed visitor to the island.

"Who was that?" Austin asked as Jesse climbed onto the porch.

"I don't know." He looked back to the street to confirm she'd moved out of sight. "Gigi and I were having lunch at the cafe today, and your sister mentioned a well-dressed woman who'd come in asking questions about Callie. That lady fit the description."

"I'm sure it's a curious tourist." Austin shrugged. "And what were you and Gigi doing at lunch together? Was Callie there too?"

"No, she can't just go eat lunch out in public," Jesse said. "I went to see Gigi about handling the historic commission for me."

Austin let out a long whistle. "Boy, how did that go? Did you tell her everything?"

"Yep. Went about like you'd expect."

"See, told you she was scary now." Austin shook his head, smiling.

"She agreed to a bit of a compromise. I have to show her

the contract, and as long as she's satisfied that Callie's being taken care of she'll help me with the commission when the time comes."

"That was mighty nice of her. And she won't tell Callie?"

"She says she won't." Jesse shrugged. "It was a calculated risk, but I think she respects Uncle Lonnie enough to wait for him to speak with Callie. I'm just not sure what he's waiting on." It would be nice to get a heads up from Uncle Lonnie when he decided to unveil his grand plan. Now that Jesse and Callie were getting along again, he was beginning to worry more and more about how she was going to react when she found out the news. He'd visit Lonnie first thing tomorrow. Maybe this was something they needed to do together.

Jesse and Austin worked in tandem, getting the railing back up in place and drilling it into the posts on either end. It was definitely a two-man job, and Jesse had to admit it was nice to have someone else around. He could certainly knock out his to-do list faster with Austin helping.

Every time Jesse heard a car drive by though, his attention was diverted. Callie should have been back by now. She was coming back, wasn't she? He realized how much the need to be near her had been growing with each of their interactions. He knew he shouldn't be feeling this way, but he couldn't seem to stop.

"Who do you keep looking for?" Austin asked. "You worried that lady is casing the place?" He laughed at the idea.

"Nah." Jesse stopped to wipe his brow with his forearm. "I thought maybe Callie was coming back. She was here earlier. She actually went inside for the first time."

"Wow, you have had a big day." Austin stopped to take a swig from his water bottle. "How'd that go?"

"It was different than I thought it'd be." Jesse paused to chug from his own water. "I thought it would bring her nothing but pain and heartache, but instead it was like a weight was lifted off her shoulders. She sat in her room for under five minutes and was already writing a new song. She was running back to Gigi's to get her guitar. I thought she'd be back by now."

"So now you want her to be here? Because I thought you were trying to keep her away. Doesn't having her here complicate things?"

"No, we're grown adults. We can be together without being... *together*." He was being overly defensive, but he wasn't going to admit to Austin how he'd started feeling about having Callie nearby.

He thought back to the morning on the beach, the way it had felt to wrap his arms around her and comfort her again. He'd been shocked when she'd told him how much she needed his forgiveness. But the breakup hadn't been easy for her either. She'd carried it around all these years like he had.

"Whoa dude, I didn't even mean it like that." Austin shook his head. "I was talking about her digging around to find out who bought the house. Is something else going on?"

"No." Jesse pushed the image of her on the beach out of his mind. He busied himself with picking up the tools they'd used to reattach the porch railing. "Of course not. She'll be going back to Nashville soon enough. It's just nice that she's making peace with the house." He nodded toward the building before heading to his truck to find some sandpaper they could use to buff out the chipping paint on the delicate balusters.

"Okay." Austin followed Jesse. "Because it'd make sense if her being back here was stirring up more than just the dust in this house."

Jesse kept his back turned on his friend so he wouldn't have to meet his eyes. "I'd be lying if I said her being back has been easy, but we're good. We're different people now. She's got a whole life in Nashville, including a boyfriend." He could feel the muscles in his jaw twitching at the thought of Andrew. He began rummaging around in a bag in his backseat for the sandpaper, forcing himself to concentrate on the task at hand.

"But if she didn't have a boyfriend back in Nashville then maybe there'd be something?"

"No, that's not what I said." Jesse started throwing things out of the bag onto the floorboard of the truck. Where was the sandpaper? He was getting irritated now. He wasn't sure if it was because he couldn't find it or because images of Callie and her boyfriend on the red carpet and hanging out at football games were filtering through his mind.

"The spark's still there, isn't it?" Austin slapped him on the back. "I knew it!"

"It's like you don't hear the words coming out of my mouth." Jesse shook his head, unzipping the side pockets on the bag now, still searching for the sandpaper.

"Oh, it's not the words," Austin teased. "It's the *way* you're saying them." He leaned against the side of the truck next to Jesse. "You know what they say, buddy. First love only happens once."

Austin and his quotes. Jesse scoffed as he leaned across the backseat of the truck to grab another toolbox. What was that even supposed to mean? Of course it only happened once. That's why it was called *first* love.

But what if they'd had the conversation from the beach all those years ago? Would it be him sitting next to her in the stands at a football game? The fact that he was allowing himself to even imagine it was proof that anything could happen.

CHAPTER TWENTY-THREE
CALLIE

She asked Andrew if he wanted to sit on the back deck to talk. After all, it wasn't often either of them got to spend time on a beach. She would live on that back deck if she could, breathing in all that salt air and listening to the waves crash against the shore.

Andrew, however, declined. He said it was too muggy out and he'd rather not get all sweaty. So they went into Gigi's living room. Callie sat on the couch, watching as Andrew began pacing on the other side of the coffee table between them, like a professor preparing to lecture his class.

"Callie, I listened to your song." He started then stopped, as if choosing his words carefully.

He'd driven all the way here to give her feedback on a song?

"I think you've let this place go to your head." He gestured toward the ocean visible through the windows to his left. "That song, it was like something Jimmy Buffett or Kenny Chesney would sing."

She was so taken aback by his words, she was rendered speechless.

"How many times have we talked about your brand, Callie? I know it's not something that comes naturally to you —branding, that is—but you do trust me, right?" His eyes were on her now.

She knew she was supposed to say yes, but she couldn't will her mouth to say the word. Was he seriously giving her no credit for the success of her career?

Andrew didn't wait for her to respond; he was pacing again. "When you were sixteen, it was cute that you were a simple girl from a small town, but you're a grown woman now —a superstar. You don't sing about the wind and the waves and whatever that song was you sent me, and you certainly don't play small-town festivals. Don't you understand that your next move has to be *perfect*? That your career depends on it?" He motioned vigorously with his arms, imploring her to see his side of things.

Her jaw clenched, and she took a deep breath. The first time he'd given her constructive feedback on a song after they started dating, she'd taken it very personally. She'd broken down in tears right there in the studio. Once she'd composed herself, he'd explained that if he didn't give her the feedback, someone else at the label would, and they wouldn't care about her the way he did. He'd asked, wouldn't she rather hear it from him? Back then, maybe that was true. But not anymore. He was right. She wasn't sixteen, but that didn't mean she had to become someone else entirely.

"When did this stop being about doing it for the love of the music?" she asked. "Do you remember when we worked together on the songs for my second album? We would stay up all night in the studio jamming. Remember how much fun that was?" She searched his eyes for any sign that the guy who'd sat on the floor of the studio with her, eating pizza straight out of the box with two days' worth of stubble on his face, was still in there somewhere beneath the hair gel and slick wardrobe. When she'd met Andrew, he'd worn plaid flannel shirts and driven a Ford SUV. Now he was all skinny jeans, custom-tailored shirts, and flashy sports cars.

Andrew pinched his nose between eyes, sighing before coming over to sit next to her. His knees turned toward hers, he grabbed both her hands in his and looked her in the eye. "Isn't it fun to sell out stadiums, Callie? Don't you enjoy winning awards and landing magazine covers? Because that's what I want for you. It's a business. The satisfaction is in selling albums, packing arenas, and keeping your fans interested. The fun you're talking about is something you only get in the beginning when you're still too naive to realize this isn't about chasing some dream you had as a teenager of what it would be like to become a superstar. It's the best job in the world, but it's still a job."

The last part really hit home. He was right, it was a job. Just a job. It didn't have to be her entire life. How much money did one person really need? And what was the point in winning awards and packing stadiums if she couldn't even find time to visit her uncle and her best friend?

There was no point in broaching all this with Andrew. He'd never understand. The next step in her career would be hers alone.

"What's going on at your parents' house?" Andrew asked as he pulled out his phone, swiping at notifications. "Is that all sorted out now? I think I got us a second meeting at Epic. They want you to come this time."

Callie didn't want to commit to anything. Gigi was still combing through her contract, and she didn't want to tip him off that they were looking for a way out. She was more determined than ever to play at Beach Bash, though, and she sure as heck wasn't abandoning the first song she'd written in years that she actually liked.

"I finally went inside today," she offered, steering the conversation away from the meeting at Epic.

"That's great," he said, not looking up from his phone. "Hey, do you think I should stay at the Ritz or the Omni?" He was scrolling through something on his phone, presumably looking for a hotel on the island. The Ritz and Omni were both on the south end; sprawling resorts that attracted tourists and business conventions.

"They're both nice. How long are you planning on staying?" She assumed it would only be a night; it was too far to drive back and forth from Nashville in one day. "You could stay at the Palmer House down the beach. It's the only B&B right on the water, the others are all downtown. They're nice too though."

"I'm not a B&B guy. The Ritz looks nice, and they've still got a room left on the Club level."

Callie would have preferred the personal touch of a locally owned and run B&B. She remembered going with Gigi and Myrtle one time to visit a friend of Ms. Myrtle's who was in from Charleston for a weekend. The room had a giant four-poster bed with French doors that opened onto a private balcony with sweeping views of the beach that sat beyond the dunes.

"I guess you'll head back to Nashville tomorrow? I'm going to need to stay at least another week or two to pack things up. There's a little more to do in the house than I thought." Even though the Beach Bash was fast approaching, she needed to buy Gigi some time to find a way out of her contract.

"No, I'm going to stay a few days. I heard about this guy—Colt King—who's opening at the amphitheater down in Jacksonville tomorrow night. Bart wants to sign him to the agency, so I said I'd meet with him while I'm down here. He agreed to have dinner with me tonight. In fact"—he glanced down at his phone again—"I need to go get checked in so I can change before meeting him."

So this visit wasn't about her? That was a relief.

Callie watched until Andrew had pulled out of the drive and disappeared down Fletcher Avenue. Then she ran back inside long enough to grab her guitar and a bigger notepad. She caught herself hoping Jesse was still at the house, but told herself it was only because she was scared to be there alone. Her parents had always teased her with stories that the house was haunted by the pirates that used to roam the island, but she knew deep down her desire to see Jesse was less about the ghosts in the house and more about the ghost of their past, still lingering between them.

CHAPTER TWENTY-FOUR
JESSE

Jesse's pulse quickened each time he heard a car pass by. He and Austin were doing the tedious work of sanding the balusters in the porch railing by hand, and he was thankful it wasn't a job that required much concentration. With only a few daylight hours left, they'd each only sanded down a couple of balusters. He hadn't counted, but there must be at least a hundred in the giant railing that formed an L-shape around the porch.

When her car finally pulled up to the curb in front of the house, it was close enough to dinnertime he told Austin he could knock off for the day.

"Yeah, I wouldn't want to be the third wheel." Austin laughed as they walked around the porch to greet Callie.

Jesse gave him a warning look as she approached the porch stairs, guitar in hand.

"Hey, Cal." Austin tipped his baseball cap in her direction. "I was just leaving."

"Don't leave on my account." She took off her sunglasses and put them on top of her pink baseball cap. "I'm going to go up in my room and write for a little while.

I'll stay out of the way and let you guys get your work done."

"I've gotta get home and watch a game or two to get ready for my show tomorrow." Austin patted Callie's shoulder as he passed her on the sidewalk. "Good to see you."

She turned to Jesse, smiling. "And then there were two."

Her blue eyes were piercing his, as if she was trying to read his mind. It was unnerving, and he shifted uncomfortably, shoving his hands into the pocket of his jeans.

"Yeah, I've got some work to finish up out here, but I'll come check on you before I leave. You can lock up when you're done."

A car Jesse didn't recognize drove by slowly and he was reminded of the woman he'd seen earlier and what Chloe had told him at the diner. Even with the hat on, he didn't think it was a good idea for Callie to hang out in front of the house where someone might put two and two together.

"Actually, I'll come in too. I need to grab another water." He followed behind her, blocking the view of anyone who might be watching. When they were inside the house and the door was safely shut behind them, Jesse stopped her before she headed up the staircase. "Hey, just a heads up. Chloe said a woman came into the diner asking about you—about where you used to live. Then there was a woman I didn't recognize standing out on the sidewalk staring at the house earlier. I wouldn't hang around outside too much if I were you."

Her eyes had widened, and her posture was suddenly stiff. "Did she have a camera?"

"No, she didn't look like a paparazzi—at least not what I think one would look like."

"You'd be surprised." Callie shook her head. "They don't always look like the sleazy guys you see in movies with a camera hung around their neck. Cell phone cameras are so good these days, they're a lot sneakier than they used to be."

"It was probably just someone who knows this is where you grew up." Jesse shrugged. "Tourists have always come by and taken photos and such."

"I know, it's so weird." Callie sighed. "It's a house, not an amusement park. Wouldn't people rather spend their time at the beach or something?"

"Well, let's be careful," he said, putting a hand in his back pocket. "You know what? Let's not leave your car parked out front with those Tennessee plates. Might get people thinking."

The truth of it registered on her face, her mouth falling open as she looked toward the door.

"Give me your keys." He held out a hand. "I'll go park it in one of the lots downtown and walk back. No one will think anything of it over there, there are plates from all over the place this time of year."

"But I can't risk walking through downtown at night when everyone is out for dinner and walking around—"

"You won't have to." He motioned with his outstretched hand. "I'll stay until you're ready to leave, then I can go back and get it. I have plenty to do around here."

"Okay, if you're sure it's no imposition. Thanks." She fished her keys out of the pocket of her shorts.

As she handed them over, her fingers brushed against his, sparking a wave of electric current he could feel shooting through his body. Her eyes met his as if she'd felt it too, and for seconds that seemed like minutes they stood there, fingers touching, neither wanting to break the trance.

He swallowed hard, taking a step back as an image of her with Andrew smiling on the cover of a magazine drifted into his consciousness. *She's not available, remember?*

"No problem at all." He forced himself to turn away from her and head out the door.

After he parked her car in the lot by the marina, he decided to walk down Main Street to clear his mind before crossing over into the numbered streets where he and Callie had grown up. He gave a little wave to a few locals he passed, but most of the traffic on the sidewalks was tourists.

Even if he didn't know everyone who lived on Big Dune Island, you could spot the out-of-towners from their sunburned skin and fancy clothes. Women wore colorful sundresses and men donned khaki or seersucker shorts and carefully pressed polo shirts. Although locals patronized the Main Street restaurants during the offseason, most stayed away during the spring and summer, when the restaurants were so busy they could only seat reservations.

It was still a couple of weeks from the peak season. Beach Bash would mark the opening on Memorial Day weekend and then the island would fill with couples and young families looking to escape the rat race and relax on the beach. These earlier weekends in May got a little busy with day-trippers because it was already plenty warm enough for sunbathing and a cool dip in the ocean, but the weeks were still quiet. It was the calm before the storm of the summer season.

Making a left turn on 6th, he walked the remaining two blocks back to the house on autopilot. He fought the urge to head around back and watch Callie up in the window like he had so many times as a teenager. He'd feel ridiculous if she caught him, but seeing her write music again earlier had reminded him how magical it had felt to watch her at work. As much as she was an engaging performer up on the stage, nothing lit her up like writing new music. He wondered if she'd ever written songs for anyone else since moving to Nashville. Rarely was an artist as talented a songwriter as they were a vocalist.

He'd need to find work to do inside the house now that it was twilight and too dark outside to work on the balusters. He didn't want to disturb any of the belongings inside the house, so he grabbed a bag of tools out of his truck to test the electrical outlets around the house to see if any would need replacing.

Methodically making his way from room to room with the receptacle analyzer, he jotted down a few outlets that were loose and several others that were dead. Once upstairs, he skipped the master bedroom—he still hadn't felt right opening the door and entering yet—checked the guest bedroom and the hall bath and then paused outside Callie's door. She'd left it open, but he couldn't see her from where he stood. She tested several chords, similar but with slight variations, before all was quiet again. He tried to slip away quietly in the hall, but the old floorboards creaked beneath his feet, giving him away.

"Jesse?" she called out.

He popped his head around the doorframe, but didn't step inside, afraid to intrude on her work. "Yeah, I'm testing the electrical outlets." He held out the receptacle analyzer as if he needed to prove he hadn't been eavesdropping.

"Hey, come listen to this for a minute," she said, sticking her pencil in her mouth before knitting her brows together and playing a few chords.

"Sounds good." He stepped more fully in the doorway to lean against the jamb.

Taking the pencil out of her mouth and laying it on top of the pad at her side, she played what sounded like one of the same chords over and over again, singing softly.

The way that we were

His heart stopped and he stiffened against the doorframe. Was she singing about them?

Seemingly oblivious now to his presence, she scribbled down a note and then started playing once again.

It's porch swings and high tide
It's the way that we were

He felt as if his heart was trying to beat out of his chest, and he was certain it was so loud she must be able to hear it too. None of the songs on her last few albums had included anything that seemed personal. Nothing about the island or the beach, and certainly nothing about him.

No, there hadn't been any songs that reminded him of their relationship since those ones on the first album about breaking up. He was sure those had been about the end of their time together, although he'd found it hard to believe at the time that she'd given him a second thought once she'd gotten to Nashville.

She was writing as fast as her hand could move across the piece of paper, so he slowly backed out of the room before walking quietly down the hallway. He began to feel as if he couldn't breathe, so he grabbed a beer from the fridge and took it out on the back deck to get some fresh air. He hadn't been outside long when she appeared at the back door.

"Hey." She crossed the back deck to sit next to him with her pad and pen in hand. "What was the name of that ice cream place we used to go to up near Main Beach? The one that was next to the water slides?"

She was sitting so close he could smell her coconut-scented shampoo, and the dizzy feeling from before started to come back. Forcing himself to concentrate on the single porch light mounted by the back door, he tried to remember the name. He could picture the little clapboard shack next to the water slides that had sold ice cream to sun-burned tourists and locals alike, before the land was sold to one of his competitors and paved over so a restaurant on the mainland could open an outpost on the island. The outpost wasn't popular with locals, most of whom still refused to eat at the restaurant. Unfortunately, their boycott had done little to curb the steady stream of tourists who kept the place plenty busy. It was the kind of thing Gigi had moved back to prevent from happening in the future.

"Beaches and Cream," they both blurted out at the same time.

Laughing, their eyes locked and his whole body was suddenly alive, electricity feeling like it would spark right out of his skin.

"That's it." She held his gaze a beat longer before breaking the trance to write down the name.

Swallowing hard as he composed himself, he asked, "You writing about the island?" He looked down at the bubbly handwriting that had once penned him love notes she'd handed him by his locker between classes. She'd always signed them with a big heart and then her full name, Callie Jackson. It had always seemed so formal, but maybe she'd been preparing for a life of signing autographs.

"I am. I think it's becoming a love letter of sorts." Her eyes twinkled.

His heart had to be nearing tachycardia at this point it was beating so fast. "So we've made you fall in love again?" He said it jokingly, but he found himself hoping she'd say yes. That she not only loved the island again, but that maybe she could love him again too.

"I don't think I ever stopped loving it." Her voice was breathy and her eyes locked onto his again. "I think maybe I just forgot who I was until I saw it again."

The house. She was talking about the house. He repeated this to himself, trying to slow his heart and stop the buzzing in his ears. He swallowed hard, but his eyes stayed on hers. He was afraid if he turned away from her the magic would break. Time stood still as he searched her eyes for more, his breathing coming heavier now. Her lips were inches from his, all he had to do was lean in. He could feel the magnetic pull as he reached up to brush back a tendril of hair that had escaped from under her hat. His hand lingered, moving to cup the back of her head before he realized what was happening—

Woof!

Fen came bursting through the back door Callie had left open, running over to Jesse to nuzzle up against his leg.

"Sorry," Jesse's mom said as she appeared in the doorway, her eyes moving between them.

Jesse felt Callie scoot a few inches away.

"I wanted to bring him back. Your father and I are heading out to see a movie."

"Hi, Mrs. Thomas." Callie gave a little wave and busied herself clipping her pen on the spiral binding of her notebook.

"Hi, Callie, honey. I didn't realize you'd be here." His mother's face lit up with joy at the sight of them together. He was embarrassed by how openly she was displaying her pleasure at finding them together. "Don't let me interrupt anything, I've gotta run anyway. Bob is waiting in the car."

"No, it's okay," Callie said. "I was getting ready to head back to Gigi's. I just came by to write in my old room for a little while."

"That's lovely, dear. Anything we might get to hear at the Beach Bash? Myrtle said she thought we'd be able to announce you as our headliner today." His mother smiled expectantly, her hopes clearly pinned on Callie's participation in the festival.

"Maybe." Callie smiled politely. "I'm still working on it."

His mother excused herself after hearing his dad honk from the driveway, but the spell was broken. Callie asked him to drive her to her car and retreated upstairs to grab her guitar and other belongings. They rode in silence along the few blocks to the marina.

At the parking lot she started to open the truck door and then turned to him. "Thank you."

"Of course." He toyed with the lid of a cup in the console between them. "I wouldn't want anyone to find out you're here until you're ready for it."

"No, not for that."

He looked up to meet her eyes as she continued.

"For helping me remember who I am and where I come from." She leaned across the truck and kissed him on the cheek.

Her warm lips against his skin made his breath catch in his throat. Before he could say anything more, she was already hopping out of the truck and waving goodbye.

"Goodnight." She shut the door behind her and unlocked her car.

On the short drive back to his house, Jesse found himself hoping maybe there was some crazy scenario where they could try again. Where she saw him restoring the house as his version of a love song to her. He'd told himself all along that he'd bought the house because Uncle Lonnie had made him such a great deal, but he knew deep down it had always been more than that.

CHAPTER TWENTY-FIVE
CALLIE

The song she'd written the night before was still playing in her head as Callie dressed and got ready the next morning, before joining Gigi on the back deck for coffee. She told Gigi about going inside the house and how easily the songs had been flowing out of her the past few days.

"Hmm, isn't that interesting." Gigi smiled as she sipped her coffee and looked out at the ocean.

"What's interesting? That I went back inside the house? I mean, it was bound to happen. That's why I came back."

"No, that's not what's interesting." Gigi turned to Callie and pulled her sunglasses down to look her in the eye. "It was the part where *Jesse* went inside with you. And then the part where *Jesse* was there when you were writing your song. Oh, and then there was *Jesse* again helping you hide your car and working into the night alongside you."

"He was not 'working alongside me,'" Callie said, mocking Gigi's tone. "I was there working on my song, and he was there working on the house. We were barely even in the same room."

What she didn't tell Gigi was how she'd listened out for his footsteps the whole time she was in her room. How her heart had sunk when she'd hear them moving further away and then leap in her chest when they came closer.

Pushing her sunglasses back up in place, Gigi turned to the ocean again. "Okay, if you say so. How was it being back in the house?"

"It was oddly comforting. Not at all how I thought it would be. I thought it would make me sad, that it would make me miss them more. But it was kind of the opposite. I feel better, not worse." Callie was still surprised by how at peace she'd been once she was back inside. It made her feel silly for avoiding it all these years. For avoiding Uncle Lonnie and Gigi and the rest of the town—even Jesse.

"Hypothetically, what if Uncle Lonnie hadn't sold the house? What would you do then?"

Callie paused to consider what her friend was asking. What would she do with it? It wasn't as if she could get any real use out of it herself. Regardless of which label picked her up next, they were all in Nashville or even New York or LA. She'd be lucky if she could make it back a week or two a year. She'd seen the effect of leaving the house sitting empty without any inhabitants to keep it in shape. Of course, she could hire someone to take care of it from now on. But it was silly to keep it just to house all her memories.

"I'm not sure." Callie sighed. "My first instinct when I heard Uncle Lonnie sold it was relief. Sure, part of me was sad to say goodbye, but at least when I was done packing I'd never have to face it again. But being there yesterday made me realize there's still a piece of me there I'm not ready to say goodbye to. It's the place where I feel most like me."

Gigi reached over and squeezed her hand, and they sat like that for a while, holding hands and listening to the waves crashing against the shore in front of them. Callie had never been able to meditate, her thoughts always intruding while she tried to concentrate on keeping them at bay. But listening to the ocean, that was what calmed her mind. On the road and in Nashville she had to settle for an app that played sounds of the ocean. Although there were dozens of tracks to choose from, none sounded like the ocean on Big Dune Island. They either lapped at the shore like a lake or crashed against rocks like on the Pacific Coast. She'd never been able to find one that was quite right, but she'd made do with one that sounded like a tamer version of the waves back home.

"I forgot," she said flatly, "Andrew is here."

"Here where? Big Dune Island?" Gigi sat up in her chair and whipped around to face Callie.

"Yep." Callie nodded. "I came back yesterday to grab my guitar and he was waiting in the driveway."

"Where is he now?"

"He's down at the Ritz. Apparently, he's staying a couple of days to try to help Bart sign someone down in Jacksonville."

Gigi's forehead wrinkled as if she was trying to work out a complicated math equation. "I pulled the SEC's filings in the case against Marco, and I think I might know a way you can find out if Andrew really was involved."

"Really? How?

"I'll tell you exactly what to ask him, and we'll record the conversation on your phone. It's not something we could use in court, but he won't know that. Then you, my dear, are free. You can sign with whomever you choose, and you can play Beach Bash without any repercussions."

It took Callie a minute to catch up with what Gigi was saying. If her best friend was right, she could wipe the slate clean and start over.

Callie had never been a risk taker, but now she realized that was because no one had ever given her any room to roll the dice. Maybe it was finally time to take some risks in her career. Maybe in her love life too.

———

ANDREW HAD ARRIVED AT THE DOOR IN HIS running clothes the next morning. He was an obsessive runner, going out alone in the mornings on tour or hitting the hotel gym late at night after a show. He'd never invited her along because he said it was his time to think, but she didn't understand why people ran—unless they were running away from something.

"You cooked?" Andrew surveyed the bowls and pans spread haphazardly around the kitchen as he wiped sweat from his brow with the towel draped around his neck. "I don't think I've ever seen you cook."

"Well, I'm not ever home long enough to buy groceries, much less cook." She placed fresh berries on their plates next to biscuits, scrambled eggs, and bacon. Handing the plates across the kitchen peninsula to Andrew, she asked the question she figured she already knew the answer to, "Want to take it outside?"

Andrew started in the direction of Gigi's back porch, and she was shocked when he balanced the plates in one hand and opened the door. Maybe it was early enough in the day he wasn't worried about the humidity he constantly complained about in the South. Following him out, she grabbed a small table that was next to Gigi's usual chair and placed it between them so she could set down the big bowl of her mom's gravy. It was a little lumpier than her mom's had ever been, but she thought it wasn't bad considering she hadn't made it since she was a teenager.

"Gravy?" he asked, staring at it like something might jump out at him.

"My mom's recipe." She smiled. "I haven't made it since I lived at home. Try a little."

She hadn't been able to picture health-conscious Andrew smothering a biscuit in gravy when she'd been making it, but she'd made it for herself as a special treat. She was shocked when he picked up the spoon from the bowl and spread a thin layer on top of one-half of a biscuit. Seeing him eat a biscuit was rare enough.

"So what do you think?" She put a generous portion of gravy on her own biscuit.

"Maybe stick with your day job." He winked in her direction.

Fair enough, it was a little lumpy. "Speaking of my day job..." She looked down and used her fork to push a few berries around her plate. "I got another call from that SEC guy. He asked if I remembered the name of the guy we met with from the marketing company when we were working on the branding for the label. I had to dig through my emails to find his name. Levi Richards," she said, her heart pounding as she let the name hang in the air for his reaction. "I need to call back today and let him know I found it."

Andrew cleared his throat, reaching for his glass to take a sip. "Why is he asking about him? What else did he ask?"

Callie shrugged. "I don't know. He just asked what I remembered about the meeting."

"And what did you tell him?" Andrew was using the sleeve of his shirt to wipe his forehead now, which was glistening in the morning sun.

"Just that we met and talked about the logo and the website and that sort of thing. I think he really wants to get in touch with him. Why? Is he someone Marco knew?"

"Callie." Andrew scooted forward, grabbing her hand where it was resting on the arm of her chair. "You cannot give him that name."

She feigned surprise. "Why? Who is this guy, Andrew?"

"Just promise me you won't give him that name. Just tell him you couldn't find it anywhere. And delete the email you found with his details. And don't forget to delete it from your trash. You can't give them that name."

She pulled her hand back. "Why not, Andrew? I thought we agreed that Marco made his bed, and now he has to lie in it."

He sighed, not meeting her eyes and instead focusing on the beach in the distance. "It's better if you don't know anything more." Turning back to her, he said, "I'm protecting you here, Callie. Trust me."

"It sounds like you're protecting Marco. I have no interest in doing that. He deserves what he gets for what he did to both of our careers. I'm not going to lie, and I'm definitely not deleting emails."

Andrew practically tossed his plate onto the table between them as he leaped from his seat and started pacing on the deck, running both hands through his sweaty hair.

Turning back to face her, his tone was pleading. "Callie, please don't give them that name. You can't. It will implicate me."

Acting surprised, she said, "Implicate you? How? You said you didn't know anything about what Marco was doing." Seriously, maybe she should consider a career on the big screen if music didn't work out, because she was doing a great job of pretending Gigi hadn't nailed every bit of this conversation.

"I just wanted us to be successful," he said, dropping back into his chair and reaching again for her hand. "I wanted to make you the biggest star the music world has ever seen."

Again removing her hand from his grip, she frowned. "Andrew, are you telling me you did know about this? That you were in on it with Marco?"

Rubbing his neck with his hand, he looked off in the

distance for a long time before he answered. "It's best if you don't know anything else. I'm begging you. If you ever cared about me at all, please don't give them that name."

It was gutting to learn Gigi had been right. Andrew had been involved. Callie didn't need any more details. She'd gotten what Gigi had asked her to get, the recorder on her phone silently running on the table where she had it face down to capture their conversation.

Andrew finally left after she told him she'd think about how she wanted to proceed. Truth was, the SEC hadn't called and asked for anything. Gigi had acted on a hunch based on the evidence publicly filed in the case already. She was pretty certain Marco and Andrew had been funneling money into a marketing firm through what looked like a legitimate marketing expense, which was later paid back to them by the marketing firm by licensing Callie's songs. Apparently, it was called a "round-trip transaction," and artificially boosted revenue numbers.

Gigi had found the name of the marketing firm's registered agent, done a web search, and happened to recognize a certain dark-haired man named Levi she'd flirted with once in the VIP seats at one of Callie's concerts. Levi Richards, who'd been introduced to her by none other than Andrew. He wasn't a good enough friend of Andrew's for Callie to have ever met him, but Gigi never forgot a handsome face. A little more digging, and she was pretty sure she knew how the whole scheme had worked, but she couldn't be certain until Callie confronted Andrew.

Now they knew, it was time to decide what to do with the information. Of course, only after they used it to get Andrew to let Callie out of her contract.

CHAPTER TWENTY-SIX
JESSE

J esse's feet felt like lead as he walked back to his truck in Gigi's driveway. He'd rung the doorbell, but Gigi had answered the video doorbell from her phone and told him to go on in, giving him the door code. They both knew Callie could get lost in writing music, so when he knocked once more and got no answer, he punched in the code Gigi gave him.

He called out Callie's name as he entered, but there was no reply. Continuing into the living area, he saw her out on the deck. He was almost to the door when he realized there was someone in the chair next to her, holding her hand. His stomach turned over as if he'd eaten bad shellfish. Was that Andrew? He could only see part of his face, but it was enough. He turned and bolted for the front door.

How had he let himself believe this time they could have a different ending? Just because she'd opened up to him about how she was feeling about her career and returning to Big Dune Island didn't mean she still felt anything for him. Sure, they'd almost kissed last night, but they'd been caught up in the moment. She still had a boyfriend waiting for her in Nashville. A boyfriend who was here now.

Jesse was embarrassed by the idea that he might have shown up and spilled his guts only to have her tell him she was heading back to Nashville. Or maybe she wouldn't have told him. After all, she'd abandoned him once before without any real explanation.

As he drove back to the Lyman house, where he'd left Austin to accept a delivery from the lumberyard, his mood turned from sadness to anger. Not at Callie, but at himself. He should have known better. They couldn't possibly have a future together. She was an international star, and he built houses on a tiny island in the middle of nowhere. They couldn't live in two more different worlds, and he'd just let his heart and his hormones override all common sense because she showed up wearing his hat.

Changing the radio station to a hard-rock channel—where there was no chance of accidentally hearing her voice come through his speakers—he turned up the volume and tried to drown out the voice in his head telling him he'd lost her again. The fast-paced music fueled his adrenaline, and he nodded in time to the beat. It was time to focus on *his* goals, chase after *his* dreams. She was going back to Nashville. It was a good thing. No more distractions.

There was barely room to pull his truck into the drive with all the new lumber stacked up in it. Austin was over on the side porch, sanding down more balusters. Since it was Sunday, they'd have all day to work on the house and could hopefully finish up the porch so he could move on to other projects.

Austin looked up as Jesse approached. "Hey, that dude with the slicked-back hair you work with came by. What's his name? Myles?"

"Michael," Jesse said, frowning. "He came here?"

Jesse didn't like the idea of Michael sniffing around. He knew Michael was due back to finalize the purchase of some land up on the south end, but he hadn't expected him to come by the Lyman house. It made sense, he wanted to check in on his investment, but it made Jesse nervous. He might be upset, but he still didn't want to see the investors exploit Callie's name just to make a quick buck. He'd promised Uncle Lonnie he wouldn't let that happen, and Jesse intended to keep his word.

"Yeah, I told him you'd be here any minute, but he said he'd catch up with you later."

"Be right back," Jesse said, dialing Michael's number as he walked to his truck to grab some tools. It rang through to voicemail, so Jesse left a message. "Hey, man, heard you came by. Let me know if you want to grab a bite or something later."

He would prefer to meet Michael somewhere other than the Lyman house, and Michael loved grabbing fresh seafood while he was in town. Jesse figured that would keep him away, at least for the day.

Yelling out to Austin to ask if he needed a water, Jesse headed inside to the fridge, but the sight of all the furniture in the living room stopped him in his tracks. He wasn't done with her yet. She still had to come in and get rid of all this stuff.

Jesse felt so stupid. He couldn't wait until this nightmare was over and Callie was back on the road to Nashville where he didn't have to see or think about her. He wouldn't listen to pop radio anymore. Or look at the magazines in the checkout line at Publix.

When he reached the fridge, he pulled so hard on the handle that it came right off in his hand. Tossing it onto the counter, he pried the fridge open from the top, tugging at the edge of the door until the rubber seal gave way. He found a water and slammed the door shut.

Without a word, he went back to the porch and started sanding a baluster alongside Austin. He was being so rough with the baluster his hand slipped on the sanding square and it fell to the porch.

"Hey, you kind of seem like you're in a mood. Something you want to get off your chest?" Austin paused his sanding to turn toward Jesse.

"Nope. There's nothing to say."

Austin nodded. They worked side-by-side for a good twenty minutes before Jesse exploded, no longer able to keep it in any longer.

"Her boyfriend's here. That Andrew guy."

Austin let out a whistle. "So that's what's got you all in a snit." He lowered himself from a crouched position to sit on the cement of the porch. "How'd you find out?"

"I went to Gigi's to talk to her. She was here last night, and I thought we were making some progress..." His voice trailed off, not wanting to embarrass himself further by admitting to Austin that he'd almost kissed Callie. "Whatever, it's not important. He probably came to help her. Maybe it's a good thing. Then they can get done inside faster."

"It doesn't sound like you really believe it's a good thing." Austin wiped his forehead with the sleeve of his t-shirt.

"It is." Jesse was trying to convince Austin as much as he was trying to convince himself. "We'll finish this up out here, and then we can get started on all the work inside. No need to tiptoe around in there anymore."

As he turned back to focus on the sanding, he saw someone at the road in front of the house out of the corner of his eye. His breath caught in his throat for a second until he turned to see it wasn't Callie. But it was the woman from the other day, the one who matched Chloe's description of the person who'd been asking about Callie's house.

"Hey!" Jesse shouted, jumping to his feet and storming

across the porch to the stairs. The woman was still frozen in position on the sidewalk when he bounded toward her. "Who are you? And why do you keep coming by here, huh? She doesn't live here anymore. This isn't a tourist attraction."

"I-I'm—" the woman stuttered. "I'm staying down the street here," she said, pointing toward Main Street. "I was just out for a walk. I'm sorry." She turned and rushed off before Jesse made it halfway across the yard.

"Dude." Austin came up and put a hand on Jesse's shoulder. "You have got to chill. You scared that poor woman half to death."

"She looks like the woman Chloe said was asking about Callie down at the diner. And we've already seen her out here before. Callie said paparazzi don't look like they do in the movies, they're sneaky."

"Well, good thing she's not staying here." Austin put his hands in the pockets of his jeans. "Won't be any reason for the paparazzi to hang around once she leaves. Although I doubt that woman is coming back around here anytime soon after that. I've never seen you so angry. You sure there's not more you want to talk about?"

"I'm sure," Jesse growled, turning back toward the porch. "These balusters aren't going to sand themselves."

Jesse and Austin managed to finish the sanding before it got too dark to see any longer. Jesse was thankful the conversation had focused on the Florida Gators recruiting class and the start of the Atlanta Braves season, which helped keep his mind off Callie.

Michael texted him as he headed into the house to wash his hands, passing on dinner, but letting him know the closing had been scheduled for two weeks from Thursday. Jesse resolved to see Uncle Lonnie in the morning to update him. Although he didn't really care when or what Uncle Lonnie told Callie anymore.

Austin shook his head as he washed his hands in the sink. "I'm sorry, man. I thought..." He paused as if searching for the right words. "Well, I guess I thought maybe she'd find a reason to stick around or at least come back more often. She seemed to be having a good time here, and I sure thought the sparks were starting to fly again between you two."

"Yeah, well, we were both wrong, I guess. She doesn't fit in here anymore. She's a superstar. She belongs back in Nashville with her producer boyfriend and all her fancy things." Jesse hung his head, the weight of admitting out loud that Callie had left him once again sinking in. How had he let himself believe that Callie Jackson could ever be his again?

Chapter Twenty-Seven
Callie

L ater that afternoon, Callie returned a missed call from Ms. Myrtle and confirmed that she and Sienna were nearly ready for the performance next weekend.

"Everyone is so excited," Ms. Myrtle gushed. "It's time to make the official announcement that you're our headliner. With only a little more than a week left, there's no time to lose."

"I'm going to call my publicist to make sure she's working simultaneously to get some buzz going."

"Thattagirl! What about Andrew? Georgia said he was in town. Will he be staying for the festival?"

"No, he's headed back to Nashville tomorrow."

"Oh, what a shame. Beach Bash is simply the best time of year on Big Dune Island. It's his loss."

"Yes, it is," Callie said, exchanging pleasantries with Ms. Myrtle and promising to call her back after she'd spoken with Piper. Callie would ask her for advice on how to get Big Dune Island the publicity it needed without getting mobbed by the paparazzi in her hometown. She knew she already had a publicity strategy ready to go.

Callie tried reaching Piper but had to leave a message.

Lying down on the couch while she waited for Sienna to come over, Callie thought about how nice it would be to let everyone in on the secret that she was back in town. No more baseball hats and sneaking around in the shadows. She could go check out Chloe's coffee shop—she'd been dying for a latte since she arrived, and she couldn't wait to see what Chloe had done with the place—and she could eat at her favorite restaurants without fear of being spotted.

She could almost taste the fried shrimp basket from The Marina Restaurant over on Main Street. Maybe she could even grab an ice cream a couple of blocks down after dinner. The idea of it was so freeing she caught herself smiling like a crazy person as she sat out on the deck alone. It made her think about how much she wanted to share her excitement with someone. With Jesse.

Callie had to text Gigi to get Jesse's number after realizing she had no idea what it was anymore.

> Call when you can. I got what we needed! Can you send me Jesse's number when you have a sec?

For a moment, it saddened her to realize she and Jesse had grown so far apart and spent so many years away from one another that she didn't even have his phone number. The promise of a second chance hung in the air now though, and it made her feel she could do anything—even reinvent her career. The possibilities were dizzying.

Sienna arrived before she could give it too much thought, and they dove into the set list for each of them, including the song they'd perform together.

"What do you think? What's your favorite song of mine to sing?" Callie asked her.

Sienna bit her lip before she answered, not meeting Callie's eyes. "'Our Song' is my favorite," she said quietly.

Callie let a deep breath whoosh out of her. "Okay, maybe not that one." She forced a smile. She'd written it about Jesse, and everyone on Big Dune Island knew it. It had ended up on her debut album despite her protests, because it had also been a favorite of Jim Wiseman, the record executive who discovered her at Beach Bash. By the time she was recording it, her relationship with the man it was about was long over, and she could barely get through it without crying. She hadn't sung it on stage in years.

"Yeah, I kind of thought you might say that. Sorry. What about 'This Summer'?" Sienna named a song from Callie's second album, a light-hearted tune that came without emotional baggage.

"Perfect," Callie said. "Want to try it?" She picked up her guitar from where it leaned on the chair next to her.

Sienna was shaking her head as she took her guitar out of the case at her feet. "I cannot believe I'm about to sing with Callie Jackson. I don't know whether to be terrified or thrilled."

"Welcome to being a performer." Callie laughed. "I still feel fifty-fifty every time I go up on stage."

Sienna scrunched up her face. "Seriously? It never gets any better?"

"Oh, it gets better." Callie nodded as she started to tap her foot at the right rhythm for the song. "So much better than you could ever imagine."

As they started to play together, Callie remembered what it had been like when she lived to go out on the stage every night. When young girls lined up after the show to meet her. When she sang songs that meant something to her. She wanted that feeling back. Could she find another label that would let her return to recording country music? Could she tell them she didn't want to tour as much? She didn't have her future mapped out entirely, but she was pretty certain she now knew what she didn't want.

———

"I'm so proud of you," Gigi gushed after Callie recounted her conversation with Andrew that night over dinner. "I wish I could have seen his face."

"I'd be lying if I said I wasn't a little nervous." Callie followed Gigi out onto the deck so they could take their usual seats facing the ocean. She'd been getting ready to go find Jesse when Gigi had returned from her board meeting, so she'd stayed to catch her friend up on the day's events. "He basically told me I'm going to ruin my career at Beach Bash."

Gigi waved off the idea as if it was no bigger problem than a fly. "Ridiculous. Labels will be lined up around the block to sign the great Callie Jackson when they find out you're back on the market."

"What if this is all a blessing in disguise?" Callie said, staring out at the ocean. "What if I could find someone who shares my vision?"

"The world is your oyster, Callie Jackson." Gigi spread her arms out wide as she leaned back in her chair to indicate the vastness of the possibilities. "You just wait and see."

Callie took in a deep breath to let the salt air do its magic. Closing her eyes, the mix of waves crashing on the shore in front of them and laughing gulls circling overhead provided the soundtrack of her childhood. Whatever came next, she knew one thing—she wanted to spend more time on Big Dune Island.

"Oh, I totally forgot." Gigi sat up in her chair and dug her phone out of her back pocket. "I saw you texted me for Jesse's number, but we were right in the middle of the meeting, and I forgot to answer you. Here, I'll send it to you."

"It's so strange to not have his number anymore." Callie swiped at the notification on her phone that Gigi had sent her Jesse's contact card. "I was going to tell him I'd finally talked to Andrew and was closer than ever to getting out of my contract."

"He's going to be happy for you. Will you have to go right back after Beach Bash, or can you stay longer now? *Mi casa es su casa*," she said, sweeping her arms around.

"I'm not sure." Callie realized it was the first time in more than a decade that she had no idea about her schedule. "I guess it depends on what happens with the festival and what Piper advises as far as making it public that I'm back on the market." She'd probably have to go back to Nashville or fly out to L.A. for meetings with labels, but maybe she could fly in and out of Jacksonville and stay here a little longer until she had to be back in the studio.

Callie's phone began vibrating in her lap. She found herself hoping it was Jesse—even though she knew he didn't have her number—but it was Piper. Her heart sank a little, but she was anxious to talk to her publicist too.

"Sorry I missed your call earlier," Piper said as Callie answered. "I've had so many calls I haven't even had time to eat today." Piper let out a long whistle.

"One of your other clients get themselves into trouble?" Callie asked. Piper had a couple of younger artists who partied a little too hard sometimes and wound up on the front page of papers for all the wrong reasons.

"No, everyone is buzzing about you," Piper said, laughing. "Next time, give a girl a little warning. I knew you were planning to play the festival, but I didn't think it was public yet. But no worries, I'm going to whip something right up. I don't want to call it a comeback, because you've always been a hot commodity in my mind, but a 'homecoming' has a nice ring to it."

Piper was from the south, but she talked a mile a minute like a New Yorker. Callie was struggling to sort through everything she was saying. Why were reporters calling her? Had Andrew leaked the news? Why would he do that?

"Andrew told the press?" Callie asked. Gigi was mouthing for Callie to put it on speaker so she could hear too, so Callie hit the button and held the phone between them so they could both listen.

"Oh, no—well, I don't think so. It was just some press who got wind of what you're doing down there. There hasn't been much news about you lately, so they're all eager to find out what you've been up to."

"So the press knows I'm here? That I'm playing the Beach Bash?" Callie tried to calm her breathing. She wasn't ready for a media frenzy quite yet. She'd still hoped she could sneak in a meal or two in town before the paparazzi descended and made it impossible for her to go anywhere.

"Actually, the reporters are all asking about you selling your house, not the Beach Bash. One of my guys at *Us Weekly* said he was going to forward me an email he got. Hold on, let me check my email on my phone real quick."

Callie gave Gigi a confused look and asked her quietly, "How does anyone know about the house? Besides, it's not for sale—Uncle Lonnie already sold it."

There was some rustling on Piper's end. "Here, let me put you on speaker so I can read this," Piper said. "'*Grammy award-winning artist Callie Jackson's childhood home on Big Dune Island in Florida will soon be for sale. After a painstaking restoration, this Victorian treasure will allow one lucky buyer the opportunity to roam the same hallways and sleep in the same bedroom where the starlet was born and raised. From the heart pine floors to...*' You get the idea. It's not the best worded press release I've ever seen. Who'd you get to write it? I would have written it for you."

Callie's heart was pounding in her ears and a wave of nausea washed over her. The idea of strangers buying her childhood home to live out some sort of fantasy to get closer to her was sickening. She gave Gigi a panicked look, which prompted Gigi to reach over and pat her hand. The look on Gigi's face wasn't all that reassuring, but Callie turned back to the phone.

"I have no idea what that is," she said to Piper. "My uncle sold the house to some sort of investor or something. That's why I came back home, to pack before the closing. Jesse…" She paused, realizing Piper didn't know who Jesse was. "A local guy has already started fixing it up, but my uncle hasn't even closed on the house yet. I haven't even cleaned it out."

"It looks like the email is from a man named Michael Russo. That name mean anything to you?"

Gigi's face went white, and Callie realized the name meant something to her. "Piper, forward me the email. Can you stall the reporters? Get them to hold off on the story?"

"I can try. I'll tell them I haven't been able to get in touch with you yet. They won't run a story they haven't been able to confirm. That'll buy you a little time, but it sounds like someone is trying to exploit your name to drive up the sale price after the flip."

"Thanks, Piper. Forward me the email, and I'll call you back as soon as I have this figured out."

After she'd hung up with Piper, Callie turned to Gigi. "Who is Michael Russo?"

"Callie." Gigi looked down at her hands. "Michael is an investor in Thomas Construction."

CHAPTER TWENTY-EIGHT
JESSE

Jesse set out Wednesday morning for Main Beach. They only had a few days left to finish the setup at Beach Bash, and he was a little further behind than he'd like to be thanks to having to split his time between the festival and the Lyman house renovation. He'd sent over crews from Thomas Construction to work on much of the buildout, but there was still plenty left to do.

He was unloading tools from his truck when Ms. Myrtle's little white Mercedes pulled up next to him. Great, she was here to check up on him. He was in no mood to be lectured about how behind they were on the project.

"Jesse, my dear." Ms. Myrtle came around the back of her car and opened her trunk. "I'm glad you're here. I picked up the banners this morning." She plopped down several rolls of vinyl on the open tailgate of his trunk. "The big one is for the main stage, and the smaller ones can go up at the entrance to this lot and the one down the road for overflow. I've got the mayor hanging banners on the light posts downtown this morning too. I hope that producer of hers didn't give her too hard of a time about the Beach Bash." Ms. Myrtle clapped her hands together, grinning ear to ear.

Jesse stepped around Ms. Myrtle to grab a toolbox from the back seat of his truck, shaking his head. "So Callie got the okay from that boyfriend of hers to do the festival?"

Ms. Myrtle slid down her oversized sunglasses so she could look Jesse in the eye. "You don't know, do you?" She seemed delighted she would be the one to deliver some unknown news.

"Know what?" He opened the door of the truck and then wiped sweat from his forehead with the back of his hand.

She smiled at him for a long moment before answering. "He's not her boyfriend anymore. Georgia told me all about it last night. They've been broken up for months, but she didn't want it in the press while they were dealing with their legal troubles. He came down to try to win her back and drag her to Nashville to sign with some horrible label, and my brilliant daughter figured out how to get Callie out of her contract. They'll have him packed up and out of here in no time." She smacked her hand on the car for emphasis.

Jesse had turned back to face her, his mouth hanging open and his hand frozen above the handle of his toolbox inside the truck. Callie had been broken up with Andrew for months? He'd seen them holding hands. Or maybe it was just his hand on hers as he pleaded with her to come back with him? It had all happened so fast.

Ms. Myrtle was talking about picking up more banners, but Jesse wasn't listening. He could feel the corners of his mouth turn up into a smile. Callie was single.

"So she's staying?" he said, bracing his arm against the truck over his head. He was feeling a little lightheaded at the realization.

"Why, yes, I thought she would have told you by now." Ms. Myrtle frowned. "She's probably just busy working out plans with her publicist. They're going to help us get the word out. I knew Callie would help us save the festival!"

Jesse wondered if Callie had gone looking for him to clear up the confusion. If she'd tried the beach first, wouldn't she have tried the house next? He and Austin had been there all day, and she definitely hadn't looked for him there.

"Are things almost ready?" Ms. Myrtle asked, stepping a few feet from the truck to get a better view of the beach. "I know you can't put up the tents until later in the week, but is the stage done? I thought I'd be able to see it from here. I can't walk in these down in the sand," she said, pointing the toe of one of her shiny black heels out in front of her to indicate she had on the wrong shoes for beach walking.

Thankful she'd overdressed for the occasion and couldn't see his lack of progress, Jesse reassured her. "It's all right on schedule. I'm finishing up the stage today and then getting the footings in for the tents." He held up one of the metal footings as evidence work was progressing along as planned.

"Fantastic!" She clapped again. "I'm headed down to the newspaper to make sure our big news hits the front page tomorrow morning, and then I'm calling the paper down in Jacksonville." Although Big Dune Island had its own newspaper, there wasn't enough happening in town to warrant a daily newspaper, so it published bi-weekly on Mondays and Thursdays. Although Jacksonville was under an hour away, it rarely bothered to cover news on the island. This wasn't just any news though, and he was sure they'd gladly give the festival a little free advertising about its local celebrity coming home to be the headliner.

Ms. Myrtle turned back to Jesse as she reached the driver's side of her Mercedes. "Make sure you get those banners hung today. We want everyone to know our girl has come home!"

Jesse couldn't help but smile as Ms. Myrtle climbed back in her car and took off on her mission to publicize the news.

He unrolled one of the smaller banners on the tailgate of his truck. Seeing Callie's name emblazoned in bright-white print against the ocean-blue background made his chest swell with pride. Their star had come back home to Big Dune Island. And maybe this time she wouldn't want to leave.

He knew she couldn't stay forever, but he couldn't help imagining scenarios where she spent more time here. Maybe when she wasn't in the studio or on tour she'd come back here instead of Nashville.

As Jesse worked to finish the stage, which wouldn't be ready today as he'd told Ms. Myrtle—even if he worked until sundown—his mind kept drifting to the Lyman house. Did he have time to turn Callie's old bedroom into a recording studio? He'd gotten the information on what he'd need to soundproof the room, and it was definitely doable if he had some help. Michael and the other investors would never approve it, and he'd have to use his own money. But what if she didn't decide to keep the house after Lonnie told her about their deal? And who would want to buy a property on Big Dune Island with a recording studio inside?

He tried to force himself to concentrate on securing the flooring for the stage, but every time he heard footsteps in the sand he caught himself looking up to see if it was her, his heart sinking each time he merely saw another beachgoer plodding their way down to the shoreline. Callie was probably busy planning her set for the Beach Bash or getting ready to field press requests once the word got out. No doubt, the island would be mobbed as soon as everyone read the news.

Maybe she wouldn't have to hide out anymore, though, sneaking around in hats and sunglasses and wigs. Although he did like seeing her in that Red Sox hat.

He'd been fighting off feelings since she first stumbled upon him in her backyard, telling himself she was no longer his. And as much as he knew he was setting himself up to potentially have his heart broken by her again, he couldn't help hoping for a different outcome.

Pulling his phone from his back pocket to check the time, Jesse saw a missed call from Gigi. Maybe Callie was calling him from Gigi's phone since they hadn't exchanged numbers. His hand was jittery as he pushed the button to return the call and nervously waited for Gigi—or better yet, Callie—to answer.

Disappointed, he hung up after the call went to voicemail. He turned the volume on his ringer up as high as it would go before sliding the phone into his back pocket. He didn't want to miss any more calls. He contemplated running by Gigi's house to see Callie, but he'd never finish the stage on time if he didn't stay and work until dark. Surely Callie would call or come by to see how everything was coming along.

———

JESSE COULD BARELY SEE TO GATHER UP HIS TOOLS as the sun fell beyond the horizon to the west of the beach toward downtown. His back ached, and the disappointment that had crept in with each passing hour without word from Callie had made for a long day. Even so, he still needed to stop by the Lyman house.

As he eased his truck onto 6th Street, he caught himself hoping he'd see Callie's car in front of the house. If it weren't so late, he'd stop by Uncle Lonnie's, but it was already past 9 p.m. Had he told her yet? He kept envisioning the worst-case scenario where she knew and was furious with him, first for buying her house and then for not telling her the truth.

Once inside the house, Jesse sat at the kitchen table and rolled the plans back out, smoothing the creases as he studied the walls he'd planned to remove to create the more open floor plan desired by most buyers these days. Although the historic commission would insist things like the doors and windows be replaced with period-appropriate materials, Jesse didn't need approval for interior changes that weren't visible from the outside. He decided to stick with his plan to remove the wall on either side of the fireplace in the living room so you could pass from the living room to the kitchen on either side. He was also going to open the fireplace on the kitchen side to make it double-sided, which he thought would give the kitchen a much homier feel.

The kitchen was on the smaller side, so he'd planned to lengthen it through the breakfast nook where he currently sat and open the wall it sat against so the kitchen would flow straight into the dining room. Taking down the wall adjoining the kitchen and dining room, along with removing the walls on either side of the fireplace, would make the kitchen appear much bigger than it was and take away the galley-style feel.

It was the second floor where he was rethinking his plans. Initially, he'd wanted to keep the four bedrooms upstairs the same, updating fixtures, refinishing the floors and applying a fresh coat of paint. Now, however, he considered removing the wall between the master and a small bedroom adjacent to it where Mrs. Jackson had a sewing room. The master bedroom closet was woefully inadequate, closets having been smaller or nonexistent in these older homes where clothing was stored largely in dressers and armoires. He'd planned to leave it in order to stay on budget, but now he imagined turning the sewing room into the kind of walk-in closet women drooled over.

After he finished sketching out the grand closet, with its center island for her jewelry and accessories and shoe racks that ran from floor to ceiling on one side, he realized he was designing it for Callie. He was picturing her keeping the house.

Jesse pulled out his phone to reread the emails the music store in Jacksonville sent him about building a home studio.

He was making a list of the materials he'd need when his phone rang. His heart leaped, hoping Callie had somehow gotten his number, before he saw Michael's name on the screen and his hopes were dashed.

"Hey, man, what's up?" Jesse said, settling back in the little wooden kitchen chair, resting his head against the faded yellow wall behind him.

"I know marketing isn't your forte," Michael said, "but you could have told me that house is Callie Jackson's! We could double the asking price based on that fact alone—I've already got a press release out. I wish we hadn't agreed to that buy-back clause because if she decides she wants it back, we'll be leaving a pile of cash on the table, but the exposure will be priceless. You can't buy this kind of publicity."

Jesse had shot up in the chair at the mention of Callie's name and was sitting on the edge now, his lower back screaming in reply after his afternoon spent bent over, putting together the stage. His head was pounding. How did Michael know it was Callie's house?

Michael was talking so fast about his plans for the marketing Jesse couldn't get a word in edgewise.

"Slow down, Michael. Who told you that? I made a deal with her uncle. He was trusting me—trusting us—to do right by her and not exploit her name to make a buck. I gave him my word."

"I should have known you weren't ready to be out there making deals on your own," Michael said, not answering the question. "I thought that contract was kind of screwy, but I figured that's the way you guys do it down here. I would never have agreed to that buy-back if I'd known whose house we were talking about, at least not at that price. And that friend of yours Austin showed me the hand-carved mantel and stair-case and, frankly, gave me more of a history lesson on the house than I needed. You know I hate old houses, but even I have to admit there's a market for that sort of thing. A *high-end* market."

"Michael, did you say you put out a press release?" Jesse ran his free hand through his short-cropped hair, pacing the length of the kitchen now. "What were you thinking? What did it say?"

"That Callie Jackson's historic childhood home would soon be hitting the market, renovated and ready for its new owner. If she decides to keep it, we'll put out another release saying she was so thrilled with the renovation that she bought it back from us. We'll be the builders who renovated the childhood home of a pop superstar. It's got glamour, it's got glitz, and it'll punch all those sentimental fools right in the heart. Honestly, it might be better than putting it on the market. What do you think? Is she going to want it?"

Michael's New York accent was in full force now that he was talking a mile a minute. "Do you actually know her? I knew she was from this sleepy little hamlet, but I heard she never came back."

Jesse had put the phone on speaker while Michael was talking and punched Callie's name into his browser to see what came up. He stared at the phone in disbelief. It was everywhere.

Callie Jackson Returns to Big Dune Island to Sell Her Childhood Home

Callie Jackson's Childhood Home Will Soon Be for Sale

You Can't Go Home Again: Callie Jackson to Sell Childhood Home

Every major entertainment site in the country had the story up already.

"Hey, that's Vincent on the other line. I gotta run," Michael said, cutting the line to go talk to one of the other investors before Jesse could grill him about how he'd found out it was Callie's house. Had Michael done a public records search for the closing? No, that wouldn't have done it. The house was under a trust with Uncle Lonnie as the sole trustee, nothing linking it to Callie Jackson unless you dug around enough to find out her mother's maiden name was Lyman.

Jesse was replaying everything he'd ever said to Michael about the house when he heard his phone start ringing in his hand. It was Austin. He was about to push the Accept button to take the call when it all clicked together. Michael had stopped by the house that morning while Jesse was at Callie's. He'd run into Austin. He said Austin showed him the hand-carved mantel and staircase and told him all about the history of the house.

Jesse hit "Decline" on the call before throwing it down on the counter. He leaned over the sink bracing against the edge, his knuckles turning white. Austin and his big mouth had ruined everything.

CHAPTER TWENTY-NINE
CALLIE

C allie had spent the entire day on the phone. There'd been multiple calls with Ms. Myrtle about publicity for the Beach Bash and an interview with a writer for the local paper, *The Newsleader*. Between those calls, she'd been on the phone with Piper trying to simultaneously manage the news about her headlining the festival and combat the reports that she was selling her childhood home. So much for reporters waiting to confirm the news with her.

Even more disappointing was that it was true. Gigi had spilled everything the night before, from Uncle Lonnie's deal with Jesse to Jesse coming by her office for help. The list of people who'd misled and hurt her seemed to include everyone she cared about the most.

After sleeping on it, she'd decided Uncle Lonnie deserved a chance to explain himself. Based on what Gigi had been able to tell her, Uncle Lonnie had been trying to help Jesse while also ensuring Callie could have the house if she wanted it. She couldn't blame him for not knowing whether it was indeed something she wanted or not, it was her fault she hadn't come back and dealt with it sooner.

She couldn't believe Gigi hadn't told her about it the second she'd learned, but Gigi had pleaded with Callie to try to put herself in Gigi's shoes. She didn't feel like it was her secret to tell. She'd wanted to respect Uncle Lonnie's wishes to reveal his plan in his own way and in his own time. Gigi didn't agree with it, but she'd been taught to respect her elders.

As for Jesse, he'd only been trying to chase his dream and get out from under the thumb of the investors. Gigi had felt bad for him, knowing she and Callie had both been able to go off and achieve their goals. Plus, Gigi had read the contract he'd brought her. It was as he'd described. Callie could easily buy the house back—if she wanted it.

Callie didn't know what she wanted anymore. Part of her had been imagining herself living in the house again. Being with Jesse again. But knowing he could keep something like this from her, even after all the time they'd spent together, made her feel foolish.

She'd barely slept, but had waited until Gigi left for work the next morning to go to Uncle Lonnie's. She hadn't wanted to rehash anything with Gigi, so she waited until she heard the lock on the front door turn after 8 a.m. before she emerged from the bedroom. She'd go straight to Uncle Lonnie's and hear him out because he was her only living family, but she wasn't ready to confront Jesse yet.

Jesse had lied to her over and over again, ever since that very first day when she'd found him in the backyard. First, he'd led her to believe he was only doing a little work for Uncle Lonnie before the sale. Then he'd admitted being hired by the new owners. Why hadn't he told her then *he* was basically the new owner?

It made sense he'd had his guard up on the first day; after all, he'd been as surprised to see her as she was to see him. But by the time he'd admitted to working for the new owner, they'd grown closer. Apparently not close enough to be honest though. She fumed on the drive to Uncle Lonnie's house, thinking about how vulnerable she'd been with Jesse—first on the beach and then going inside the house. She'd let him back in, and she thought he'd done the same. Now she felt foolish. He was no different than Andrew, putting his career first and her second.

Uncle Lonnie hadn't been on his porch drinking coffee as she'd expected, and he didn't answer his door. She was thankful to have a few minutes to calm down. She decided to sit on the porch and wait, certain Uncle Lonnie must have walked into town for coffee and would be back soon.

She'd almost drifted off, rocking herself in a chair, when she heard a car pull up in front of the house. Opening her eyes, she saw Uncle Lonnie climb out of the passenger side of the black Buick with some effort and slowly make his way up the drive to the path that led to the front door.

She was still taken aback at how much he'd aged since she'd last seen him. Callie shifted in her seat, suddenly unsure of what she wanted to say. She'd saddled him with a lot, from the physical needs of the house to the decisions regarding what to do with it. Sure, it was technically his house, but she knew he had always been waiting on her to be ready to face it.

"I guess we need to talk." Uncle Lonnie's voice was soft as he lowered himself slowly into his rocker.

He knew she knew. She tried to summon the anger she'd felt when she found out the night before, but now he was in front of her she faltered. She shrunk back in her rocker. "Yeah, I think maybe we should."

"I imagine you've seen the news by now." His gaze was fixed on his hands in his lap. "You know I don't go online, but Jesse called me last night. I had Hal next door drive me to Gigi's looking for you, but obviously we missed each other."

"Yeah, I haven't been here long." She studied a spot on the painted green concrete flooring of the porch that was chipping away to reveal the layers underneath. He wasn't even taking care of his own house anymore; how could she have expected him to tackle the projects at the Lyman house?

"How much do you know?"

"Everything." She paused. "At least I think so."

"Well, maybe I should begin at the beginning."

She nodded. Where anger had resided an hour earlier, she was now curious. What had Uncle Lonnie hoped would happen when he sold the house to Jesse and negotiated for her to buy it back?

Uncle Lonnie told her about how Jesse had come by one night to help him rewire a light in the hallway. Jesse had confided in Uncle Lonnie that he was still holding on to his dream of renovating older homes, and how unfulfilled he felt building increasingly bigger homes on the natural land that gave Big Dune Island its unspoiled quality.

Uncle Lonnie had long debated what to do with the house —and how to gently nudge Callie into coming back to face it so she could decide what she wanted to do with it—and that night the answer had seemed so clear. He could help Jesse achieve his dream while also getting the necessary work done to save the house from complete disrepair. Uncle Lonnie had gambled Callie would return when she heard the news and that between him, Jesse, and Gigi, they could help her go back inside. He'd sat quietly and watched her gamble away her future on Andrew and his label, but he couldn't just be a spectator anymore. He thought if he could get her to come home to Big Dune Island, he could remind her who she was and help her get her life and career back on track.

"Well, it worked." Callie leaned her head against the rocker as she processed everything. "I came back."

"Went inside the house too." Uncle Lonnie nodded. "I know that wasn't easy, but I'm glad I was still alive to see you do it. You've been avoiding this place and all those memories for long enough. Sugar," he said, his accent so thick the "r" was imperceptible, "you can't run from who you are forever. Haven't you ever heard that song? 'Wherever you go, there you are.'"

"There's a song for everything, isn't there?" A small smile formed on her lips. "You were right, Uncle Lonnie." She leaned over to pat his hand. She could feel the deep wrinkles on his sun-worn skin, and she thought about all he had faced in his life. First losing Doris before they'd even been able to start their own family, then losing his sister and brother-in-law, who were his best friends. He'd been left with no one except a niece who was off globe-trotting and too busy to check in on him as often as she should have.

"It was time for me to come back. Not just to Big Dune Island, but to who I am. Did you hear I'm playing the Beach Bash?"

Uncle Lonnie chuckled. "Hard to miss. There's a banner on every light post in town. Myrtle's handiwork, I'm sure. That woman is something else."

"A force of nature, that's what Momma always called her," Callie said, smiling. "I wish I had a little more of that in me."

"Oh, sugar. It's in there. You just have to give it permission to break free."

"I think maybe I already did. Andrew told me I was gambling my career on the festival, but I think he's wrong. I'm betting on myself, and I think if I stay true to myself, that's a sure winner."

"Well, it'll be mighty nice to have you here a bit longer." Uncle Lonnie reached down in the basket by his chair to pick up a sea turtle that was beginning to emerge from a block of wood. With its head and front flippers already carved, it looked like a baby coming out of a square-shaped egg. Pulling a knife from his pocket and flipping it open, he began to chip away at the block. "Whataya reckon you'll do about the house?"

"I'm not sure what I want to do." She picked at the pink polish on one of her nails. "Now I've been back, part of me wants to find a way to spend more time here. I don't know what's next for me in Nashville, and I think I need to figure that out first. I'm not even sure how much I could get back down here if they want me in the studio and touring again."

"As long as you're happy, the decision is yours. Don't feel you have to keep the house on my account, your parents' either. It's just a house. Your memories are here." He held the turtle and his knife in his left hand while he lifted his right over his heart.

Was it only a house though? Her tiny handprints were still on the first step going up to the front door. Her childhood dog, Murphy, was buried in the backyard under the big oak tree. She'd written a hundred songs or more in the window seat in her little back bedroom. But, most importantly, it was where she felt most like herself.

"He's a good guy, you know." Uncle Lonnie interrupted her thoughts.

"Who?" she asked before realizing who he must mean. "Jesse?"

Uncle Lonnie nodded, continuing to shave away at the block of wood from which the sea turtle was being birthed.

Callie scowled, anger bubbling back up to the surface. It had been one thing for Uncle Lonnie to withhold the truth. He'd never lied; he'd only declined to give her more information. Jesse had actively lied. He'd let her pour out her heart, let her lean on him for support, all the while not returning any of the vulnerability or trust.

"Uncle Lonnie, he lied to my face." Callie swallowed hard to keep from tearing up. "I thought we were..." She couldn't bring herself to finish the sentence, to admit what she'd wanted to happen. "Well, it doesn't matter what I thought, because I was wrong."

"Life was tough for him after you left. He had to watch all his friends—you, Austin, Gigi—go off on a new adventure and chase after their dreams while he stayed here trying to dig his family out from under one heck of a mess. He had to become a man before I reckon he was really ready."

Callie's jaw was clenched. That might be true, but all she could think about was how he'd told her he was hired by the new owner to do a few repairs prior to closing. How he'd watched her struggle to even go inside the house and hadn't bothered to tell her it could be her house again. How could you watch someone you cared about suffer like that? She'd been raw and real, exposing herself like a ship left out on anchor in a storm and he'd barreled right on through like a hurricane with no regard to the destruction he left in his path. That was what happened when you let someone get too close; you opened yourself up to getting hurt.

"It's too bad all that happened to him, and it was nice of you to want to help him, but it's no excuse for lying to me. I've had enough of that back in Nashville to last me a lifetime. But I guess I should learn not to expect anything out of anyone. Manage my expectations better." Callie couldn't help but wonder what it was about her that made her so easy to lie to. It made her feel disrespected at best, stupid at worst.

"What those people did to you wasn't right, and I'd like to pick up that little Andrew and see how far I could throw him." Uncle Lonnie chuckled. Had it been twenty years earlier, he probably could have tossed Andrew across a room. "But I think the real problem is that you threw yourself into work after what happened to your parents."

He wasn't wrong. It had been a distraction at first, and then because she felt like she had something to prove. That all the sacrifices and the loss hadn't been in vain.

Uncle Lonnie's grey eyes were gentle when they met hers. "You want to know why I think you had writer's block until you came back here?"

"Because Big Dune is the most inspiring place in the world?" She smiled weakly.

"No, because you weren't letting yourself feel anything anymore. It's the lows that give the highs their meaning. Nobody ever wrote a song about just sittin' around lettin' life happen to them. You know as well as anyone that you have to make people feel something inside. How you gonna do that if you can't feel anything yourself?"

He was right about that too. She'd compartmentalized and focused on writing songs about other people's lives. She'd written about the teenage girls she'd seen in the front row at a concert singing along together, arms slung over each other's shoulders. One of her other hits had been inspired by a flower she'd seen improbably growing in the concrete outside the back entrance of an arena in Oklahoma City. Writing about other people's lives—or at least about the stories she made up for them in her head—had been good enough to get by, but it had also caused her to drift away from herself.

Uncle Lonnie had seen it though. And he'd brought her home so she could see it herself. Sure, he could have asked her to come home, but she would have made excuses, like she had for nearly a decade. She didn't blame him for the events he'd set in motion, in fact she should thank him.

But she still wasn't sure about Jesse. Had he only been out to do what was best for him?

CHAPTER THIRTY
JESSE

Jesse stared at the text on his screen, seething with anger as he clenched his jaw and gripped the phone tighter in his hand.

> Need help today? I can come by after my show.

It was from Austin, whose help he definitely did not want. He'd done enough. Jesse still couldn't believe he'd opened his big mouth and told Michael the house was Callie's. Served Jesse right for trusting anyone else with his secret. He'd known when he struck the deal with Uncle Lonnie it was a delicate situation that he couldn't afford to screw up, but Austin was like a brother to him. Jesse grimaced. He, more than anyone, should know you can't trust your own brother. Had he learned nothing from watching his uncle almost destroy Thomas Construction all those years ago?

Jesse had called Gigi after he cooled off the night before to find out if Callie knew. She did. Gigi had been whispering from another room and didn't have time to share much, only that Callie knew, and she was furious. She was going to see

Uncle Lonnie, but she wouldn't even talk to Gigi about Jesse. That couldn't be a good sign; Callie told Gigi everything.

Running his hand through his hair, Jesse surveyed the work that still needed to be done on the beach. The stage was nearly complete, and he could get all the footings in for the tents today and tomorrow, but it was a two-man job. Teddy, one of the guys on his crew at Thomas Construction, always loved having a little extra cash in his pocket. Jesse was sure he could get him to come lend a hand after he was done on the job site Thursday. Vendors would arrive early Saturday morning to start putting up their tables and displays, selling everything from fried shrimp baskets to seashell jewelry.

"Hey."

Jesse turned to see Gigi approaching, heels in hand as she walked across the sand barefoot.

Jesse stuffed his hands in the front pockets of his jeans. "Hey, yourself." This couldn't be good.

"Sorry I couldn't talk last night. She was in the next room, and I couldn't get caught speaking to the enemy." Gigi moved to his side, hoisting herself up on the edge of the stage to sit. The stage was as high as his chest, so it was a pretty impressive jump. Jesse remembered Callie telling him once that Gigi could have been a competitive gymnast, but Ms. Myrtle hadn't been willing to engage in the sort of schedule that would have demanded. They'd compromised on cheerleading, where no doubt Ms. Myrtle thought Gigi could be popular and date the star quarterback. It was the Southern version of a Norman Rockwell painting.

"You here to tell me you can't help us with the historic commission?" Jesse leaned his back against the stage next to where Gigi sat, letting out a long sigh.

"That depends."

Jesse looked over his shoulder at her. "On what?"

"Did you leak the story to the press?"

Jesse turned to face her. "Of course not. I wouldn't do that to Callie."

Gigi nodded in reply, reaching up to tuck her brunette hair behind an ear. "So who did?"

Jesse looked at the ground, kicking a seashell over with the toe of his boot. "I'm pretty sure it was Austin." He frowned when he saw what had looked like a full conch shell was only the broken off top of one.

Gigi's eyebrows knitted together as she pursed her lips. "Why would he do that? It doesn't sound like him."

"I dunno," Jesse said, stuffing his hands back in his pockets. "He gets paid to talk for a living. Heaven knows his sister can't keep her mouth shut. Maybe it runs in the family."

"Maybe Michael heard it around town? It's not like it's a big secret that she grew up there."

"You don't want it to be Austin, do you?" Jesse was still plenty mad at Austin, but he smiled at the thought that Gigi was defending him. He'd always thought the two of them would make a good couple if they could ever get past their own egos.

Gigi bit her lip, which was painted a shade of red that seemed to have been made to go with the blouse she was wearing. Did women have a hundred lipsticks so they could match all their shirts? He was glad to be a guy. It was so much simpler.

"It's not that I don't *want* it to be Austin. I just don't think he'd do that. Do you remember that time we all snuck off to Peter's Point to swim after curfew? Austin's dad caught him coming in that night and told him he would knock off half the time he was going to be grounded if he told who he was with, and Austin never outed the rest of us. Mr. Beckett for sure would have called all our parents, and we all would have been grounded."

Jesse laughed as he remembered them sneaking out well past the 10 p.m. closing time at the beach, just weeks before Callie had been discovered at the festival. He and Callie had been in the water up to their knees, kissing in the moonlight as waves crashed into them. He'd had to pull her closer so she didn't get her legs swept out from under her. Austin and Gigi had walked down the beach to give them privacy, and he had been sure Austin would finally make his move on Gigi. Jesse had asked him later, but he'd never admitted to anything. It was surprising because Austin was usually happy to kiss and tell.

"And if we'd been grounded," Gigi continued, "Callie's parents probably wouldn't have let her play Beach Bash that year, and then where would we all be?" Gigi looked sideways down the beach, as if trying to picture how their lives might have played out differently.

"I don't know about you, but I'd still be here." He moved next to Gigi and put his elbows on the stage.

"Would you have really gone with her? If she hadn't broken up with you, I mean." Gigi was studying his face now, looking for his answer even before he spoke.

Just like back then, he wasn't sure. It wasn't as if he hadn't felt some obligation to stay and help his family. But instead of settling for being angry at his uncle for putting them in that position, Jesse had spent years blaming Callie for not letting him make a choice. What had started as anger when she first left turned to bitterness months later and then eventually being resigned to his fate. When she'd asked him for forgiveness, he'd given it freely, ready to be rid of the burden of blame. But what he hadn't done was ask himself if his life would be any different had she let him choose.

"I don't know," he said honestly to Gigi. "I'd like to think I would have stayed here and helped my dad, but the allure of college and Nashville and being with Callie would have been hard to resist. Eighteen-year-olds don't always make the best decisions." He shrugged.

"Watching her go off and do what she did, it gave me the confidence to believe I could go after my dreams too," Gigi admitted, brushing off sand that had blown onto her skirt. "Maybe I wouldn't have gone to law school. Ms. Myrtle would be a whole lot happier." Gigi smiled now, clearly pleased she could rankle her mother.

Callie, Gigi, Austin—they'd all gone off, but he'd stayed behind. Then it had finally felt like his turn when Uncle Lonnie made him the deal on the Lyman house. He'd thought that was what would make him happy, what would give his life meaning finally. Nothing was turning out like he'd planned though.

"So what now?" Jesse didn't look Gigi in the eye.

"She wants to go by the house today, but she doesn't want you to be there."

Jesse winced. He could have taken her yelling at him, but refusing to see him? Having Gigi tell him to stay away from the house while she was there? It felt as if a rock was crushing his chest, he could barely breathe.

"I'll be here all day. In fact, I should get back to work." He turned from Gigi so she wouldn't see the tears stinging in his eyes and walked to his nearby toolbox. He hadn't cried since that day she'd called to say he shouldn't come to Nashville. He hadn't cried on the phone, but he'd been unable to stop the tears from falling after he'd hung up.

"Hang in there." He heard Gigi dismount from her seat on the stage. "I'm sure she'll come around."

Jesse grunted in reply as he dug around in his toolbox for a tool he didn't need, avoiding her gaze.

"And, hey, why don't you ask Austin what happened before you decide to play judge, jury, and executioner?"

He grunted again, willing her to leave him alone so he

could wallow in peace and quiet. He heard her footsteps retreating in the sand and waited until all was quiet around him before turning to make sure she was gone.

Alone, he threw the wrench he was holding in his hand back in the toolbox, the sound of metal on metal piercing the quiet morning as it connected with the other tools inside. He was developing a headache, and the noise punctuated the pain in his temples.

Whatever flicker of hope he'd had that Callie had been feeling the same things as him when they were together was gone. He'd spent the past thirteen years avoiding serious relationships so he'd never be heartbroken again, but he hadn't counted on Callie being able to break his heart twice.

————

THE AFTERNOON SUN WAS BEATING DOWN ON JESSE'S back as he secured the vinyl banners that encircled the bottom of the stage to hide the supports. The beach was filled with sun worshipers and families frolicking along the shoreline. He'd put in headphones to try to drown out the thoughts in his head, which kept him from hearing the person who'd approached and whose shoes he now found himself looking at as he kneeled at the edge of the stage. Shielding his eyes, he glanced up to find the one person he didn't want to see. Jesse took off his headphones as he rose to look Austin in the eye.

"Hey, man." Austin put a hand on Jesse's shoulder. "It's starting to take shape out here. Need some help?"

Jesse shrugged off Austin's hand. "Not yours," he said under his breath as he turned to grab the box of vinyl coverings he needed to finish the last of the skirt around the stage.

Clearly not hearing the comment, Austin followed Jesse as he walked further down the stage to the next unfinished section. "You seem like you're in a mood. What's up?"

"As a matter of fact, I am 'in a mood,'" Jesse spat out as he whipped around to face his friend.

Jesse was shorter by several inches, but he was considerably more muscular given his daily labor. Austin was tall and lean, a pitcher who'd never had to spend much time lifting heavy weights. They'd had their disagreements over the years, but they'd never come anywhere close to an altercation. Jesse knew he'd never get physical with Austin, but he let himself picture how satisfying it would be to land a punch right in Austin's perfect jawline right now.

"What did you say to Michael when he came by the house?"

Austin took a step back, surprise registering on his face. "What do you mean? He just came by looking for you. I told him you weren't there, and he said he'd track you down later. He asked to see your progress, and I showed him around the downstairs before he was running out the door again."

Jesse clenched his fists by his sides. "Walk me through the whole conversation. Did he ask you questions about the house?"

"I don't know, I was out sanding the balusters after the shipment came and he appeared on the porch looking for you. He remembered we'd met once or twice before, and I told him I was helping you out some. He took a look around and said he hoped you knew what you were getting yourself into. Then he left." Austin shrugged.

"What about Callie? Did you tell him it was her house?" Jesse took a step forward and pointed at Austin.

"Whoa." Austin held up his hands and took another step back. "What's happening here? Does Michael know it's Callie's house?"

"Yes, Austin. Yes, he does. And since Uncle Lonnie, Gigi, Callie, and I are the only other ones who knew about the house, and I know none of them told Michael, I know something you said tipped him off. And now he's put out a press release to the whole world about it and Callie's furious." Jesse's arms flailed around as he talked, emphasizing his points and drawing the attention of several people nearby.

"You think I told him?" Austin's voice rose to match Jesse's. "Why would you immediately think I'm the one to blame? Maybe he searched the public records or heard it from someone around town. Everyone knows that's Callie's house."

"I think it's awfully convenient that he just happened to come by the house and talk to you the very same day he found out and shared it with the world."

Austin shook his head. "Unbelievable, man. After everything we've been through together over the years. When have I ever sold you out about anything? I know things have been stressful with the house and Beach Bash and Callie being back, so I'm going to give you a pass this once and leave so you can cool off. Why don't you take a walk or something." He pointed down the beach.

Jesse couldn't believe Austin wouldn't man up and admit he'd let something slip. But before he could say anything else, Austin had started walking back to the parking lot. Fists still clenched, Jesse returned to the stage. He had too much work to get done to deal with this betrayal right now.

As he tried to put up one of the final sections of skirting around the side of the stage, Jesse was distracted by a young family playing near the surf's edge. The parents didn't look much older than him, and they had a towheaded toddler between them, each grabbing a hand and swinging her up over the water. The little girl shrieked in excitement each time they lifted her, pigtails flying in the wind.

Jesse hadn't really given having a family a lot of thought, since he'd never dated anyone long enough to get that serious. He imagined the dad had a solid job back home, a 401(k), a house with a little white picket fence. Although they were fifty yards away, Jesse could see the smile on the man's face as he turned to his wife. They looked very much in love.

What had that guy done right that Jesse had done so wrong? Why was Jesse being punished? He'd stayed home, helped his dad like a good son. When was it going to be his turn to be happy?

CHAPTER THIRTY-ONE
CALLIE

Callie was still stewing over what she learned when she woke on Thursday. After visiting Uncle Lonnie the previous afternoon, she'd come back to Gigi's house and sat on the back porch, staring at the water. Any time she'd ever needed to think as a teenager, she'd come to the beach and sat alone on a towel, letting the sound of the waves wash over her and clear her mind.

By the time Gigi came home from work, Callie felt the sounds of the beach had smoothed out her frustrations. They'd ordered pizza and sat on the deck until well past dark, talking about what Uncle Lonnie and Jesse had done. Callie forgave Gigi for not telling her, understanding why she'd deferred to Uncle Lonnie to handle things in his own way.

But she hadn't forgiven Jesse. He'd made her feel like a complete fool. He'd cared more about protecting the project than her. She wasn't going down that road again. One career-obsessed boyfriend was enough for this lifetime.

"What would you do? With the house, I mean," Callie had asked Gigi the night before. She had started to feel she belonged on Big Dune Island again. She wanted to see Uncle

Lonnie more and Gigi. She wanted to feel the sand between her toes and listen to the waves crashing against the shore. But the memories of her parents were thick here. And those of Jesse.

"I'd listen to my gut," Gigi said. "That's why I'm back here. I stopped listening to what everyone else thought I should be doing. Just because I *could* live in New York and work in a big firm doesn't mean it's the right thing for me. Life is too short not to live somewhere you love." She shrugged as if the decision had been a no-brainer for her.

Callie did love Big Dune Island, and being back hadn't brought the painful memories of her parents she'd always thought it would. Sure, something reminded her of them multiple times a day, but it was comforting instead of crushing. If anything, she regretted spending so many years away from the place where she felt most like herself. Uncle Lonnie wasn't getting any younger, and she wanted to spend more time with him while she still could. It'd be nice to see Gigi more often too, and she hadn't even gotten to see so many of the other people on the island she remembered fondly from her childhood.

Then there was Jesse. She'd started to want to see more of him too, but now he was the last person she wanted to see. She pictured trying to avoid running into him around town, which was all but impossible. How long would it take before she could see him without feeling the sting of the knife in her back?

Maybe it would be better for everyone if she went back to hiding in Nashville. After all, that's what she'd been doing all these years: hiding. Sure, she'd been busy, but that's what she'd wanted. Artists took time off to raise a family or focus on songwriting. Few in the industry operated on the record, release, tour, rinse-and-repeat schedule she had for so many years.

Callie made her way across the island to her childhood home. If she saw Jesse's truck, she wasn't going to stop, but she was hoping he'd be at the beach working on the setup for the festival. Last she'd seen, he still had a way to go, and they were only two days away from the festival. Besides, Gigi had promised to talk to him this morning.

Jesse's truck was nowhere to be seen, so Callie parked and headed to the front door with a key Uncle Lonnie had given her in hand. She needed some time in the house alone to think. Could she picture herself here? Even if she decided to spend more time on Big Dune Island, did she want to be here or have a fresh start over on the beach? She could buy something near Gigi.

Callie stopped at the first step, kneeling down to put her right hand on top of the print she'd pressed into the cement when she was five. The hand in the cement fit inside her palm now. She remembered when her dad and Uncle Lonnie had spent a whole weekend rebuilding the porch stairs. Her father had found her in the backyard on the old wooden swing that hung from the big oak tree and walked her around front where the cement was beginning to dry. She could still feel the cool wetness as she'd pressed her hand in it, like sand after a wave washed over it.

"Do the other one next to it," her father had coached.

She'd placed them side by side, the left a little crooked.

"Now a little piece of you will always be here," he'd said, grabbing a stick and giving it to her to hold while he wrapped his big, strong hand around hers and helped her carve her initials in the step beside her hands.

Callie traced the letters now, a tear falling down her cheek. Since returning it had become apparent that a piece of her was still here, and it wasn't just the tiny handprints in the cement.

Would a new owner cover this up one day and erase her from this place? She remembered what Uncle Lonnie said about the memories being in her heart, but it was the house that was pulling them out from where she'd long ago stuffed them in the file cabinets of her brain, locked the drawers and thrown away the key.

Pushing open the front door, the creak of its hinges echoed in the two-story hallway as Callie stepped inside. She hadn't come over with a real plan in mind, she just needed to be here.

Feeling drawn back to her room again, Callie climbed the stairs, each one crying out in a pattern that was as familiar to her as the chords of her songs. She fell into her favorite spot in the window seat, and looked out over the yard, trying to shove thoughts of Jesse to the side.

She considered what Sienna had said about her music, about how she hadn't liked Callie's newer songs, and then she thought about what Uncle Lonnie had said. Now she was the one who was embarrassed. How had she let herself stray so far?

Her last few albums hadn't been like her earlier ones. They weren't about her life, or about what she was going through. In the beginning she'd taken people on an emotional journey, making them cry in the front row when she played one of her ballads as an acoustical set and then launching into a more upbeat song to end the concert with them jumping around, smiling ear to ear.

Even though touring was exhausting, Callie had always enjoyed the meet-and-greets after her concerts. She'd always thought it was because she enjoyed meeting her fans in person, but now she realized it was more than that. She loved hearing about how her words had touched their heart, how she "got" them. Being a teenage girl was tough, from the impossible standards on social media to first loves and the inevitable heartbreak that followed.

On her last country tour, she'd been celebrating her tenth No. 1 hit and the band had put together a little musical montage of all her No. 1 songs. She remembered being surprised when she went to the after-party that night and a young girl—who must have been a toddler when Callie's first album had come out—rushed up to ask about her first No. 1.

"Did you really have a boyfriend back home when you first went out on the road? You know, like that song 'Missing You'?" asked a young girl, who'd introduced herself as Madison and looked to be about fourteen.

The girl's mother started to interject, embarrassed her daughter was prying into Callie's private life.

"It's okay," Callie said, waving off the mom. Turning back to the young woman, she said, "I did. You know, I wasn't much older than you when I was first signed. I was sixteen and dating and going to prom and doing all the other things teenage girls do."

"That's so cool," Madison gushed, turning to smile up at her mom.

Callie had a feeling the girl had dreams of her own and was imagining right now all the ways in which her life would be amazing if they came true.

"Were you afraid to move away from home like that?" Madison asked, no doubt picturing what it would be like to no longer live with her parents. It was probably something that both excited and terrified her. Callie remembered feeling that way.

"It all happened super fast," Callie said, "but Jim, the gentleman who signed me, took great care of me. And my mom was able to move to Nashville with me for a couple of years."

She'd discussed her surprising signing to the label at sixteen what seemed like a million times over the years in media interviews, at backstage after-parties and everywhere else she went. Her origin story wasn't a hot topic anymore, but talking about it still came automatically, even though it felt as if she was describing someone else's life, a story she'd heard one day and simply memorized.

Of course, it kind of was. The label had hired a media specialist to teach her how to give interviews in the beginning. At only sixteen and straight out of small-town America, they weren't about to just let her loose to see how it would go.

As Madison's mother turned away to talk to another mom, the girl asked, "What about your boyfriend? Did you ever see him again?"

Callie remembered the genuine curiosity in Madison's eyes that night. Callie had been surprised at how the question threw her for a moment. Back then, no one had asked her about Jesse for a very long time and she'd long ago learned to detach herself from lyrics to songs like "Missing You." She'd performed them so many times she could sing them in her sleep, so although the crowd clutched their hands over their hearts as they swayed and sang along to the dreamy lyrics about first love, they'd become only words to her. She'd trained herself not to think about anything when she sang them. Not to think about anyone.

Now it occurred to Callie that maybe Uncle Lonnie had been onto something the day before about her music suffering because she wasn't letting herself feel anything anymore. But he didn't know what it was like to stand on stage every night and rip your heart wide open in front of 50,000 people. You built up defenses over time. You had to in order to survive.

That's not what she'd told Madison that night. No, she'd said to her, "I think getting your heart broken is part of life. If you don't ever get your heart broken, it probably means you aren't really living."

Callie's response mirrored her hit song "We Were Living." That one had come on album three, when she'd learned to look back at her relationship with Jesse more fondly, choosing to believe that first love is meant to be fleeting, something that teaches you lessons and allows you to outgrow it. People in the real world didn't find happily ever after at sixteen.

But being around Jesse again had challenged that belief. She'd started believing the old saying about setting something free and that if it came back it was meant to be.

Now what was she supposed to write about? How then sometimes you find out that person bought your childhood home so they could exploit your name for profit? Nah, that wasn't very catchy.

Letting out a huff, Callie stared back out the window at the Spanish moss that had so many times helped her find the right lyrics. What were the words to express how she was feeling right now?

> This is a song about nothing
> Nothing at all
> This is a song about springtime
> Winter and fall

Callie had to laugh to keep from crying at the absurdity of it. It rhymed, but that was about all it had going for it. Maybe coming back to Big Dune Island had been a bad idea after all.

CHAPTER THIRTY-TWO
JESSE

When Jesse entered the coffee shop Friday morning to grab some caffeine to get his day going, he could tell the whole town was abuzz about Callie's return.

"I heard she's already here," Alice Barker told a table full of her garden club members as Jesse walked to the counter.

"Come back to help Lonnie sell that house," Lorna Dillon said in reply, nodding as she sipped from a pale-yellow teacup. "Heaven knows it's time."

"Oh, Jesse." Alice motioned to him as he pretended to examine the pastries in the case by the register. "We have a question for you."

Reluctantly, Jesse walked over to the table of women. "Good morning, ladies." He plastered on a smile as he stuffed his hands in his pockets.

"Dorothy said she's seen you working over at the Lyman house," Alice said, nodding toward the woman who lived diagonally across the street from Callie's childhood home. "What's going on over there? Have they got you fixing it up for the sale?"

"Something like that," Jesse mumbled, looking around for Chloe in the hopes she'd interrupt, and he could politely leave the conversation. She was at a table near the rear, her back to him. He willed her to turn around and notice his presence.

"Has Callie already arrived?" Lorna asked, teacup poised midair as her eyes searched his for an answer.

"She's not staying at the house, if that's what you're asking." Jesse shifted uncomfortably, looking around for Chloe again.

"Are you sure?" Dorothy said, her eyes narrowing at him. "I thought I saw a car with Tennessee plates there yesterday." This elicited a chorus of gasps from the table.

Forget gardening. These women could give the Big Dune Island detectives a run for their money. In fact, they were probably investigating far more on the island than the police, although the worst crime they'd uncover was someone whose lawn was overgrown with weeds.

"We should cook her something," Lorna said. "It's not like she can just go out to dinner. I bet the paparazzi and the reporters will be here in no time."

Everyone at the table nodded and started talking at once about casseroles and pies and potato salad. Feeling he had outlived his usefulness, Jesse quietly excused himself and went to meet Chloe as she stepped back behind the pastry display to grab an order for someone.

"Oh, Jesse, I'm so sorry," Chloe said as she lifted out two scones and placed them on mismatched plates she'd sat on top of the case.

"It's okay, I made my escape," he said, glancing back at the garden club deep in planning behind him before turning back to smile at Chloe.

She leaned to look behind him before recognition dawned on her face and she realized he was talking about his conversation with the ladies.

"No, not about that." Chloe bit her lip. "About Callie. I think maybe I spilled the beans."

"Nah, it wasn't you. Ms. Myrtle's been hanging banners all over town. I think it's supposed to be the front-page story in *The Newsleader* today. Everyone knows she's back to sing at the Beach Bash."

"No, about the house, I mean." Chloe looked down as she fidgeted with the tie on her apron.

"That's all over the news now too, Chloe. Don't worry. Hey, while you're in there can I grab a couple of bear claws? And I'm going to need an extra coffee for Teddy too. He's coming out to help me on the Beach Bash stuff." Jesse pulled out his wallet and rifled through to find a ten-dollar bill.

"That's what I mean," Chloe said, quieter now as she placed his pastries in a bag. "I think maybe I told Michael something he didn't already know."

Jesse's hand froze on the bill he was about to pull from his wallet. "Wait, you talked to Michael about the house? When?" He already feared what her answers would be.

"Sunday." She sat the bag on the counter without meeting his eyes. "It was my day off and I was over at the Ritz for a spa day my friends got me for my birthday. I ran into Michael at the bar when we were getting our mimosas, and we started talking. He said something about how he didn't know why you wanted to renovate that house, and I may have accidentally told him about how you and Callie used to date. I didn't even know you were restoring her house until Michael told me where you were working, and then I just assumed that was part of why she came back. Michael acted so surprised to learn it was Callie's house. I told him he should talk to you about it."

Jesse pinched the bridge of his nose. It had been Chloe—not Austin. Gossip didn't run in the family after all. He was a terrible friend. He needed to see Austin before he left for the radio station.

"I didn't know he didn't realize it was Callie's house. I'm so sorry," Chloe said, her forehead wrinkled as she searched his face for forgiveness. "I feel terrible. Maybe I should go apologize. Is she at the house?"

"No, she's—" Jesse stopped himself from revealing she was staying at Gigi's or that would get out too. "I don't know where she is, but I'm sure you'll run into her sometime this weekend." Meanwhile, he wasn't sure he could say the same. She'd sent Gigi to make sure he didn't go by the house yesterday. Now he was nervous to go anywhere near it.

"Here." Chloe pushed the coffees and bear claws across the counter. "These are on me."

"Thanks," he said, putting the cash in the tip jar instead. He practically ran out of the cafe.

He was going to drop off the coffee and pastries with Teddy and get him going on the tent footings, then he needed to start his apology tour, first with Austin and then with Uncle Lonnie. He needed to apologize to Callie too, but he knew it was going to take more than just words to repair the damage he'd done there. He might have an idea though.

––––––––

Jesse waited outside Austin's front door after he knocked. Usually, he'd punch in the security code on the deadlock and let himself in, but it felt a little weird after the fight they'd had the day before.

Austin's house was on the west side of Fletcher Avenue, the beach road. Instead of backing right up to the ocean like Gigi's bungalow, it was a two-story frame house with a third-floor rooftop deck with a great view of the ocean over the top of the single-level house across from him on the beach. Austin had made decent money during his short stint in the Major Leagues, but he'd always been very conservative about spending it. He'd invested a little into this fixer-upper, a little into Chloe's business, and tucked the rest away. He and Jesse had spent weekends fixing up his house over the last couple of years, and it had gone from 1970s crash pad to a more modern, if masculine, home befitting a young bachelor.

Austin's truck was in the drive, and it was way too early for him to have left for work. Jesse knocked again, louder this time.

His hair pointing in several different directions and wiping sleep from his eyes, Austin finally answered the door.

"To what do I owe this pleasure?" Austin leaned against the doorway.

"I've come hat in hand to apologize." Jesse bowed dramatically.

Austin stepped back. "Come in."

Jesse entered the hallway and ran a hand through his hair. "Man, look… I'm sorry. I shouldn't have accused you of telling Michael. Chloe told me it was her when I went in to get coffee this morning."

"Figures," Austin said, shaking his head. "Need another cup? I haven't had mine yet."

"Yeah, sorry if I woke you. I thought you'd be up by now." He followed Austin toward the kitchen on the back side of the house.

"Late game last night." Austin yawned. "I stayed up until after midnight just to watch the Braves give it away in the twelfth inning." He grabbed filters and a bag of coffee out of a cabinet before setting the machine to brew. "So it was Chloe who spilled the beans? How'd she know? I swear, man, I never told her what was going on."

Jesse leaned his back against the granite countertop. "Nah, she didn't know what she was saying. You know she has a thing for Michael, right? She was probably trying to impress him, let him in on a little insider knowledge."

"My sister has the hots for Michael?" Austin scrunched up his nose. "My mother will die if she finds out her sweet little Southern girl wants to date a guy who looks like an extra from *The Sopranos*."

"Don't set a place at the dinner table for him just yet." Jesse laughed. "I'm not sure he thinks of her in that way. She flirts with him every time he comes in the cafe, but he doesn't seem to notice."

"Good, maybe there's still hope." Austin pulled two mugs out of the cabinet as the coffee pot began to fill.

"Hey, what are you up to after your show?" Jesse knew he didn't deserve his friend's help, but he also knew Austin would give it if he asked. And it was time to start calling in some favors, even if it made him feel a little cringy. He owed Callie that much.

"What do ya have in mind?"

Jesse laid out his plan for the grand gesture he hoped would show Callie how sorry he was for lying to her and how much he wanted her to consider spending more time on Big Dune Island. Austin agreed to pick up some things in Jacksonville after his show and meet him back at the house that afternoon.

As Jesses climbed back in his truck in Austin's driveway, he dialed Gigi's cell. There was one more thing he needed to do.

"Hey, Thomas," she answered.

"Is Callie at the house today? There's something I need to do."

"No, her publicist flew in and they're running all over town with Myrtle doing interviews and working out plans for the Beach Bash. But maybe you oughta tell me what you're up to. You know, keep the surprises to a minimum going forward."

"That's the thing," he said, backing out of Austin's drive. "I kind of need this to stay a surprise, and I don't want to tell you and ask you to lie to her again. Could you keep Callie away from the house until after Beach Bash? I promise you, it's something she's going to love. It might even be something that convinces her to come back to Big Dune Island again."

The line went silent on Gigi's end as she likely contemplated putting her trust in him. He silently pleaded with her to go along with his plan.

"Okay, fine. She's too busy getting ready for the festival, so I doubt she'll go back before Sunday or Monday. And, you're right, I don't want to know. I'm not sure any of us will survive lying to her again. Don't make me regret this."

"You won't, I promise," he said before exchanging goodbyes.

Jesse had one more thing to do before he went back out to the beach to help Teddy. They'd get the rest of the footings in for the tents, and then he could meet Austin at the house that afternoon. But right now he needed to swing back through downtown to the hardware store for a can of green paint.

CHAPTER THIRTY-THREE
CALLIE

C allie was in her fifth interview of the morning. Everyone from *Rolling Stone* to BuzzFeed had sent someone to cover Callie Jackson playing the hometown festival where she'd been discovered and gone on to make it big. Ms. Myrtle had been right; the headline wrote itself.

"This next one looks like she's a music blogger. Surprised she had the budget to come out here, but she seemed nice on the phone," Piper said as she returned from ushering the Buzz-Feed reporter out of the gate at the end of the porch and reviewed her clipboard on the table.

They were sitting outside at Sandy Bottoms, the beach-front restaurant at Main Beach fifty yards south of where the festival stage was built. Callie had tried sitting with her back to it so she wouldn't be distracted every time she saw movement, but Ms. Myrtle had insisted she sit with her back to the ocean instead so the photos reporters took would have her framed by the island's pristine beach. That meant the stage was sitting to her right and her peripheral vision caught every movement.

Someone by the stage drew Callie's attention again, but she

didn't recognize the man who was scurrying around working that morning. She should have been glad not to see Jesse, not to be reminded of his betrayal, but her pulse betrayed her each time she saw someone by the stage out of the corner of her eye. If he wasn't here, did that mean he was at her house? Or was it his house?

Frustrated, she shifted in her seat and busied herself with straightening her skirt and pushing her curls back out of her face as Piper approached with the blogger. Ms. Myrtle was stationed next to her in case the reporters needed any details on the festival itself.

"This is Wanda Savage," Piper said as she escorted a tall woman who seemed much older than the average music blogger to Callie's table. Their group was the only one out on the porch, which Ms. Myrtle had arranged for them to have until 11 a.m. when the restaurant would open for lunch.

"Hi, Wanda." Callie extended her hand. "Nice to meet you."

"The pleasure is all mine." The woman smoothed her dark shoulder-length hair behind one ear. "I appreciate you working me into your schedule."

Callie nodded and smiled politely, resisting the urge to turn and look toward the stage again, instead forcing herself to focus on the woman in front of her. Wanda had simple diamond studs in her ears, manicured nails, and a big emerald ring on her right hand. She wore a white linen suit that was perfectly pressed. Wanda was the best-dressed blogger Callie had ever met. Usually, they wore concert t-shirts and jeans.

Wanda went on to ask the same questions everyone who came before her had asked Callie. How long had it been since she'd been back? What was it like to return to sing on the same stage where she'd been discovered? How did it feel to know she was playing a role in saving the island's beloved festival? What was happening with her label?

Callie gave all the answers Piper had coached her to say, each half true and half crafted to ensure nothing was taken out of context. Most of the reporters had asked gentle questions about how it felt being home without her parents and then had ventured into asking about the sale of her childhood home. She assured each of them that no decision had been made yet on the house, she was just back taking care of some maintenance and a local builder had gotten a little overly excited about the prospect of her selling.

Jesse was only fifty yards away. She had half a mind to march off the porch, across the sand, and demand he tell her why he lied to her. Force him to tell her why he had targeted her house and what he intended to do with it.

She was so lost in thought, she missed Wanda's next question, and Piper nudged her with an elbow.

"I'm sorry, long morning." Callie reached to take a sip from the water glass in front of her. "What did you ask?"

"The songs you sang back then." Wanda raised an eyebrow. "They're a little different than what you sang on your last album. What can we expect to hear on Saturday? I'm told you might debut a new song."

"We're keeping the playlist a secret for now." Callie smiled at the woman. "We want to give the fans something to look forward to."

"Well, I hope you don't mind me saying, but I'm a little partial to your earlier work." Wanda's tone was warm and friendly. "It was like you read my diaries, and for a moment I was right back in high school again. Obviously, I'm a little older than you, but I guess first love is a universal experience that transcends time."

Callie winced as she remembered some of the lyrics she'd written about Jesse. She stole a glance toward the stage, but he was out of sight again.

Wanda followed her gaze. "Does it look like it did when you played here as a teenager?"

"Mostly, but we moved the stage this year. The back used to face this way, but we turned it this year so the audience can take in the ocean while they listen to the acts." She turned back to Wanda, ready to wrap up the interview. She needed to go to the bathroom and hide for a few minutes. She'd forgotten how exhausting it was doing interviews.

"That stage was actually built by Callie's teenage sweetheart," Ms. Myrtle cooed from her seat next to Piper. "How's that for a full circle moment?"

Callie whipped her head in Ms. Myrtle's direction and gave her a look that she hoped sent a stern message, since she couldn't say anything out loud and risk Wanda writing something negative about her reaction.

"Really?" Wanda asked. "Well, how sweet. I love how small towns are so... small. That could be a little awkward though I guess." She turned back to Callie, raising an eyebrow.

"It's fine." Callie gave a tight smile. "Thank you so much for coming to town and for writing about the festival. I know we all appreciate it. If you'll excuse me, I need to go use the ladies' room. Piper can get you anything else you need."

When she pushed back her chair, it clanged against the metal railing behind her, surprising the women at the table. She murmured an apology and rushed to the bathroom.

Locking herself in the accessible stall, her heart pounding, Callie leaned over the white porcelain sink, gripping the edge for stability. Taking deep inhalations, she fought to return her breathing to normal while she thought about how many reporters Ms. Myrtle might have told about Jesse. Did everyone know his name now? Would the storyline be about how the first love in her songs was now building her stages? That made it sound as if she'd left him behind in the dust, and now he was only good enough to erect the stages upon which she sang.

She looked up in the mirror and barely recognized the face that stared back at her. She hadn't worn this much makeup since she'd returned to Big Dune Island, opting instead for a daily routine of tinted moisturizer with SPF, a quick swipe of mascara, and her favorite cherry lip balm. She felt suspended somewhere between the girl she had been last time she'd stood on that stage and the woman she'd become. She couldn't go back to the girl she'd been—the experiences and the lessons she'd learned were a part of her now—but it had become clear that she could no longer be the woman her last label and Andrew had carefully crafted either.

Callie took her time in the quiet restroom, waiting until her breathing had returned to a more normal pace before exiting into the empty restaurant. She had almost made it to the patio door when a familiar voice behind her spoke her name. She turned to see Jesse walking toward her from the front door.

She held up a hand. "Stop right there. I can't deal with this now. I'm in the middle of interviews." She turned to take the few remaining steps to the patio. Suddenly, she couldn't wait to get back to the media.

"Callie, wait. Who was that woman? The one you were just talking to in the white suit?"

Callie whirled back around. "Some music blogger, Wanda something. Why?" She stood, hands on hips, wondering why he was so interested in who was interviewing her.

"That's her," Jesse said. "The woman Chloe said was poking around the cafe. The one I told you walked by the house."

"Are you sure?" Callie's mind raced. The woman had been in the cafe long before anyone knew Callie was back on Big Dune Island.

"Yes, I'm sure. I saw her in the parking lot."

"I'll have Piper look into it." Callie dropped her arms by her side. "She said she was with some music blog. But how'd she know I was here before the news broke?"

"I don't know." Jesse shook his head. "Be careful, okay? Something's not right about her."

He ran his hand through his short, sandy hair, a nervous tick he'd always had that she'd thought was cute when they were younger. Callie forced her eyes to the floor, she had to remember she was mad at him.

Jesse was right though. Something didn't add up about Wanda. She was too mature, too polished to be a music blogger. And what had she been doing snooping around town? How'd she know Callie was there?

"I'll be fine." Her tone was firmer than she'd meant, so she softened as she continued. "But thank you. I'll talk to Piper."

He nodded, but didn't move. She could see him studying her face, her hair. Her body betrayed her, tingling as his eyes moved to hers.

"I've gotta go," she stammered, pointing toward the patio. "I have more interviews."

Jesse held up one hand in a wave before turning to leave.

"Hey," she called after him. When he turned around, his face expectant, she fought to muster up the anger she'd felt earlier. "We still need to talk."

He hung his head now. "Yeah, I know. I'm here whenever you're ready."

When she didn't reply immediately, he stuffed a hand in his pocket and turned to push the door with his free hand. She watched as it opened, sunlight flooding into the dimly lit interior. The restaurant had closed all the blinds facing the patio to give them privacy as workers prepared for the lunch rush. She watched his figure retreating until the door slowly closed again. She tried not to notice how tight his jeans fit, or the muscles peeking out from under the short sleeves of his deep-green t-shirt.

Shaking her head, she reminded herself once again how he'd lied to her. But that part of her brain was fighting with the part that basked in feeling protected by him. That's where it got complicated. The only thing he couldn't protect her from was him.

Chapter Thirty-Four
Jesse

Jesse and Austin were almost done putting the second coat of paint on Uncle Lonnie's porch as the sun slipped behind the trees, darkness falling on 6th Street like a curtain closing. Act One of Jesse's apology tour was complete.

Sure, he didn't necessarily owe Uncle Lonnie an apology. After all, he hadn't been the one to spread the word about Callie's connection to the Lyman house, but he'd been the one to bring Michael into Uncle Lonnie and Callie's lives.

"Back to the house?" Austin asked as he came around from the side of the house where he'd been washing out the rollers and brushes.

Jesse nodded, grabbing the paint cans and heading to his truck in the drive. Uncle Lonnie would be back from the pre-festival dinner at the American Legion any minute. Jesse pulled out caution tape that said *Wet Paint* and went to tape off the entrance to the steps so Uncle Lonnie wouldn't step in the wet paint when he got home.

They made the quick drive back to the Lyman house and started unloading Austin's truck, which they'd left in the driveway. Austin had met Jesse after work, stopping to pick up some supplies on the way back to the island. They'd moved all the furniture out of Callie's bedroom after putting the first coat on at Uncle Lonnie's house, then they'd rushed back down to put on the second coat before he made it home.

Jesse had a little hesitation about touching Callie's things, not that she had much left in her childhood bedroom beyond furniture, stuffed animals, and trinkets, but he remembered Gigi's words about Callie not wanting him there. He'd decided to take the risk though. She was already mad at him; how much worse could it get?

Act Two of his apology tour involved transforming Callie's bedroom into a recording studio. It was the riskiest thing he'd ever done in his life. It had taken virtually all his savings to buy the equipment and sound-proofing materials Gus, the guy who owned the music store in Jacksonville, had suggested. And there was also the risk that Callie wouldn't buy the house and he'd have to rip all this out later to transform it back into a bedroom before they listed it on the market. Then he'd be out the money on the things he couldn't return, and he would have blown a lot of man hours.

But the real risk was that the gesture wouldn't be enough. Not enough to make Callie forgive him. Not enough to make her stay. Not enough to heal the broken heart he'd been served once again.

Jesse and Austin brought in loads of lumber, fabric, fiber-glass insulation, bass traps, and diffusers. Jesse had all but wiped out the store's supply of acoustic materials. Luckily, Gus had emailed Jesse instructions for building his own acoustic panels. Now he and Austin stacked up all the supplies by the window seat in the bedroom, where it quickly mounded up as high as their heads.

"Do we just cover it all up?" Austin asked, motioning

toward the wall, scratched and marked from years of neglect with its peeling wallpaper border at the top.

"Yep. Sure beats having to steam off wallpaper."

"Tell me about it." Austin wiped sweat from his brow. "Do you remember the weekend we spent stripping that awful pink wallpaper out of my master bath?"

"What about the pink toilet and matching pink sink and bathtub?" Jesse shook his head, laughing at the memory.

"Dude, there was so much pink. It was like living in a Pepto-Bismol bottle until we got done."

"Looks great now though. I was planning to put that same slate counter in my master. It's pretty slick."

"Let me know when you're ready and I'll lend a hand. I still owe you."

"Nah, I'm calling in my favor right now. Besides, I won't be able to afford it after this anyway." Jesse shrugged. He didn't need a new master bath to be happy. This project though—it might be the key to his future happiness.

Gus told him the biggest mistake rookies made in building home studios was forgetting about the bass traps and going straight to hanging acoustic panels. Jesse had emailed him photos of the room, along with measurements, and Gus had made some recommendations about where to place some corner bass traps. Jesse consulted the email as he walked around the perimeter of the room.

"Grab those wedge-looking pieces first," he said.

"These black foam thingies?" Austin held up the bass trap.

"Yeah, grab a few of those. We'll start in this corner."

They worked side-by-side late into the night. If Jesse wanted to finish this up while Callie was busy with the Beach Bash, there was no time to waste.

———

Jesse had pulled in two more from his crew to help Teddy finish up the Beach Bash setup on Friday, but he swung by first thing Saturday morning to check that everything was ready for the concert that evening.

"It looks great," Jesse said, slapping Teddy on the back as they walked down the main thoroughfare of the festival, each side lined with bright-white tents that reflected the afternoon sun overhead. Shopkeepers, local craftsmen, and restauranteurs had started to unpack their displays, filled with everything from jewelry and handbags to brightly painted canvases and small wooden sculptures. The smell of funnel cakes filled the air, which would mix with the more savory aroma of fried seafood later in the day.

"I can't thank you enough, man." Jesse shook Teddy's hand. "You really saved my butt."

"Whatcha been working on?" Teddy asked. "Not that it's any of my business."

Jesse chuckled. For better or for worse, everything on Big Dune Island was everyone's business. "It's a surprise, but hopefully one I can let all of Thomas Construction in on soon."

"Fair enough. You need me to stay and do the sound check with Sienna?"

By the look on Teddy's face, and the anxious way he kept glancing back toward the stage where Sienna was adjusting a microphone, Jesse could tell that Teddy wouldn't consider the sound check work. Smiling, he said, "You know what, that would be a big help. I'm going to run to finish up one other project before we get this thing started tonight."

Teddy almost tripped as he ran to the stage and then nervously fumbled with the microphone stand, getting it adjusted to Sienna's height as she gave final instructions to the band behind her warming up.

Jesse knew what it was like to fall in love with the girl on the stage. Poor Teddy. He didn't stand a chance.

———

By the time Jesse got back to the Lyman house, Austin was already there working on the sound panels. They were having to skip the pancake breakfast and downtown parade that ushered in Beach Bash each year, but Callie would be busy with interviews all morning, and Jesse was eager to complete the project. Today they'd finish lining the walls with the acoustic panels they'd built the night before. The mixing desk and its equipment would arrive later today thanks to overnight shipping, along with reflection filters and diffusers.

Gus had mapped out what he thought the room needed, but he'd warned them they'd likely need to make adjustments once Callie—whose name Gus did not know, Jesse only telling him the homeowner wanted to play around and record some demos—got in and could test the sound.

Jesse would happily rip it all down and do it again any way she asked him to if only the studio was enough to make her not only forgive him, but want to spend more time on Big Dune Island. More time with him.

CHAPTER THIRTY-FIVE
CALLIE

When Callie woke up the Saturday morning of the Beach Bash, she felt like a kid on Christmas morning. Friday had gone by in a blur of interviews, both with the writers who'd come into town and with half a dozen radio stations in Northeast Florida. The hard part was over and all she had to do was eat her weight in fried foods and put on a simple concert on the beach.

Piper had suggested doing all the interviews Friday so she could enjoy the festival the rest of the weekend without being hounded by the press. It had been exhausting, but she'd sat down with every single writer, including that woman, Wanda. Piper was looking into who she was, but in the meantime Ms. Myrtle had an off-duty police officer who was going to wear plain clothes and walk around the festival with her so she could try to enjoy it like a normal person. The part of the job she hated—answering all the prying questions, plastering on a smile for twelve hours straight, carefully choosing each word she said—was over and now she was free. Well, as free as you could be with an off-duty police officer escorting you and photographers following you around all day.

Callie knew the photographers would be at every event trying to get candid shots, so it wouldn't be completely like the old days, but she was glad they'd see her in her element. This version of Callie Jackson—the small-town girl from Big Dune Island—was the real her, and now they'd all get to see that too.

She was dressed and ready a half hour before she and Gigi had planned to leave the house, impatiently waiting for Gigi to finish applying her makeup.

"I'd tell you to go get the coffee pot started, but I don't think you need the caffeine," Gigi said, looking at Callie's foot bouncing in anticipation as she sat perched on the edge of the clawfoot tub.

Callie burst into a wide smile. "I can't help it. I think it's going to be a great weekend."

"Did you decide what you're singing?" Gigi asked as she carefully applied mascara to her impossibly long lashes.

"I did," Callie said as she stood, punctuating the "did" by tapping Gigi on the nose before bursting out in laughter.

"Oh, boy, aren't we in quite the chipper mood? I'm definitely going to need coffee to catch up to that."

"Grab it to go," Callie said as she skipped out of the bathroom. "We still have to swing by to pick up Uncle Lonnie."

Callie and Gigi pulled up to Uncle Lonnie's to give him a ride to the annual pancake breakfast that kicked off Beach Bash. He wasn't in his usual spot on the porch, so they went to the door. While they were waiting for him to answer, Callie glanced around and felt something was different, something she couldn't quite put her finger on.

The front door creaked open, drawing her attention.

"Well now, aren't I lucky? I have the two prettiest girls in town taking me to the pancake breakfast. All the young men will be green with envy." Uncle Lonnie winked at them as he stepped out onto the porch and embraced each woman in a hug.

"Puh-lease," Gigi said, taking the arm he offered her. "If there were any young men like you in this town, I wouldn't be single anymore. They don't make 'em like they used to." She exchanged smiles with Uncle Lonnie, who'd always been as much her family as Callie's, the girls being inseparable growing up.

As she turned to follow him and Gigi down the stairs, Callie realized what looked different about the porch. "Hey, did you paint the porch, Uncle Lonnie?"

He stepped onto the path, letting go of his hold on Gigi's arm, but as he turned back to Callie, she could see the corners of his lips begin to turn.

"No, Jesse did," he said.

The information smacked Callie in the face. When had Jesse found the time to finish up the Beach Bash preparation and paint Uncle Lonnie's porch?

"He did, did he?" Gigi asked.

Callie saw Uncle Lonnie and Gigi exchange glances, each accompanied by a knowing smile.

"So what? He painted a porch. Let's not go knighting him or nominating him for sainthood or anything." She plastered a scowl on her face even though she felt a warmth spreading in her chest.

"Austin helped him too," Uncle Lonnie said to Gigi, whose cheeks flushed pink at the mention of the name. "Maybe there are some good guys left around here after all. Now come on, we gotta get there before they run out of blueberry pancakes. Those are my favorite."

As she followed, Callie watched Uncle Lonnie open Gigi's door for her, something he'd done for Aunt Doris every time they went to the car. She thought about how it's the things people do for someone that show they care. That had been the problem with Andrew; he'd never done anything for her—he'd only ever done things for himself—she'd simply benefited as a side effect sometimes.

And then there was Jesse. Buying and renovating the house had been all about him. Sure, he had no reason to do anything for her at that point, they hadn't spoken in over a decade. But then she'd come back, and they'd reconnected, or at least she thought they had. What had he done to show her he cared? He'd agreed to the right of first refusal, but that had been all Uncle Lonnie's idea.

Callie began to make a list in her mind. On the one side were the good things he'd done. He'd helped her go inside the house again. He'd warned her about Wanda. He'd painted Uncle Lonnie's porch—but did that even count? It was more for Uncle Lonnie than for her.

She worked on the other side of her mental list as Gigi drove them the short distance to the pancake breakfast in Central Park, at the edge of the historic downtown corridor. Jesse had lied about buying the house. It had been mostly lies of omission, but lies just the same. He'd even gone to Gigi behind her back.

Callie realized she was disappointed to find the scales tipping toward the things he'd done behind her back. Making the list had only proved to her that her heart and her mind had been hoping for two completely different outcomes.

———

The pancake breakfast was followed by the annual parade through downtown, which led trucks and trailers made into makeshift floats to the west, down Ash, before they turned at the marina and headed east up Main Street. All the businesses on the island shut down for the day, and with the exception of those who were over at the beach setting up their booths, seemingly everyone in town lined the streets, pointing and waving at the floats and decorated vehicles.

Callie had been perched on the back of a red Corvette convertible at the end of the parade, embarrassed she'd been asked to sit and wave like a pageant winner. She'd made Gigi sit beside her, not that it had taken much convincing. After all, Gigi had held each of the titles in the Pirate Pageant, from Tiny Miss Pirate Princess as a four-year-old to Teen Miss Pirate Princess at sixteen.

As they climbed out of the convertible at the end of the parade, Callie's arm aching from the nonstop waving she'd done for the hour they'd slowly crawled through downtown, three young girls raced up to her side from the crowd. Officer Carter, the off-duty policeman who'd been tasked with escorting Callie around town, stepped between them and Callie to stop them, but she placed a hand on his arm and told him it was okay.

"Hi, girls," Callie said, flashing a grin that made her cheeks ache after a morning spent with a permanent smile on her face.

The girls looked to be around eight and were all trying to talk to Callie at once. "Would you sign this for me?" a girl with a long brown side braid asked, as she tried to unroll a Beach Bash poster while balancing two scoops of ice cream on a cone in her other hand.

"Here," Callie said, taking the poster from her and unrolling it the rest of the way. "Do you have a pen?" The little girl began to look around, panicked. "It's okay, I have one. In my purse," Callie said to Gigi, pointing to the back of the convertible.

Gigi tossed the pen she found the few feet to Callie, but Callie missed and it landed on the ground. As Callie bent to retrieve it, one of the other girls said, "I've got one." Callie looked up just in time to see the girl with the pen stepping forward and bumping into the girl with the ice-cream cone. Callie's head was at the perfect height to be on the receiving end of the ice cream as the girl's arm shot forward.

"Omigosh, I'm so sorry," the girl with the ice-cream cone said, covering her mouth, tears springing to her eyes.

The other two girls stood still, their mouths open.

Callie felt the side of her hair, pulling away a hand covered in sticky blue ice cream. Seeing the girls all now on the verge of crying, she stuck a finger in her mouth as she stood. "Yum! Is that Superman ice cream from Island Ice? It was my favorite as a kid." She winked at the girls, their faces still frozen in shock.

Gigi and Officer Carter looked at each other and then at Callie, unsure what to do as all three girls started apologizing at the same time.

"Girls, it's okay," Callie assured them. "Here, let me sign your posters before I go wash this out."

The girls reluctantly handed over their posters, too afraid to speak until it was done. They all gushed more apologies and thank-yous before running back toward Main Street.

Gigi came closer to inspect Callie's hair. "What are you going to do now?" She checked her watch. "We only have forty-five minutes before we're supposed to be at the luncheon."

"We'll run over to my house. It'll only take me a minute to wash out this section of my hair, and then I can just let it air dry."

"Air dry?" Gigi said with a laugh that came out a little too loud. "It'll get all frizzy. Let's just run to my house so you can use all your product and stuff." Gigi motioned for Callie to follow her and started walking in the direction of the car.

"No, we don't have time. Traffic getting across the island will be a nightmare on parade day. My house is right there," Callie said pointing down 6th Street. "My hair will be fine, it's only one little section. Besides, there's no avoiding frizz in this humidity."

Gigi was picking at her nail polish now, not meeting Callie's eyes. "What about Uncle Lonnie's? There's probably not even shampoo at your house."

"I don't have a key to his house. I'm not going to wash it; I just need to put some water on this bit." She pulled at a sticky clump of curls.

"You don't want to run into Jesse though, right?" Gigi stuffed her hands in the pockets of her dress as she intently examined a crack in the sidewalk, poking at it with the toe of her wedge shoes.

Callie gave Gigi a questioning look. "Jesse? He's not going to be there today. I'm sure he's helping get everything ready for the big opening at Main Beach. What are you not telling me?"

"Nothing." Gigi took her hands out of her pockets and crossed her arms. "I told Jesse I'd keep you away from the house until Beach Bash was over."

Heat rose in Callie's face. "Why, Gigi? Why doesn't he want me over there? What is he doing now? Razing the whole thing to the ground?" She was practically shouting. She looked around to see if anyone had overheard. Thankfully theirs had been the last car back into the staging area and everyone had cleared out and moved on to the next event.

"No, I'm pretty sure the house is still there." Gigi gave a small smile. "Look, he promised me it was something you would like. We both decided I shouldn't know so I wouldn't have to lie to you about whatever it is."

"Well, we're about to find out." Callie grabbed her friend's arm. "Come on."

As they entered the house, Callie heard a drill coming from somewhere upstairs. What were they doing? Her pulse quickened as she thought about the men tearing apart her bedroom or—worse—her parents' bedroom. She rushed up the stairs, Gigi on her heels. The drilling stopped before they reached the top, and she heard footsteps and a door opening and closing from the direction of her bedroom.

"Hi," Jesse said, clearing his throat as he stood in front of the closed door to her room. "I wasn't expecting you today. Did you need something?"

"What are you doing in there?" Callie asked, charging down the hall to stand toe to toe with him.

"Uh, nothing." He leaned an arm against the doorjamb to further block entry. "Just freshening things up a bit."

"Where's my stuff? You never said you were working in there yet." She reached around his side to grab the door handle.

But Jesse shifted quickly to the side, blocking her attempt. "Please don't go in yet. Not until it's finished." His eyes pleaded with her before looking to Gigi for backup.

"G," Callie said, turning to her friend. "A little help?"

"I'm not getting in the middle of this one," Gigi said, holding up her hands in surrender.

"This is still *my* bedroom. Now let me in." She clenched her teeth and willed the tears not to fall. What were they doing to her room? To her stuff? How could Jesse go in and touch her things after what he'd already done to her? It was a violation.

He finally stepped aside, saying quietly, "I wanted to surprise you when we were done."

Callie burst through the door and then froze at what she saw.

Gigi came up behind her. "What is it—" Gigi said as she

started to push Callie's hand away from where it was still outstretched holding the doorknob. "Whoaaa."

There were still hammers and drills and lengths of 2x4 and fabric scattered on the floor, but one glance at the acoustic panels on the walls and the box with the mixing table in the middle told Callie exactly what this was. It was a studio. They were transforming her bedroom into a professional recording studio.

The tears flowed freely, and she cupped both hands over her face, suddenly sobbing. Her shoulders heaved as she struggled to catch her breath.

Gigi put an arm around Callie's shoulders. "Cal, it's okay. We can put it back like it was."

Callie tried to slow her breathing, using her hands to wipe away the tears streaking down her face, but they kept coming.

"Beckett, get her some tissues," Gigi said to Austin, who was standing awkwardly in the corner of the room. He rushed out, probably thankful for an excuse to leave.

"Cal, I'm sorry," Jesse said, stepping toward her from the doorway. "I—"

Gigi held up a hand to cut him off. "Hey." She smoothed Callie's hair away from her face. "Let's sit down." She ushered Callie over to the window seat, which was the only thing in the room that remained untouched. Gigi rubbed circles on Callie's back as her breathing began to return to normal.

Austin came in the room and walked with his head down, an arm extended toward them with wads of toilet paper in his hand. "This was the best I could do."

Gigi snatched it from him, exasperated with his inability to produce proper tissues.

"Thanks," Callie said quietly as she swiped at her face with a wad of toilet paper Gigi handed her. "I'm not upset," she said once she could speak again, looking toward Jesse, who stood in the middle of the room looking apologetic. "It's beautiful."

She looked around at the soft sand-colored panels on the walls. She'd never seen any acoustic panels like it. And the ceiling was like a pale-blue morning sky.

"It's supposed to make you think of a sunny day at the beach," Jesse offered. "But we're not finished yet."

Callie laughed as a stray tear traced its way down her cheek. "It's perfect."

"Why don't we give you two a minute," Gigi said as she looked to Austin, nodding her head toward the door.

When Callie was alone in the room with Jesse, Gigi having closed the door as she and Austin exited, she stood to face him. "Why'd you pick my house?"

He took a long moment to think before giving his answer. "Because I've always loved this house and Uncle Lonnie gave me a good deal."

"That's all?"

"Of course it isn't." He swallowed hard. He took a step toward her. "I bought it because it was all that was left of you here. And because maybe deep down I hoped Uncle Lonnie was right and that it would bring you back."

"You wanted it because it's my house?"

He nodded. "Is it? Still going to be your house, I mean?"

He took a step closer, and she didn't back away like she had when they'd been alone together those first few days she'd been back home. He searched her eyes, and she knew in her heart what he wanted her to say. What *she* wanted to say.

"I'm not sure." She bit her lip, making him wait to hear it. "I think maybe it could be. Seems like it would be awfully tough to sell with one bedroom turned into a studio. How many buyers around here need a home recording studio?"

"I can think of one," he said, taking another step closer.

He reached out and took one of her hands, pulling her toward him, the gap between them closing.

"It's Miranda Lambert, isn't it? I heard she vacationed in one of those private cottages on the south end last year."

He shook his head. "No, it's not Miranda Lambert. It's another blonde country music singer I hear might even be on the island right this very minute."

She smiled up at him as her heart threatened to break through her chest, threading her fingers through both his hands. She was fifteen all over again, willing him to lean down and kiss her.

Then, as if he could read her mind, he finally did. She closed her eyes as his mouth met hers. His lips were warm and soft, and she could smell his familiar woodsy scent. It made her tingle all the way to her toes, just like their very first kiss.

Maybe some things really didn't change. She knew her feelings for him hadn't, not in thirteen years.

CHAPTER THIRTY-SIX
JESSE

J esse never wanted to be apart from Callie again, but he was called back over to Main Beach for an unexpected delivery, and Callie had to get her hair washed and head downtown for part of her hosting duties. So they finally parted, an anxious Austin and Gigi waiting downstairs, no doubt curious for details. Jesse filled in Austin on the way to Main Beach, his friend sharing his excitement at the way things had turned out.

Once at the concert site, Jesse began directing a truck driver with a trailer to relocate the additional portable bathrooms Ms. Myrtle had ordered at the last minute after finding out the mayor of Jacksonville and a local senator were attending with their wives. Next thing Jesse knew, a new "VIP area" was taking shape to the south of the stage.

These portable bathrooms were like nothing Jesse had ever seen before: the size of mobile homes, complete with stalls and sinks like a real bathroom. A far cry from the porta-potties on the north end of the beach that were brought in for the masses.

Jesse kept replaying Callie's words in his mind. She'd said

the studio was perfect. He knew he had a stupid grin plastered on his face, and he didn't care. His heart was bursting, he was so happy. She'd forgive him. Maybe she'd even stay now.

"I've never seen someone so happy to get a bathroom before," the truck driver said as he approached Jesse, having already unhooked the restroom trailer from his truck.

"What?" Jesse said, confused for a moment. "Oh, yeah. The bathroom." Jesse glanced past the driver to make sure he'd dropped it in the right place. "Looks good."

"We'll pick it up Monday morning." The driver shoved a clipboard into Jesse's hands for him to sign the delivery receipt. Shaking his head as Jesse signed and handed the clipboard back, the driver said, "Hope it won't break your heart to see it go."

Jesse laughed as the surly truck driver left. No, Jesse was hopeful he'd never have his heart broken watching something go ever again.

———

CALLIE HAD OBLIGATIONS ALL AFTERNOON, BUT HE'D find her after the pirate invasion. She was scheduled to make the big announcement downtown warning that pirates had been spotted and were making their way into the marina. The whole town would gather to watch dozens of pirates—in very elaborate costume—arrive in replica pirate ships and dock, before running into the town, plastic swords in the air as they came to claim it for their own.

From there, everyone would make their way the two miles straight down Main Street until it ended at Main Beach, some walking, some biking, and others riding the island trolleys. It was the official kickoff of Beach Bash, and acts would take the stage for the remainder of the evening while locals shopped and ate and staked off their spot in the sand to watch the performers.

Ms. Myrtle had called twice more to check everything was ready for the crowd to flood. Usually, it would have annoyed Jesse, but he was practically vibrating he was so excited about seeing Callie later. He assured Ms. Myrtle everything was under control and that he was personally on site to supervise as the last things were put into place. He had seen the pirate invasion enough times over the years. There was only one person he wanted to see, and he knew right where she'd be. As soon as Callie made the announcement about the invasion, Officer Carter would be waiting for her in his cruiser by the docks and whisk her down to Main Beach while the rest of the town was watching the pirates invade. Two trailers had been brought in that morning and placed on the north edge of the parking lot, one for Callie and one to be shared by other performers throughout the weekend as they prepared to go on stage.

Jesse went to the trailer to wait. He paced the length of it waiting for her to arrive, checking his reflection in the bathroom mirror twice to fix the collar of his shirt—which was inexplicably flipping itself up on one side—before he heard the police cruiser pull up.

When Callie opened the door to find him, her face lit up in a smile. "Miss me?" she teased.

"Every day for thirteen years," he said as he closed the gap between them. There was no sense in holding back now. He'd built her a recording studio in a house he was supposed to be flipping. She had to know already that she was his whole world. He swept her into him with one arm, his other hand getting lost in her curls as he cupped the back of her head and pressed his mouth to hers. Her frame fit perfectly against his, like a final puzzle piece snapping into place.

"Thank you," she said after their lips had parted and she was staring up into his eyes.

"For the kiss? There's more where that came from." He pulled her closer for another.

"No." She laughed as she leaned back to look at him again. "Thank you for bringing me home. You buying the house, it's what brought me here. And coming home..." She stopped, her eyes glistening as she smiled up at him. "That's what brought me back to me."

Jesse wanted to push for more. He wanted to hear her say she'd come back to him too. But he didn't want to spoil the moment by asking for too much.

They walked hand in hand out onto the beach, where they found Austin and Gigi. Officer Carter trailed them for the rest of the evening as the four friends sampled everything from fried shrimp to fried cheesecake balls—Chloe's latest dessert creation—and ensuring Callie got to enjoy the festival like any other town resident. Locals were respectful and said their hellos to Callie, exchanged pleasantries and hugs, and then went on taking part in the festivities.

The foursome had seats near the stage when it was time for Sienna to start her set. Darkness had fallen on the beach, a full moon bathing it in soft light that was punctuated by strings of big round bulbs that zig-zagged overhead attached to poles Jesse's team had driven into the sand the day before. He looked around for Uncle Lonnie, but he must have found a seat with his friends.

After swaying and bobbing their heads around to several songs from Sienna, Callie leaned over and whispered to Jesse, "I'll be right back." She gave him a quick kiss on the cheek and then disappeared around the side of the stage toward the VIP restrooms he'd help place earlier in the day.

Officer Carter had hopped up from a nearby chair and was right behind her. Hopefully he didn't have to actually go into the bathroom with her. It must be irritating to feel you were being babysat all the time.

Jesse was still looking at the spot where Callie had disappeared when the crowd around him began to roar. He looked on stage to see what the fuss was all about and saw Callie was up there whispering in Sienna's ear, Officer Carter standing in the shadows in the back corner of the stage.

"I hope y'all don't mind if a friend of mine joins me for this next one," Sienna said into the mic.

The crowd's response was deafening approval.

As Sienna strummed the first few chords, she stepped to the side to allow Callie up to the mic. It was a song Jesse hadn't heard since the last time Callie had been up on that stage. A song he hadn't been able to bear listening to since she'd left.

And this is Our Song
Every time you hear it
Know that you're the one
For now and for always
For worse or for better
You and me, darling
We're in this together

And with that, he thought he knew the answer to the question he'd been too afraid to ask.

CHAPTER THIRTY-SEVEN
CALLIE

Callie hadn't been this nervous about taking the stage in years. The last time she remembered feeling this way was before the first stop on her tour as a newly minted pop star. She'd felt uncomfortable in the short, form-fitting dress her stylist had chosen; her red lips painted to match her attire. Wobbling on impossibly high heels, she'd nearly tripped on her way across the stage.

At least tonight she was at no risk of tripping. Not from her heels anyway. She looked down to admire the cowboy boots Gigi loaned her, thinking about how Dorothy felt when clicking her heels together had finally brought her home. It must have felt like this.

After their song together, Callie asked the crowd to give it up for Sienna one more time, and they didn't disappoint. She searched the sea of faces for the ones she knew would calm her. Jesse, Uncle Lonnie, Gigi, and Austin were all standing at the front of the stage smiling and cheering.

"Hey, Big Dune Island," Callie shouted into the microphone over the roar of the crowd. "It's good to be back!" She punctuated the end of her sentence with the first chord of the biggest hit off her freshman album.

The band kicked in behind her and they were off.

Callie felt as if she floated across the stage the entire evening as she went through her country hits, sprinkling in a couple of her pop songs—they weren't all bad. But she saved the one she knew the crowd really wanted to hear for last.

"Y'all have been real patient with me," Callie said to the crowd, surprising even herself with how quickly her drawl was coming back now she was singing her old songs again. "I know what y'all wanna hear, but I wonder if you might let me try out a new song first. What do you think? I wrote this one right here on Big Dune Island."

Callie was breathless as she grabbed a water bottle and took a quick swig. The crowd roared in response.

"Some of y'all know I grew up down on 6th Street in the house my great-grandfather Lyman built, so this one is a kind of an ode to that." Callie nodded to the bass player to bring her over a stool like they'd practiced that morning. The spotlight dimmed on cue, and she climbed on the stool, guitar in her lap. "My Uncle Lonnie once told me you're not a real artist if you can't write and play your own songs. In fact, Uncle Lonnie has taught me a lot and continues to. So, Uncle Lonnie, this one's for you."

Callie had woken up that morning with "Saltwater Revival"—the first song she'd written back on the island—in her head. So much had happened in the short time since she'd written it, she'd decided it needed a different second verse, and she knew exactly what it would say. She'd scribbled it down in mere minutes. Although she'd dedicated it to Uncle Lonnie for helping her find her way again, there was another man in the crowd who'd inspired it too. She kept her eyes on Jesse as she sang.

We drew our names in the sand
When they washed away
I said I'd move on, but I can't
Thought I'd forget your name in time
But it turns out I've forgotten mine
I'm trying to find my way again

She was elated to see everyone in the audience swaying to the music. By the final round of the chorus, people were starting to sing along to the words they'd picked up.

I was chasing dreams that ran away with me
And now I'm right back where I started
Oh, I should have known I couldn't build a home
So far away from where my heart is
There's a difference between living and survival
Oh, how I miss this
Saltwater revival

By the end, Callie had tears streaming down her face, and she could see matching ones on Uncle Lonnie's. Jesse, Austin, and even Gigi—whom Callie had never seen cry about anything—all looked as if they'd shed tears as well. She didn't think her heart could swell any bigger than it already had that night, but she felt so full she feared she might burst.

"Alright, y'all. I hope you don't mind if I end with a very special song," she said as she stood and walked back up to the mic stand that was being brought to the center of the stage. She reached behind her to flip off the mic pack attached to the belt of her dress and turned on the mic on the stand.

"This was my very first No. 1 single, and it holds a special place in my heart." Callie looked directly at Jesse. As the first chords began to play, she saw the recognition on his face as he burst into a smile.

The crowd sang along to every word of "Me and You Someday," the song Sienna had been singing in Breakwaters when they'd first met. Looking to the side of the stage where she knew Sienna was sitting with her friend Teddy—who apparently worked for Jesse, talk about a small town—Callie motioned for her to come up on stage. Sienna joined her for the last verse, belting out the chorus along with what had to be five thousand people in the crowd.

> On the tailgate of your truck
> Young love and a little luck
> Sometimes we laugh, sometimes we play
> It's gonna be me and you someday

Callie turned to Sienna as the final chords faded, exchanging smiles with her. It had only been a few days, but they already felt like old friends. Two souls connected by a love of country music.

After taking her final bows and waving to the crowd, Callie joined Sienna at the bottom of the stage stairs. Piper and Officer Carter were there to meet her, although she was in no danger of being swarmed thanks to the fences that had been erected around the side and back of the stage, and the officers posted just beyond them. It felt like overkill, but Callie knew everyone meant well.

"Want to sign a few autographs?" Piper asked, nodding toward the area of the fence closest to the front of the stage where at least a couple of dozen people were waiting, waving and calling out her name.

"Sure," Callie said, smiling. She looked over to Sienna. "I'm pretty sure they're going to want yours too. Come on." She waved at Sienna to follow her.

Jesse, Gigi, and Austin were let through the fence and

stood off to the side talking to one another. Callie looked around for Uncle Lonnie, but didn't see him. She and Sienna stepped up to the fence and started signing autographs, smiling and offering thanks to everyone who stayed to meet them. She was signing the final autograph when she saw Uncle Lonnie approaching with Wanda Savage.

Why was that woman with Uncle Lonnie? Was she trying to get more fodder for her story? Some people really had a lot of nerve.

Callie turned to look for Piper, but didn't see her. Piper had looked up the woman after Jesse warned Callie about her at Sandy Bottoms, and she hadn't found a single piece written by the woman on the music blog she'd claimed to write for. Piper had been very apologetic, saying she approved the woman's interview request because it was an outlet she trusted; she'd merely thought the woman was a freelancer, a common practice with music blogs.

They'd both told Officer Carter who to look out for as he was escorting Callie at the festival Friday and Saturday, but he was nowhere to be found now either.

Jessie rushed to Callie's side. "Uncle Lonnie, that woman—"

Uncle Lonnie cut him off. "It's okay," he said, holding up his hand. "Callie, I want you to meet Jacqueline Sharpe. I believe you may know her as Wanda." He smiled, as if taking part in a surprise unveiling.

Jacqueline Sharpe. The name sounded familiar, but Callie couldn't quite place it.

"I don't understand," Callie said, looking from Uncle Lonnie to Wanda—or Jacqueline, whatever her name was—as Jesse stepped beside her and put a protective arm around her waist. "How do you know her? Jesse said she's been hanging around the house, and Chloe said she was at the cafe asking questions. She told us she was a music blogger named Wanda, but she knows things she shouldn't—"

"Yes," Uncle Lonnie interjected again. "You must have a lot of questions, but why don't you hear her out?"

Callie looked to Jesse, who shrugged, but kept his arm tight around her. Uncle Lonnie and Jacqueline stood on the other side of the fence.

"I'm sorry," the woman said. "I didn't mean to scare you. I just couldn't tell you who I was and why I was here until I knew more."

"Knew more about what?" Callie asked.

Austin, Gigi, and Sienna had all moved closer, curious about the exchange.

"I heard rumors you might be in the market for a new label soon. Those new songs, they were fantastic. But they don't fit with what you've been singing lately, huh?" Jacqueline asked, an eyebrow raised. She continued before Callie could answer. "Have you ever heard of Sharpe Music Group?"

It all clicked into place. Sharpe Music Group was a small label that started in Nashville back in the 1950s. They didn't have any big names, but they were a respectable label that gave a lot of country artists their first deal. Most of those artists moved on to bigger labels who could offer more resources once they had a hit or two under their belt.

"You're Arthur Sharpe's daughter," Callie said. "You and your sister took over the label earlier this year when he passed." Jacqueline nodded. "I'm sorry about your dad. I heard he was a great man."

"He was." Jacqueline smiled. "He had a vision for the label that we intend to uphold. We've intentionally stayed small over the years. Sure, it means some of our best artists move on from us and graduate up to bigger labels, but that's okay. My dad turned down dozens of offers over the years to sell the label to one of the giants. He wanted to be the place where artists could take charge of their own careers, sing what they wanted, how they wanted. We give our artists complete control, from song selection to distribution channels and even pricing. So when I heard your clock would run out soon on your current contract... Well, I couldn't live with myself if I didn't at least try."

"You miss one hundred percent of the shots you don't take," Austin said, winking at Jacqueline.

Callie caught Gigi rolling her eyes at his ability to find a quote for any situation.

"Yes, exactly." Jacqueline smiled at him.

Callie was speechless. Was this woman offering her a new deal? She looked at Uncle Lonnie, who was beaming at her and standing awfully close to Jacqueline.

"Jacqueline came by to see me," Uncle Lonnie said. "Sort of asked for my permission to talk to you."

"Yes, I know your manager—" Jacqueline started in a tone that said she knew she didn't need to explain the rest. "I wasn't sure he'd bring you my offer."

She was making Callie an offer. But for what?

"I'm sorry," Callie said. "I'm a little surprised. I'm not sure what to say. What is it you're offering?"

"Your uncle here," Jacqueline said, turning to smile at Uncle Lonnie, "he thought you might be ready to make a change. I can get you the formal offer letter in the morning, but we'd like to bring you over to Sharpe. I know we need to wait out the rest of your current contract—"

Gigi cut her off, stepping forward. "Actually, we've already taken care of that. Callie is no longer under contract." She winked at Callie. "I received written confirmation from Andrew this morning."

Jacqueline looked relieved. "Well, that was easy. Now you just have to decide if you want your next contract to be with us. You'd have complete control—if you want to go back to country, that's fine by us. Want that song you sang tonight on your next album? Done."

Callie's mind was racing. She shrugged off Jesse's arm around her and then reached for his hand, gripping it for support.

"What if I wanted to live here?" she asked, swallowing hard.

She saw the surprised look on Gigi and Austin's faces, and felt Jesse squeeze her hand tighter. Uncle Lonnie had a smile that stretched ear to ear.

"Who am I to tell you where to live?" Jacqueline asked. "I certainly understand the appeal of being here." She looked at Uncle Lonnie and they exchanged glances.

Was Jacqueline flirting with Uncle Lonnie? Callie hadn't seen her uncle look at anyone like that since Aunt Doris passed. It warmed her heart; she couldn't imagine how this weekend could get any better.

"In fact, I think I'm going to hang around for a few more days," Jacqueline said. "So we'll have plenty of time to chat. You don't have to make a decision tonight. And, Sienna," she said, turning to where the girl stood on the edge of their group, "I'd like to sit down with you as well. I think you might have a future at Sharpe too."

Sienna's face went from surprised to ecstatic, and Callie remembered what it had felt like when her life had changed on this very beach thirteen years ago.

As Jacqueline and Sienna continued their conversation, Callie pulled Jesse away from the group. "I don't know what kind of deal they're going to offer me, but if it's enough to buy the house back, I'd like to do that."

"Of course. Uncle Lonnie made sure you'd have the right of first refusal if you wanted it back. But does that mean…" His voice trailed off.

She saw the expectant look in his eyes. The question he was too afraid to ask her.

"Yes, that means I want to live here. With you."

As Jesse picked her up and spun her around in celebration, pressing his mouth to hers, Callie realized Thomas Wolfe was wrong. You can go home again after all.

EPILOGUE
SIX MONTHS LATER

"I t's time to get ready," Jesse said, opening the door and poking his head into the studio that had once been Callie's childhood bedroom.

She now slept down the hall, in her parents' old bedroom, which made her smile every morning when she woke up and thought about them as she put on her makeup at her mother's old dressing table or placed a book she was reading on the nightstand her father had built.

Jesse tapped an imaginary watch on his left arm when neither Callie nor Sienna moved.

Callie turned to Sienna. "We really need a *Recording* sign that lights up outside that door."

"Or a lock." Sienna giggled.

"Seriously, you two, we're going to be late for the wedding. I'll wait for you downstairs."

Callie went to the closet Jesse had made her out of her mom's old sewing room and put on her dress and shoes. She met Sienna in the hallway as she exited the guest bedroom where she'd changed.

"You ready?" Sienna asked.

"I can't wait." Callie smiled.

The simple wedding on the beach was perfect. Uncle Lonnie was dapper in his khaki-colored suit with a pale-blue tie that matched Jacqueline's blue dress and the perfect robin's-egg-blue sky. Callie and Sienna sang "Saltwater Revival" together with nothing but their guitars and the waves crashing behind them for backup before Uncle Lonnie and Jacqueline said "I do" in front of their closest friends and family. They'd only been dating for a few months when Uncle Lonnie popped the question, saying they were old enough to know what they wanted, and that they'd found it in each other.

After the nuptials, the group made their way up to Gigi's for an elegant reception. A long table stretched the width of the deck, set with fine china and tall glass vases filled with calla lilies. Gigi was bickering in the corner with Ms. Myrtle over whether the chargers under the plates should have been blue or gold, and Callie caught Austin sneaking glances at Gigi over Jesse's shoulder as she and Uncle Lonnie came back from the photos they'd been taking down on the beach.

"You can come by and sign Monday morning," Gigi was telling Sienna as Callie walked up. Gigi had negotiated both Callie and Sienna's new contracts with Sharpe Music Group. Callie had fired her former manager, Bart. He had sided with Andrew, telling her it was career suicide to move to Sharpe. But that was okay, because she was ready to kill off the Callie Jackson they had created.

Callie had signed her new contract weeks earlier and only had two songs left to write to finish off her new album. Piper already had a media blitz planned to reintroduce Callie to country fans. Callie would do a small domestic tour next year, and Sienna would open for her before going out on her own longer tour, which meant they could both record and prepare here on Big Dune Island. Jacqueline was moving to the island after the wedding, leaving her younger sister in charge back in Nashville. They'd all laughed, joking that Big Dune Island was now Sharpe's defacto Florida studio.

As the group on the deck made their way to their seats, Callie lightly tapped her champagne glass with a knife before standing.

"I'd like to propose a toast." She held up her glass. "To Uncle Lonnie and Jacqueline, who took time out from changing everyone else's lives and decided to make some changes of their own. Uncle Lonnie, no one is more deserving of happiness than you. And, Jacqueline, welcome to Big Dune Island. We're lucky to have you here."

Jacqueline smiled as she raised her glass in Callie's direction. "Next time it'll be your turn."

Callie looked down at the diamond on her left hand. The same diamond her mother had worn. As she sat, Jesse wrapped his arm around her, squeezing her closer.

She was finally back where she belonged. On Big Dune Island and in Jesse's arms.

WANT MORE BIG DUNE ISLAND?

The story continues in book two: *If I'd Have Known*! Here's what's next on Big Dune Island...

Chapter 1
Gigi

"Who's ready to get married?" Gigi Franklin said in a sing-song voice as she slid into a chair across from her best friend, country music superstar Callie Jackson.

Callie beamed. "I still can't believe it's really happening."

"Oh, it's happening," Gigi said as she pulled a three-ring binder out of her oversized purse and plopped it on the table between them for emphasis.

"Omigosh, you still have this," Callie practically shrieked as she pulled the binder across the table for a closer look. She trailed a finger over the puff-paint title on the cover: The Perfect Wedding.

"Don't tell Myrtle," Gigi said, referring to her mother, whose only dream for her daughter's life was a husband and children. "I don't want to give her any false hope."

Callie frowned. "You're going to find your Prince Charming one day too."

"No," Gigi said, waving a finger. "I do not need or want a Prince Charming. Do you have any idea how many divorces I did last year? No thanks." Then when she realized Callie was frowning again, she said, "That won't happen with you and Jesse, of course. You found the one man on the planet who actually doesn't mind that you have a career and that you make more money than him."

"He might change his mind if I can't get this album recorded before the wedding so we can actually go on a honeymoon." Callie laughed as she picked up her mug to take a sip.

"How's that going?"

"We're a little behind schedule, but I should be able to get caught up. Luckily, Jesse is having to work overtime at the Watson House to get it done before the wedding too, so I don't feel so guilty holing up in the recording studio all the time. Did I tell you Sienna and I are doing a two-part duet? The first one will be on my album, and then the second one will be on hers. I'm the wife in the story, and she's the other woman, and we each get to sort of tell our side of the story."

"Kind of like 'Jolene' and 'That Girl'?" Gigi asked, referring to the Dolly Parton classic that later had the other side of the story told in a Jennifer Nettles song.

"Yes, exactly. The record company thinks it'll help boost sales for Sienna when her debut comes out this winter. I don't think she'll have any trouble—you know how talented she is—but if they think it'll help, I'm happy to shine the spotlight—"

Callie stopped mid-sentence as Gigi practically leaped across the table to grab the binder and flip it over to the nondescript back side. Chloe Beckett, the owner of Island Coffee, was approaching, and she had a bit of a reputation for gossip and the inability to keep a secret.

"Hi, Gigi," Chloe said in her bright, bubbly voice. "Can I get you anything?"

"Two shots of espresso. Thanks."

Chloe glanced down at Gigi's hand still protectively on top of the binder, and it looked like it physically pained her not to ask about it. "Okay, be right back," she finally said after a long pause.

Callie raised an eyebrow after Chloe had left them. "Espresso at four in the afternoon?"

"You're not the only one who's behind schedule." Gigi sighed, sitting back in her chair. "I have a bunch of paperwork to do for the Nickersons to adopt Ty."

Normally, Gigi wouldn't have been able to share privileged legal information, but Big Dune Island was a small town and the Nickersons were high school classmates of Gigi and Callie. Callie knew they'd fostered the five-year-old boy after having two newborn adoptions fall through when birth mothers changed their minds. She also knew they had decided to formally adopt him.

"I'm totally in awe of them," Callie said. "It takes special people to welcome an older child into their lives."

"Right?" Gigi said. "It's actually the first adoption I've done for an older kid. Everyone wants a baby."

Gigi didn't add that she personally felt zero maternal instinct when she saw babies. However, she did find a small part of herself wishing she had the time or energy to help one of the kids she'd met through the local foster care system during her time as an attorney on the island. Although her mother was an overbearing helicopter parent who'd tried to orchestrate her entire life from the day she was born, Gigi knew she was lucky to have grown up with parents who loved each other and provided her with everything she could ever need.

Chloe approached with the espresso, and Gigi thanked her.

"I know this one's your favorite." Chloe winked, referring to the cup and saucer covered in pink peonies.

"It is," Gigi agreed, holding up the tiny espresso cup to admire it.

Chloe was her friend Austin Beckett's younger sister, and she'd opened the town's only Main Street coffee shop a few years prior. One of its most unique features was the china everything was served on, which consisted of pieces donated by women in town who wanted to preserve their formal china, but didn't have children interested in inheriting it. It meant every piece in the cafe had a story to tell and allowed the history of the town's families to be carried into the future.

The cookie Callie had ordered before Gigi arrived sat half eaten on a Noritake plate adorned with pink azaleas that had once been owned by Callie's maternal grandparents. She'd donated pieces of the formal china to the cafe when she'd cleaned out her parents' house last year, opting to only keep her parents' everyday china for her future in the newly renovated family home she would share with Jesse after they were married.

"Back to the task at hand," Gigi said, flipping the binder open between them. "I left all your inspiration photos at the beginning here in case there's something that still catches your eye."

"You mean like those sheer puff sleeves?" Callie said, pointing at a cut-out photo of a bright white wedding dress with the sleeves that were popular in the 1990s.

"Okay, maybe not the dress, but I do still love this cake," Gigi said, flipping the page to a three-tier wedding cake with edible pearls dotting it and a few white roses tucked into the side of the first layer. It was simple. Classic.

"Let them eat cake!" Austin declared as he approached their table with Callie's fiancé, Jesse Thomas.

Austin's trademark was his ability to find a quote or corny saying for every situation. Gigi rolled her eyes, even if it was one of his more endearing qualities.

As he sat in one of the two empty chairs at the round table, Austin motioned for his sister. Jesse leaned over to kiss Callie on the cheek before settling in the chair next to her.

Gigi snapped the binder shut again as Chloe approached. Meeting at the cafe was probably a bad idea for privacy's sake, but it had become a bit of an afternoon habit. It was almost equal distance between Gigi's office in a little historic house one block south of Main and Callie's family home, one block north of it.

Callie steered the conversation to updates on her album after the men ordered their drinks, filling the time until Chloe had delivered their order and was back at the other end of the shotgun-style cafe.

"Is this your wedding-planning bible?" Austin asked, flipping the binder open again on the table.

"Yes, as a matter of fact, it is," Gigi said, attempting to grab it from him.

He was too quick though, and swiped it from her reach.

"Look," he said to Jesse, "it's color-coded and there are even little tabs. Venue. Flowers. Caterers." Austin rattled off each tab as he flicked through them. "Dress. Sorry, dude, you can't see this one," he said, pretending he was peeking at the next page while holding up a hand to block Jesse's view. "No seeing the dress before the wedding. Right, ladies?"

"Give me that before you mess it up," Gigi said, leaning across the arm of her chair to reach for the binder, which he passed to her as he laughed and shook his head.

"Sorry," Callie said, shrugging. Her smile said she wasn't really. "I invited the guys to help us figure out how to pull this off. I want a normal wedding, but I have no idea how we can do that without someone from the media getting wind of it and turning it into a circus."

"You heard her. She doesn't want any media there," Gigi deadpanned in Austin's direction. He'd moved back to town after his brief stint as a Major League Baseball player to host a sports talk-radio show in nearby Jacksonville.

He smirked. "Someone has to make sure this shindig is actually fun. I didn't see a tab for that."

"Children, children," Jesse chided. "There's enough wedding planning to go around. Everyone will get their turn."

"There won't be anything to plan if we can't figure out where to have the wedding and how to keep it a secret," Callie said.

"Yes, that's priority number one," Gigi said, pulling a pen out of her purse and opening the binder in her lap to a blank page.

"Do we need to call the meeting to order before the secretary begins taking notes?" Austin asked her.

"I move we vote Beckett off the committee," Gigi said, looking then to Callie and Jesse, smiling. "Do I have a second?"

"Motion fails to carry," Austin said after their friends only laughed in response. "In new business, we need somewhere these two can get hitched that's worthy of the great Callie Jackson."

Despite the Country Music Awards that confirmed Callie was basically country music royalty, she blushed just like she always did when anyone on the island acknowledged her stardom. The locals had mostly let her live like a normal person since she moved back to town, but tourists still marveled at the sight of her if she ventured into town without a wig. It was why they were sitting in the back corner of Island Coffee, Callie with her back to the door and her trademark blonde curls tucked up into a baseball cap.

"I don't care where it's at or what it looks like. I just want it to be on Big Dune where everyone we love can be there to celebrate with us," Callie said, reaching over to take Jesse's hand.

"What my Cal wants, my Cal gets," Jesse said, leaning over for a quick peck.

The only hitch was they were going to have to put something together quickly if they wanted to fit in a honeymoon before Callie and Sienna had to go on the road to promote albums this winter.

"Well, obviously, I'll draft up NDAs for all the vendors to sign," Gigi said, making a note on the to-do list she'd started.

"Do you think that's enough though?" Callie asked, raising her eyebrows.

"If one of them dares break their nondisclosure agreement, I'll sue their pants right off of them."

"What if they didn't know it was Callie's wedding?" Austin asked.

"If we tell them it's for a secret bride, they'll know it's Callie," Jesse said, shaking his head. "Who else around here would be getting married secretly?"

"Actually, I hate to admit this, but Beckett might be on to something," Gigi said, ignoring the hand Austin held up triumphantly for her to high-five. "I wonder if we could figure out how to book things as if it's a different kind of event, like a surprise birthday party or something."

"Or one of those big events Ms. Myrtle always has," Austin chimed in, referring to Gigi's mother.

"Wait, isn't your parents' wedding anniversary in the fall?" Callie asked, her bright blue eyes lighting up with an idea.

"Yes," Gigi said slowly, hoping she wasn't right about where Callie was going next.

"What if we told people it was a vow renewal for your parents? It's totally something Ms. Myrtle would do, and everyone in town would be sure to show up."

Jesse nodded. "That actually makes a lot of sense. Would your mom go for it?" he asked Gigi.

"Are you kidding me? She loves weddings, and heaven knows she's not going to see me get married anytime soon. The only problem will be keeping her from planning the wedding she wants instead of the one you want. But I can ask her tomorrow. I need to go over this week to drop off some paperwork for her to sign anyway."

"We have an early morning session tomorrow because Bruce has a flight to catch," Callie said, referring to her producer, "but I could go with you any other time this week."

"Perfect. Then we can figure out if any venues have openings this fall and go from there." It was September already, but surely somewhere would have an off-peak date available. Fall wasn't a busy time on Big Dune Island after school was back in session, and Callie had already said she didn't care what day of the week they held the wedding.

"Now that that's settled, let's talk about the bachelor party," Austin said, wiggling his eyebrows at Jesse. "I'm thinking Vegas. Nothing trashy, of course," he said to Callie. "The showgirls are all true professionals. They really don't get enough credit for their artistry."

Gigi rolled her eyes. "They want a joint bachelor-bachelorette weekend away with just a few close friends. I've already scoped out some vacation rentals up in Savannah and on Tybee Island."

"My apologies. I must have missed that tab," Austin joked, nodding toward the binder. "It's a little different to the vibe I was going for, but I can work with it."

Callie laughed. "I'm not sure I want to be stuck in a house with the two of you after all."

Gigi wasn't sure it was a good idea either. She and Austin had been friends since high school, growing even closer when they both lived in Atlanta during her college and law school years while Austin was playing for the Braves. What rattled her now, however, was that she still remembered how close they'd come to kissing the last time they'd stayed in a house together for a wedding.

———

Later that evening, Gigi took a glass of wine and her laptop out to the table on her back deck to start researching local wedding venues. She'd renovated a beachfront cottage herself when she'd moved back to Big Dune Island from New York City, where she worked after law school. She spent most of her time at the office, but when she was home, she liked to be on the back deck breathing the salty air and working to the soundtrack of the waves that crashed thirty yards behind her house on the other side of the dunes.

Lighting a citronella candle to keep the mosquitos and no-see-ums away from the glow of the laptop, she opened a browser tab and began looking up the venues she knew off the top of her head. On the fancier end of things, there was the Palm Yacht Club, The Dunes—the only luxury hotel on the island—and Wilson's Landing, a private venue for residents of the island's most exclusive community. All three were on the south end of the island, where Jesse used to help developers build second-home monstrosities that wiped out one-hundred-year-old live oaks and the last of the natural land on the island. Thankfully, he now focused on preserving and renovating historic homes.

She was on the weddings page for the yacht club when she realized it was the location her mother would choose, which made her immediately exit the browser tab. Sure, it might be what people would expect for the Franklins' vow renewal, but the actual event needed to fit Callie and Jesse. And despite the fact that Callie's wealth eclipsed most of the people on the island, a stuffy, white-tablecloth affair with servers in tails and three different kinds of forks at every place setting was about as far from her taste as you could get.

The same went for The Dunes. Too buttoned up for Callie and Jesse. Wilson's Landing might work though. It was a giant wooden pavilion built out over the marsh on the river side of the island. The website showed white twinkle lights and sheer white fabric swagging across the exposed beams. She could picture Callie and Jesse there, so she sent the PDF with more details and contact information to her printer. She'd add it to her binder and give them a call tomorrow to inquire about availability.

The website featured an Instagram feed full of past weddings at the bottom of the page, so she began clicking through for inspiration. As she went down the rabbit hole of one bride's big day, she ended up on the photographer's page, that included photos from other nearby wedding venues. Gigi had been so focused on Big Dune Island that she'd forgotten about the Whispering Palms on Fort George Island just south of them. It was an easy twenty-minute drive.

Fort George Island was largely uninhabited, much of it preserved as a state park. A small portion of the island had been developed in the 1920s, including the historic Whispering Palms estate, once the summer home of a wealthy railroad magnate. It was close enough for everyone to attend, but far enough to give the couple privacy. Gigi printed out their wedding brochure to add to her binder and picked up her wine for a long sip. Something told her she'd already found the venue. Fingers crossed they'd still have an open date.

Whispering Palms had an Instagram feed as well, so she browsed the photos to get a better look at the indoor and outdoor options for the ceremony and reception. One photo in particular caught her attention because it featured the same seafoam-green bridesmaid dress she'd worn to her childhood friend Mary Catherine Morgan's wedding back in college. Apparently, it was one of those bridesmaid dresses that never went out of style—despite the fact it had never actually been in style.

Originally, she'd been planning to go to the wedding on the arm of her longtime boyfriend, Dalton, with a ring on her own finger. But then he'd suddenly broken things off, and she'd been surprised when Austin gave up the opportunity to go to the wedding of their mutual friend as a single man and instead suggested they go together. He had stayed at her side the entire evening, giving up his chance to flirt with the single bridesmaids.

What she remembered most about that weekend, however, was when, after the wedding, they'd ended up being the last two still in the hot tub at the beach house Mary Catherine's mother had rented for the wedding party. Still buzzing from the champagne at the reception, they'd ended up in a deep conversation about their overbearing parents and their impossible expectations. Austin had made it to AAA, the highest level before reaching the majors, and his dad still wasn't happy. It was Major League Baseball or nothing. Meanwhile, Myrtle asked Gigi more about the guys in her classes than her grades. The only degree Myrtle cared about Gigi getting was her "Mrs. degree." College was for finding a husband, not a career.

They'd stayed in the hot tub until their skin was prune-like, and then Austin had exited first and held out his hand to help her up the slippery steps. When she'd reached the top, he'd held her hand a beat longer than was necessary. She remembered looking up at him, water beading down his tan, muscular chest, his green eyes fixed on hers. There had been a moment, hadn't there? Then Carly Lassiter had stumbled out the back door, interrupting them as she shouted Austin's name, still feeling the effects of the shots Gigi had seen her taking in the kitchen when they returned from the wedding.

Gigi shook her head to dislodge the memory, grabbing her wine glass to take a big swig. It didn't matter, anyway, because a week later she wasn't even speaking to Austin anymore. They'd mended fences after they'd both moved back to Big Dune Island, and then Callie had returned to complete their foursome, but Gigi hadn't forgotten. Not about the almost kiss or what happened afterward.

Grab your copy!

Acknowledgments

Dear reader, thank you! If you've made it here, that probably means you've read my book. You have no idea how much that means to me!

I fought really hard for this book. I wrote it back in 2018–2019 and tried to get it published in 2020 to no avail. I put it aside and wrote *The Library of Second Chances*, which became my debut. I couldn't stop thinking about this book though, so I sent it to my publisher. I will be forever grateful that Jenny Hale and her team over at Harpeth Road were able to help me make this story even better and get it in the hands of readers.

This book has been through many edits over the years. Thank you to Bryn Donovan and Sheila Athens who read earlier drafts of this and helped me make it better. Also to my beta readers: Zoe, Sylvia, and Rubie! Special thanks to Zoe for helping me a lot behind the scenes too!

I'm lucky to have a great group of authors, editors and other publishing industry folks in my corner. Thank you to my author bestie, Lindsay Gibson, for being my sounding board, and to my Kiss Pitch 2022 group for their continued advice and support. The guys and gals in the 2024 Debuts Discord are also a constant source of insight, cheerleading and support.

To Olivia, my author assistant, you are incredible! I can't imagine doing this without you!

My college bestie, Maggie Norris, is one of my biggest cheerleaders and is always willing to read a draft and give honest feedback. Kriggie forever.

To Stephanie, my Twinny, your support and enthusiasm for my writing dreams means the world. We were meant to be together every bit as much as Callie and Jesse!

I have the best friends in the world! Thank you to my friends Michelle, Starlett, and Allyse, for always being on my team. To Teresa, Mike, Kristin and David, thank you for helping me celebrate my last launch day. I hope you can find characters you want to be cast to play in this book as well!

I also have the best family. Thank you to my parents, my brother Bo and his wife Nickki, and all my aunts, uncles, cousins, nieces and nephews for always believing in and encouraging me. I have some of the most amazing aunts: Shug, Luder Belle, Nank, Mary Ann, and Judy. Also Nancy, Gail and Vicky, my adopted aunts!

My family by marriage is also incredible. Thank you to my mother-in-law Jane, another of my biggest cheerleaders, and my brother- and sister-in-law, Scott and Tonya.

To my husband, Chadd, thank you for everything. People underestimate how important it is to have someone who believes in your dreams and gives you the time and space to achieve them. Love on!

And last, but not least, to my readers and reviewers. I still pinch myself when I think about the fact that I have readers, and so many of you posted the most wonderful reviews of my last novel. Thank you for helping make my dreams come true! I couldn't do what I love without you.

A Letter from Savannah Carlisle

Hello!

Thank you so much for picking up my novel, *The Summer of Starting Over*. I hope you enjoyed being whisked away on a mental vacation to beautiful Big Dune Island!

If you'd like to know when my next book is out, you can sign up for new Harpeth Road release alerts for my novels here:

www.harpethroad.com/savannah-carlisle-newsletter-signup

I won't share your information with anyone else, and I'll only email you a quick message whenever new books come out or go on sale.

If you did enjoy *The Summer of Starting Over*, I'd be so thankful if you'd write a review online. Getting feedback from readers helps to persuade others to pick up my book for the first time. It's one of the biggest gifts you could give me.

Until next time,
Savannah